P9-DTI-758

THE LAST COWBOY

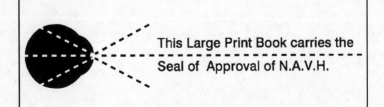

This Large Print Book carries the
Seal of Approval of N.A.V.H.

THE LAST COWBOY

WITHDRAWN

LINDSAY MCKENNA

THORNDIKE PRESS

A part of Gale, Cengage Learning

GALE
CENGAGE Learning®

Detroit • New York • San Francisco • New Haven, Conn • Waterville, Maine • London

GALE
CENGAGE Learning®

LIBRARY OF CONGRESS CATALOGING-IN-PUBLICATION DATA

McKenna, Lindsay, 1946–
   The last cowboy / by Lindsay McKenna. — Large print ed.
     p. cm. — (Thorndike Press large print romance)
   ISBN-13: 978-1-4104-4353-3 (hardcover)
   ISBN-10: 1-4104-4353-1 (hardcover)
   1. Large type books. 2. Cowboys—Fiction. I. Title.
   PS3563.C37525L37 2011
   813'.54—dc23   2011037752

Published in 2011 by arrangement with Harlequin Books S.A.

Printed in the United States of America
1 2 3 4 5 6 7 15 14 13 12 11

Dear Reader,

I love stories about the men and women of the West. They aren't always cowboys, but sometimes they are. The West has a very wild, individual energy unlike the eastern part of the U.S.A. When one considers the hardships, the risks of opening up our huge country from the east to the west, there was a very hardy group of men and women who took on the challenge. They were a group who braved the elements, the danger of Indian attacks and the wild animals. They carved something out of nothing and made it their own through hard, backbreaking daily work. And they were nature-oriented, not wanting big-city life. They craved the quiet of the days, the only music provided by songbirds, coyotes and wolves singing. They wanted wide, open spaces, not to be jammed in with one house attached to another one.

Not everyone is of that temperament or personality or constitution. That is what sets Westerners apart from the rest of the world. And that is what is fascinating about them, at least to me. What drives a person to be a risk-taker? What is the lure? The fascination? You can take the Westerner and put her or him in any environment around the world — not necessarily Jackson Hole, Wyoming — and you get the same gutsy, can-do attitude toward harsh, rugged life. It is a mindset. A way of seeing the world through that particular lens of reality.

Part of my ongoing series about the West and the people who live there, *The Last Cowboy* is about a rancher named Slade McPherson. He's had one tough life. From age five onward, he was without parents. He was torn from his fraternal twin, Griff McPherson. They were separated, one going East and one staying at the parents' ranch to be raised by dutiful uncles. Slade is barely able to make ends meet.

His hardscrabble life is nonstop and he has the bruising personality to survive, regardless of what is thrown at him next.

An endurance-riding champion, Slade enters fifty- and hundred-mile horse endurance contests. He's made a name for himself on his Medicine Hat stallion, who was once a wild mustang. Together, these two hardy survivors have carved out a stellar career across the U.S.A. and Canada. Slade offers his Medicine Hat stallion to those who want the genes passed on through their mares.

He owns the Tetons Ranch, sells endurance horses and trains endurance riders. He's seen — in that world — as a man of honesty, hard work and integrity.

And it is with this aura that Dr. Jordana Lawton, an emergency physician for the Jackson Hole, Wyoming, hospital, comes to him. She has a feisty mustang mare she feels can not only compete, but win in endurance racing. Slade is desperate for the money, but likes to teach only male students. He's had a very bad run-in with a socialite from the East Coast, who took him to the cleaners and left him nearly penniless. Slade blames himself for falling for her beauty. And it has left a bad taste in his mouth for women in general. Over time, Jordana, who is from the East Coast, slowly changes his attitude toward females.

As if Slade doesn't have enough to handle with being lured to Jordana, his fraternal twin brother, Griff, comes home. Griff, a stockbroker and banker on Wall Street, has been wiped out by the recession and the loss of his company. And legally, he owns half of the ranch. The two brothers don't get along at all. Will Slade trade in his

tough, take-no-prisoners attitude to woo
Jordana and make peace with Griff?

Lindsay McKenna

To Susan Hamilton of High Country Raptors, Flagstaff, AZ, Marchiene Reinstra, Tricia Speed, Patricia Comfort, Monica Amarillis (Milan, Italy), Sunday Larson, Naomi C. Rose and Maureen Wolverton. All strong, intelligent and compassionate women. Our world needs positive, healthy role models for women. It takes a state of mind, a confidence in yourself, to be treated as an equal in today's society around this world. I'm privileged to be a part of your lives as you are a part of mine. My wish is that someday soon, there will be equality for all women in our world.

CHAPTER ONE

"Boss! Look out!"

Slade McPherson was in a rectangular corral at his Jackson Hole, Wyoming ranch with the meanest Hereford bull he'd ever dealt with. He heard Shorty, his wrangler, give a cry of warning. There was sudden movement behind him. Diablo, the bull, had been walking toward the chute to receive his yearly set of shots. Slade never allowed any horses in such a confined area with the bull. Diablo hated men. Slade wasn't about to allow one of his prized horses to be butted and injured by Diablo.

Whirling around, he saw Diablo toss his massive white and rust head, drool flinging in all directions out of his mouth. The bull had decided not to go into the chute and, instead, wheeled his one ton body around and charged Slade who was ten feet away. The bull bellowed, lowered his head and attacked.

Slade was five feet away from the steel pipe fence. There was no way he could stop such a charge. All he could do was run like hell. And that's exactly what he did. Because he was six foot two inches in height, he had a long stride. Adrenaline shot through him as he dug the heels of his cowboy boots into the dusty floor of the corral. In two strides, Slade hit the fence, made a huge leap and landed on the third rung of the five-rung corral. The ground shook from Diablo's charge. As he jerked his leg up, still climbing to get away from the angry bull, Slade felt the brush of the bull's head against the heel of his boot.

It took a matter of two seconds before it was all over. Diablo roared and galloped around the small enclosure, tossing his head in frustration. Slade balanced himself on the fifth rung of the fence, watching his prized breeding bull bawl and race around the enclosure. *That was close!* Slade had lost count of the times Diablo had planned and waited until he'd get near enough to trample him to death. The bull had great genes for putting good meat on his offspring, but his personality sucked.

"Boss," Shorty panted, running over and looking up at Slade, "you okay? He grazed you."

Taking off his tan Stetson hat, the crown damp with sweat from the July day, Slade grinned and lifted his forearm. He wiped his brow with the back of his arm. "I'm fine," he drawled. "Close but no cigar." The sun was bright as it climbed higher in a deep blue sky. He glanced down at Shorty. The man was only five foot six inches tall, lean as a whippet and didn't look as if he could even make it as a wrangler, but he was one of the best. He came from good Irish stock with sandy-colored short hair and dancing green, elfish eyes.

"Good thing," Shorty muttered, worry in his tone. He stepped aside as Slade clambered off the pipe fence and landed on the dusty earth. "I'll tell ya, that bull seems to hate us humans more and more every year." Shorty's small face grew pinched as he watched the bull continuing to trot in circles, the drool from the corners of his opened mouth flying out like thin, glittering spider webs all around his head and massive shoulders.

"Bad personality genes for sure," Slade agreed, settling the dusty, sweat-stained Stetson back on his head. He watched Diablo. Once the bull seemed cooled down, the animal walked quietly into the chute. For the Hereford, it was a game, Slade realized as he walked around the outside of the corral. At the chute, he dropped the rear slat that would keep the bull confined. Going to his green Chevy truck, Slade picked up the syringe lying on the seat. Once a year, Diablo got his necessary vaccinations. Shorty followed him to the stout pipe chute that now enclosed the twenty-five-hundred pound bull.

"Boss, remember you got a new client comin' out here this afternoon," Shorty reminded him. The wrangler had been with Slade since he'd taken over the ranch.

Slade grunted. He really didn't want to hear that. Going to the chute, he said, "Stand by Diablo's head and distract him for a moment."

Grinning, Shorty moved to within a foot of the metal chute where the bull stood. "I'll be the decoy," he chortled.

Slade nodded and positioned himself at the rear of the bull. Diablo lived to find a human to trample. In the bull's mind, humans were a threat to his territory. And Diablo would never allow another male on two legs within the pastures he roamed with his herd of cows. If they came near, all bets were off, and he became enraged and would charge them. Good thing he thought four-legged horses were not threatening. Diablo snorted, his ears moving forward and back as Shorty slowly approached.

"Perfect," Slade murmured as he sank the needle into the thick, muscled area of the bull's well-padded hip. Diablo's entire attention was on Shorty's approach. As Slade withdrew the needle, he glanced forward to get the bull's reaction. There was none. His angry brown eyes were fixed on Shorty. "We're done," he called. Placing the emptied syringe back in the box on his truck seat, Slade said, "Release him back out into the pasture."

"Right, Boss," Shorty said with a quick nod. "He ain't gonna be happy, though. All his ladies are in the pasture across the road from him."

Pulling his leather gloves back on, Slade nodded. "Too bad. He can look, but not touch." Slade had a small herd of Herefords, fifty in all, that Diablo bred in early fall. It took nine months for gestation. In the early summer months, the calves were born. At that time, Diablo was separated from his band, a dirt road plus a stout metal pipe rail fence between them. One never kept a bull with newly born calves. The chances of them being injured or killed by the bull was very real.

And Slade needed every calf that was

birthed because after they reached a certain age, they would be sold to the meat market. And that meant money to pay a mortgage that was always a monthly nightmare to him. Above all, Slade never wanted to lose this ranch. He lived on the razor's edge of doing just that. Being a small-time rancher meant a constant balancing act with the bank mortgage on a monthly basis. Miss one payment and he'd be foreclosed upon. *It can't happen!*

Slade watched Shorty open the chute. Instantly, Diablo bellowed and shot out of it at a full gallop. The Tetons Ranch that Slade had inherited after his uncle died was only fifty acres in size. A very small ranch, all things considered. Diablo thundered out of the opened gate. Ahead of him was lush green pasture. And farther to his left was the stout pipe fence and a dirt road. All his ladies and their babies grazed peacefully on the other side. Diablo would pace for a while, walking up and down the fence line, tossing his head and reestablishing he was boss of his herd. Slade knew that the territorial bull would eventually settle down. Diablo would do his best to follow his herd, but the pipe fence and road always stood between them. Once the bull quieted, he would graze and watch his band from afar.

Shorty came back. He took off his dusty black Stetson and brushed it against his thigh. Dust poofed away from it. "Boss," he said as he pulled a crinkled piece of notebook paper from his back pocket, "here's whose comin' at one p.m."

Slade didn't like new clients, but they were his bread and butter, necessary to meet his financial obligations for the Tetons Ranch. "Okay, thanks," he grunted, taking the paper. Shorty managed Slade's endurance training appointments. Carefully unwrapping the note, he saw Shorty had scribbled a name and phone number. Frowning, he tried to read it. Shorty was thirty-five years old, single and had never been married. He'd worked for Slade's Uncle Paul shortly before he'd died, and the ranch had been willed to Slade and his fraternal twin brother, Griff. Slade was now thirty-two, and he was grateful for Shorty's loyalty to the ranch and his family. He glanced up — Shorty's thin, narrow face was set in a grin.

"I 'spose you can't read my writin', Boss?"

"Got that right," Slade growled. He handed the note back to his wrangler. "Want to translate it for me?"

Chortling, Shorty read it and said, "Dr. Jordana Lawton is bringing her mustang mare named Stormy here this afternoon at one p.m." Shorty handed him back the note.

"A doctor?"

"Yes, Boss. She's an emergency room physician, and Gwen Garner told me that Dr. Lawton is also a functional medicine specialist and has her clinic near the hospital."

Mouth quirking, Slade asked, "What'd you do? Have a cozy chat with Gwen?" Her son, Cade Garner, was a deputy sheriff. She was the town gossip, but she was careful on what she said and made sure her information was correct before she passed it on to anyone else.

Turning red, Shorty shrugged. "Hey, Gwen said Dr. Lawton was a nice lady, Boss. I guess because Dr. Lawton is used to chattin' with her patients, she's real easy to talk to."

"You weren't her patient."

"No, but when we talked on the phone, she made me feel special," Shorty said, challenging him.

Shrugging, Slade muttered, "I don't care who she is so long as she can pay for the training. What's this about a mustang mare? Is she wanting endurance training?"

"For both of 'em, Boss. The doctor wants to know if her mare is capable of being an

18

endurance horse prospect from a conformation standpoint. So, I told her to trailer the mare out here and you'd take a look at her."

In Slade's business of endurance riding, of which he was many times a champion, people often brought their horses out for him to check out. "Okay. Anything else she wants?"

Shrugging, Shorty said, "The doc said if her mare's conformation was okay, she wanted to hire you to train both of them for level one riding."

Nodding, Slade interpreted this as money coming into his coffers to keep the bank at bay. He had weekly training sessions with nine male students. He knew how to get a horse ready for an endurance ride, whether it was a twenty-, fifty- or a hundred-mile challenge. And he also knew how to get the rider in shape as well. "Okay, that sounds good. She got a background in endurance racing?"

"A little," Shorty hedged. "I really didn't get into much of a discussion with her on that, Boss. I figure you'll sort it out with her when she arrives here this afternoon."

"Okay," Slade said. Tucking the paper with the doctor's name and phone number into his dark red cotton cowboy shirt pocket, he said, "Let's get back to work. We need to start separating the calves from their mothers, branding and vaccinating them." That would be a weeklong activity. And Slade only had one wrangler. He worked from four in the morning to midnight every day. And every hour of daylight was precious.

"Right," Shorty murmured, following him to where their horses were tied to the corral fence.

As Slade mounted his buckskin quarter horse, Dude, his mind wandered back to Dr. Jordana Lawton for just a second. Slightly curious if she was a good endurance prospect, Slade hoped that it would work out so he had more money flowing in. He'd find out soon enough.

Jordana Lawton carefully negotiated the rutted dirt road. She drove her dark blue Ford three-quarter ton pickup truck as if she was driving over hens' eggs. Behind her in a dark blue two-horse trailer was her gray mustang mare, Stormy. One never took a deeply rutted road with a horse trailer at a high speed. It would bounce the horse around so much that it could either cause an injury or send the animal into a frantic emotional state akin to trauma.

And trauma was something Jordana knew inside and out as an emergency room physician. Glancing at the clock on the dash, she knew she was going to be late. She hadn't anticipated the dirt road being in such bad shape, but thunderstorms coming over the Tetons last week had made a gooey mire of every ranch road in the valley. And she wasn't going to hurry in order to get there on time. Slade McPherson, the national champion endurance rider and trainer, would just have to wait.

The windows were down in the cab, and her shoulder-length black hair flew in wisps across her face. Jordana pulled the errant strands away and then placed both hands back on the steering wheel. In the two years that she had lived in Jackson Hole, Wyoming, she had come to find that the majority of ranch roads in the valley were not paved. Most of the owners had a tractor, and they would drive out with a blade attached and smooth out the ruts.

Frowning, her focus on her driving, she worried that Stormy might lose her footing on the thick rubber mats. Jordana wanted this experience for the mare to be a good one. It only took one bad ride in a trailer to spook some horses. After that, the horse would refuse to ever enter the trailer again. That couldn't happen because Jordana had high hopes that this mustang mare would be good enough to start competing at the top endurance level in the United States. And she wanted Stormy always to look forward to entering the trailer, instead of dreading it. *Slow but sure . . .*

Slade gritted his teeth as he looked down at the watch on his thick wrist. He'd just rode in from the pastures where he and Shorty had been separating cows from calves. It was hard, sweaty work. And he didn't want to waste time. Dr. Lawton was already ten minutes late. Slade didn't like people who weren't punctual. He had gone in and checked his answering machine to see if she'd called and canceled the appointment. There were no calls. Wasn't that just like a woman? Isabel, his ex-wife, had always been late.

He hated dealing with women in general. He much preferred working with men who wanted to train for endurance riding. Ever since his divorce from city slicker Isabel Stephens four years ago, Slade had taken on a distinct dislike of the opposite sex. Isabel hailed from New York City, had rich parents and possessed the emotional maturity of a sixteen-year-old girl. She had never been on time for anything except their impromptu wedding. Slade had developed an intense dislike of city slickers, New York City types, in particular. Isabel had left a bad taste in his mouth. She'd hired a rich New York City attorney and had taken him to the cleaners during their divorce proceedings.

Grimacing, Slade kicked the red dirt with the toe of his scarred cowboy boot. Isabel was the reason his beloved ranch was teetering on the edge of foreclosure. She'd taken him for every penny he'd ever earned. All his savings that had kept the ranch on sound financial footing had gone to her. Now, four years later, Slade continued to wrestle with every penny that came in on a monthly basis. He had nightmares about losing his parent's ranch. It had been in the family for over a hundred years. There was no way he could lose it. Being a rancher was all he knew. Anger stirred in him as he relived the divorce from petulant, spoiled Isabel.

Pulling in a deep, ragged breath, Slade recalled how he'd fallen in love with the sleek, beautiful Isabel. A dressage rider from the East Coast, she'd come out to Jackson Hole for a two-week vacation with her rich corporate friend who owned a ten million dollar home here in the valley. Isabel had met Slade at the Tetons fifty-mile ride, her first endurance contest. Isabel knew her horses. And when Slade had seen her in the crowd as each rider rode up and waited to be released by the judge every five minutes, his heart had pounded. Slade could never remember a woman who had affected him so profoundly as Isabel had.

And it hadn't hurt that he'd won that race on his flashy medicine hat mustang stallion, Thor, either. Isabel had had stars in her eyes for him as he'd rode in first among a hundred other contestants. They'd had dinner and gone to bed that night. And Slade, stupid idiot that he was, impulsively married her a week later.

"What a loco decision," he groused, looking at his watch again. The dirt road to Tetons Ranch curved, so he wouldn't see a truck and horse trailer until the last moment. He saw no one driving around that corner. "Damn," he added, now walking angrily back to his ranch house. Where the hell was this woman? If she couldn't even be on time for this first meeting, what would it be like if he accepted her as a student later? If her horse had the potential? *Not good. Not good at all. Damn her. Why couldn't she call and let him know where she was at?*

Jordana gave a gasp of surprise. As she slowly pulled around the last curve, she saw

24

the iconic Marlboro Man cowboy from the cigarette ads. Oh, she'd seen photos of Slade McPherson, but in real life . . . *My God . . .*

Most things didn't unsettle Jordana one way or another. But the fierce-looking, rugged cowboy did. As she drove her horse trailer between the barn and the ranch house where he stood, Jordana felt her heart unexpectedly begin to pound. This wasn't adrenaline. She was a physician, and she knew the difference. No, this was her womanly side wildly responding to the man she saw standing there, his hands tense on his narrow hips, watching her approach.

Jordana knew Slade McPherson was a loner. Everyone in Jackson Hole had told her that. A strong, gruff, even antisocial rancher who knew more about breeding endurance horses than anyone else in the nation. She'd done her research. And in her eyes, after learning all she could about this hardened, rugged cowboy, he was the best at what he did: a champion endurance rider and breeder.

Not expecting to have such a powerful physical reaction to seeing him in person made Jordana feel giddy like a teenager. As she put on the brake, she saw his large gray eyes narrowing speculatively upon her. Suddenly vulnerable beneath that incisive, probing gaze, Jordana felt like Jell-O melting out in hot sunlight. Even her lower body was reacting to him! *Good grief!* What was this all about? Unhinged, Jordana suddenly felt unsure in this man's towering presence. He wore a set of dusty Levi's that perfectly outlined his long, powerful legs and thick thighs. His hands were long and large, draped over his narrow hips. The dark red cotton cowboy shirt did nothing but emphasize his square face that was burned dark by the sun. The slashes at the sides of his full mouth and the crow's feet at the corners of his eyes told her this man regularly challenged the weather in any condition — and won.

Her intuitive sense told Jordana he was armored up. The realization hit her in the solar plexus. Unexpectedly, her hands shook as she gathered up items from the seat in preparation to leave the truck. Jordana suddenly was taken back to when she was fifteen years old. It was at that age she had been struck by love for the first time. And how she felt then was how she felt now. Compressing her full lips, she tried to gather her strewn emotions. As hard and implacable as Slade McPherson appeared to be in person, Jordana knew she had to put on her physician's face: strong, confident and detached. It would hide her present emotions that were a mix of excitement, desire and curiosity.

Climbing out of the truck, Jordana hastily walked around the front of it. As she faced the stony looking Slade McPherson, she heard him snarl, "You're late. . . ."

CHAPTER TWO

Jordana felt as if she'd just been physically slapped by the rugged-looking cowboy who towered over her. She was only five foot six inches tall. He was like a Sequoia compared to her pine tree height. Compressing her full lips, Jordana weathered his icily spoken words. As a trauma physician, she'd encountered people in all states of anger and irritability. Knowing that a soft, steady voice and appearing unflappable calmed emotional storms, she smiled and said, "I'm sorry. I'm Jordana Lawton. The road to your ranch was a little more rutted than I'd anticipated, and I slowed down so my mare wouldn't get thrown around in the trailer." She put her hand forward.

Slade absorbed the apology in her husky voice. The sound flowed over him like melting honey. Jordana's hand was extended, and he stared down at it. She had long fingers, her hand as delicate-looking as her face. Obliquely he wondered if she had the stamina it took to gut out a fifty- or hundred-mile endurance ride. In appearance, she didn't look like much more than a pretty black-haired, blue-eyed woman with a curvy body in all the right places. The sunlight danced across her shoulder-length hair, highlighting some of the reddish strands.

"Slade McPherson, Dr. Lawton." He monitored the amount of strength as his hand engulfed hers. To his surprise, he found her hand strong and firm, just like his. Swallowing that discovery, he instantly released her hand because red-hot tingles were soaring from his hand up into his lower arm. What the hell was happening? Slade had no idea.

"Call me Jordana," she insisted. Giving him a bit of a wry smile, she added, "I am a trauma doc, but that's my job. Out here, I'm just like anyone else. Please call me Jordana?"

Slade felt as if he was being pulled into her dancing, sky blue eyes. There was warmth and understanding glinting in them like dapples of sunlight across the lakes found in the Tetons range. Her pupils were large and black, eyelashes forming a dark frame around them. Again, he swallowed hard. There was nothing to dislike about

Jordana. She appeared to be around his age, although her face appeared to be that of a young twenty-something. Slade knew that doctors didn't really get out of training until they were twenty-eight to thirty years old.

"I haven't got much time," he said abruptly, and he waved his hand toward the horse trailer. "Shorty said you have an endurance prospect you wanted me to evaluate?"

Wincing internally, Jordana had to stop the comparison between her former boss, Dr. Paul Edwin, who'd had the exact same acid, remote and cold personality as McPherson. That made her cringe inside. After a two-year sexual harassment lawsuit, Jordana had won the court case but she'd lost her position at a prestigious New York City hospital. That was why she'd decided to start all over and moved from there to Jackson Hole, Wyoming. Now, she was being tested by a man who looked as harsh as the mighty Tetons range itself.

"Yes, I have a mustang mare name Stormy. I'd like you to evaluate her conformation. See if she has what it takes."

"At what level?" he demanded, stalking around the back of the trailer and opening the latches.

Jordana quickly followed him. He flowed

like water over rock. There was a fluidity to Slade that mesmerized her. She realized he was in top athletic shape to be able to move with that kind of boneless grace. "Level one, the Nationals," she said. Jordana moved forward as the doors swung out and pulled out the ramp. Stormy whinnied.

Reaching up, Jordana patted the sleek gray rump of her mare. "It's okay, Stormy. I'm going to get you out of there." She walked to the side of the trailer and opened a smaller door. This allowed her to go inside and unsnap the hook attached to the mare's red nylon halter. That done, Jordana eased around the end and stood where the mare was tied. She attached a nylon halter lead and placed her hand on the horse's chest. "Back up," she told the mare.

Stormy obeyed. In a few moments, Jordana and her mare were standing outside the trailer.

"Bring your mare over here," Slade ordered. He walked away from the trailer into an area where the horse could be walked and trotted.

Jordana nodded and did as he asked. What a tough hombre he was! There were no articles that said anything about this man's personality. Maybe that's why, she thought. Anxious because Jordana wanted Stormy to

31

be given the good seal of approval, she took the horse about a hundred feet away. McPherson stood with his arms across his chest, his face unreadable. The shade created by his tan Stetson emphasized the harsh lines gathered across his brow. What would he say about Stormy?

"Okay," Slade called, "trot your mare in a straight line toward me."

Clucking softly to Stormy, Jordana ran alongside her mare. She knew Slade was looking at how the horse's legs moved. She knew Stormy had a good set of legs. He would be checking out whether her hooves moved straight ahead or winged out or came into a pigeon-toed formation. If the horse's hooves winged outward, it was a sign of bad conformation. Stormy would never be able to take the hard, constant stress on her legs without breaking down and becoming injured.

Slade had one hell of a time keeping his eyes on the horse's movement. Jordana wore a bright yellow tee, jeans and cowboy boots. She moved as fluidly as the mare. Slade cursed — he did *not* want to be drawn at all to this woman! He'd automatically looked at her left hand and found no wedding ring on it. That didn't mean much. Slade was sure she was hooked up in a relationship, anyway. Jordana was far too pretty, intelligent and professional to be alone out here in Wyoming. Just as well, he harshly told himself.

As Jordana drew her mustang to a halt about ten feet in front of him, Slade lifted his hand and growled, "Now walk away from me. Go the same distance and then turn around and walk back to me."

"Right," Jordana said, breathless. Stormy was feeling her oats, and she pranced as Jordana turned her around. Speaking softly to the mare, Jordana managed to get the mustang settled down and walking obediently at her side.

Slade groaned. He was watching the way Jordana swayed her hips. Her legs were long and firm. He'd been without a woman for some time now. And this one, for whatever reason, was fanning the flames of his monk-like life. Forcing himself to watch the mare, he was pleased to see she was four square. That meant that at a walk, her rear hooves would land where her front hooves had previously been. That was a sign of the type of conformation Slade wanted to see in an endurance prospect. As the horse saying went: "No legs, no horse." And in endurance riding, legs either carried you through the challenging hill and mountain conditions, or they didn't.

As Jordana brought the steel gray mare to a halt, he'd seen enough and changed his orders. "Take her over to that corral and put her on a longe line. I want to see you work her both ways at a trot and gallop." He turned on his heel and walked toward the corral.

What a terse person he was! Jordana patted Stormy's sleek gray neck, ruffled her thick black mane and said, "Come on, girl. Show-and-tell time."

Snorting, Stormy danced prettily for a few paces and then sedately walked beside her owner. Jordana saw the gate was open to the huge white painted pipe corral fence. There was a longe line hanging nearby. McPherson was already in the corral, arms across his chest, face expressionless, as if barely tolerating them being on his property. Anxious, Jordana knew, with this kind of person, the best way to defuse his coldness and bring down her armor was to do what he told her to do. Ordinarily, she wouldn't take this kind of rude behavior from anyone except a patient in shock, but today, she did. More than anything, she wanted to know if her mare had what it took to move to the national level.

Slade watched the mustang mare being

worked, first clockwise on a thirty-foot longe line by Jordana, and then the opposite direction. The mare was thirteen and a half hands tall. It was rare that mustangs were very small in comparison to other light breed horses. His own medicine hat mustang stallion, Thor, was fifteen hands tall. He was the rare exception in the mustang world. Most were between thirteen and fourteen hands tall because of hundreds of years of lean food. Not enough food and the animals never fully developed their height. In the world of endurance riding, a leggy horse meant a long stride. And a long stride meant the horse ate up more ground which was important. Mere seconds could declare a winner and loser in an endurance race. Length of stride meant everything.

For the next ten minutes, Slade critically studied the gray mare. First, he needed to see if the mustang closely listened to her owner. That was a crucial piece of information because if the horse disregarded the owner's voice, it could put them in grave danger out on the trail.

"All right," Slade called, "enough. Get her saddled up and bring her back into the arena." He needed to see how the horse responded to rider. Was there teamwork? Or not? In an endurance contest, they would have to work like a well-oiled machine. Climbing rocky hills, jumping over fallen logs, making their way through water hazards or managing muddy trails were all required of them. If the horse didn't listen or was fighting the rider, it could place them into a dangerous situation where injury would be the outcome.

Jordana quickly took her mare back to the trailer and tied her on an outside metal loop. She wasn't sure what McPherson thought. He was one of the few people she couldn't read. Wondering as she saddled Stormy if Slade ever dropped that harsh mask he wore, Jordana was shocked by her sudden interest in this man. The fact he was almost a dead ringer for Dr. Paul Edwin turned her stomach. And yet, Jordana felt a calm come over her every time she looked into Slade's rugged face. His eyes, those gray shards of ice, never gave away how he really felt about her horse. And she knew as she mounted Stormy and walked her toward the corral, he was going to be judging both of them now. Taking a deep breath, Jordana tried to calm her anxiety. She wanted so badly to have McPherson's help to go to the top of the endurance world.

Slade watched from the fence as Jordana walked her horse around the large, sandy arena. Then, she urged Stormy to a trot and then a canter. She was an excellent rider. Jordana's hands were quiet on the hackamore reins as she guided Stormy. A hackamore was a bridle without a bit. It meant Stormy was very capable of wanting to work and listen to her owner. Most horses could not go without a bit in their mouth, so this spoke highly of Stormy's desire to work with her owner.

Jordana's long, beautiful legs were quiet and rested firmly against the mare's barrel. Never once did Slade see her use her heels to ask the horse to move from a walk to a trot or a walk to a canter. He knew then that the doctor was utilizing dressage techniques, the highest art form of riding in the horse world.

As he watched them move around the arena, Slade scowled. His ex-wife had been a dressage rider, too. It was easy to recognize how quietly Jordana sat, her shoulders back, spine straight, her hands low in front of the saddle. She had the exact same posture. Yet, Slade couldn't draw a comparison between her and his ex-wife. Isabel had been a petulant child who'd used pouting and throwing temper tantrums in order to get what she wanted out of him. Jordana didn't seem fazed by his cold, hard manner. She took it in stride, listened to his orders and then seamlessly executed them. That made him curious about her. The last thing he needed, however, was to be drawn to a woman. He'd been successful the last four years of ignoring the opposite sex. His focus was trying to hold his beleaguered ranch together one month at a time.

"That's good enough," Slade called to her. "Come on in."

Jordana slowed Stormy down and guided her mare over to where Slade was standing. His face looked like stone. What did he think? Was Stormy's conformation good enough? And why was she so drawn to this glacial cowboy? Dismounting, she took the reins over Stormy's head.

"Unsaddle her."

Jordana nodded, dropped the reins and went to lift the stirrup to reach the cinch around the horse's sweaty barrel. She lifted off the saddle and the blanket, settling them across one of the rails of the pipe fence.

"Lead her out to the center of the arena."

Picking up the reins, Jordana walked, and Stormy followed her like a dog at her heels. Jordana turned and stood beside her mare's head. She watched as Slade approached. His gray eyes were narrowed, and she knew he was now critically assessing Stormy.

Crouching beside her, he spoke softly to the mustang before gently laying his hands on the top of her front right leg.

Stormy's ears switched back and forth to the softened male sounds. She stood perfectly still as Slade ran his hands knowingly down the length of her leg. He also examined the health of her hoof.

Shocked at the change in his demeanor, Jordana could only stand there keeping her mouth from dropping open. She watched as Slade's large, scarred hands moved with knowing skill down Stormy's sweaty leg. Hands that moved with such fluid ease that Jordana swore she could feel them caressing her at the same time. Shaking herself out of the shock that Slade wasn't a coldhearted bastard like Paul Edwin had been, she allowed herself to take a deep breath of relief. Slade had a soft side to him after all! Even if he only unveiled and utilized it with horses, that was fine with Jordana. She could take his military-like demeanor if only he treated her horse with loving care. And he was doing just that.

Slade moved quietly around to the other side of the mare. He placed his hands on her other front leg. One never squatted down at the side of a horse's rear. If something spooked them, they could kick out in a semicircle arc and nail the person. Slade had seen people kicked in the head for doing just that. Straightening up, he walked toward her rear legs. He placed his left hand on the animal's rump and then, with his right hand, leaned down and stood close to the mare so she couldn't kick and injure him. In this way, it was safe, and he could continue to perform a thorough examination.

Jordana watched in silence. Slade's calloused hands were sun-darkened from being outside most of his life. Stormy stood quietly. She trusted the large cowboy. More relief filtered through Jordana. After Slade had examined Stormy's legs, he then came to her face and gently moved his fingers around her ears and her poll, the top of her head. Jordana knew he was looking for bumps, scars or cuts. Once more she felt his hands flowing across her. It was a crazy sensation! *What* was it about this hardened cowboy that unstrung her as a woman?

Gulping, Jordana forced herself to remain silent. She knew Slade was tactically memorizing every part of Stormy's conformation. He was building an anatomical picture of her body in his mind. And once he was done, he would have his decision for her. She saw him slide his fingers across the black dorsal stripe down the center of Stormy's back. Mustangs often possessed this stripe. Plus, Stormy had horizontal curved black bars on the back of her lower legs. It made her look somewhat like a long lost relative from the zebra species. But she wasn't. These were genetic markers mustangs carried strongly throughout the breed.

Slade rounded the mare and then stood about six feet away from Dr. Lawton. She looked concerned and serious. He understood why. Seesawing back and forth inwardly, Slade didn't know what to do. Lawton was pretty in a natural kind of way. She had an oval face with a stubborn chin that spoke to her ability to finish what she started. There was no extra flesh on her body that he could see. That meant she was riding daily. Endurance riders put in ten to fifteen miles a day on their horse to keep it in shape for the fifty- and hundred-mile contests. She was a woman, and Slade tried to avoid the opposite sex like a plague. His other students were men. And that's the way he liked it.

"Your mare has a problem," he stated bluntly, drilling her with a hard look. Instantly, her eyes opened wider, and a stunned expression came to her features. He pointed down at the horse's front left

41

leg. "There's scar tissue on her pastern that indicates she's suffered a serious cut in that area at one time."

"But," Jordana said, "that shouldn't stop her from being an endurance horse."

Scowling, Slade said, "That cut was deep. What do you know about it?"

"I've owned Stormy for two years, Mr. McPherson. She had that cut there long before that." Watching his expression, Jordana felt frustrated. All she could see was the glittering shards in his gray eyes. It was obvious he was going to turn her down.

Not if she could help it! "Stormy was captured out in Nevada in a government roundup. She was sold to Bud Hutchinson, who lives here in Jackson Hole. He told me when I bought his house that the mare came with the deal. When I had the vet check her, he noted that scar on her pastern. Bud said the mare came to him with it. The vet thought she probably cut her pastern a year earlier, so no one really knows the extent of that injury."

Grunting, Slade said, "Well, it's her Achilles' heel, Dr. Lawton."

"What about the rest of her conformation?"

"She's sound and she had good legs. But that scar makes her questionable. If she cut a tendon as a yearling out in the wilds, and it healed, that tendon is always going to be weak and suspect of breaking down."

"But you don't *know* if it was a cut tendon," Jordana countered strongly. She wasn't going to let this cowboy run over her.

Shrugging, Slade muttered, "That's true."

"And her legs are fine otherwise?"

"Yes, they're good."

"What else?" Jordana prodded. She saw him scowl, his thick, dark brown brows moving downward in a slash because of her needling. Maybe he was the type of trainer who wanted to see his students have courage to confront him. Maybe he wasn't. She wasn't sure. All Jordana did know is she wanted a chance to train her mare with this man, no matter how sour and antisocial he appeared to be. At least he was gentle with Stormy. Jordana had gone through residency and taken plenty of blows from men who were threatened by her presence as a woman and a doctor. She'd weather Slade McPherson, too.

Surprised at Lawton's sudden backbone and fearlessness to confront him, Slade growled, "The worst strike against her is your horse is a mare."

Mouth dropping open, Jordana snapped it shut. Her hand tightened on the rope.

43

Stormy's ears flicked back and forth as she read her mistress's reaction. "A *mare?* Oh, don't tell me you're one of those people? Mares compete in endurance against geldings and stallions and *win!*"

The power and force of her tempered anger hit Slade directly. Eyes narrowing, he saw the blue fire in her eyes. "Mares are fickle, just like women. They're made up of unstable hormones."

Real anger fired through Jordana. How dare this man! Mouth tightening, she lowered her husky voice. "That's an old saw and it doesn't work anymore, Mr. McPherson. If you're going to turn me down because my horse is a mare, that's a lousy excuse."

Squirming inwardly, Slade realized Dr. Lawton wasn't going to take no for an answer. If he said, "you're a woman and I don't like training women," then she'd explode into rage for sure. "Mares are just more difficult," he snarled. "But it's your choice. I don't really care." And he didn't. His students had gone on to win major endurance rides over the years.

Brows moving up, Jordana said, "Then, you'll accept us for training?"

"You aren't going to get far," Slade warned. "Your mare has a weak pastern due to that old injury. She'll break down before she ever gets to an endurance contest."

Angry, Jordana said, "And I disagree with you."

"Just because you're a doctor of humans doesn't mean you know animal anatomy," Slade reminded her. She really got under his skin, and he recalled Isabel had exhibited that same capability. Grudgingly, Slade admired Jordana because she had fire, passion and wasn't afraid to fight for what she thought was right. Isabel always sneaked around behind him, manipulated him and then pounced. Lawton wasn't like that. In fact, he admired her fearlessness because even men didn't take him on. Slade had one hell of a reputation of winning any argument he chose to defend. And he was losing this one to this banty rooster of a woman with fiery blue eyes and a stubborn chin.

Stormy moved restlessly, and Jordana placed her hand on the mare's damp neck. Instantly, the mustang quieted. "You're correct about that, Mr. McPherson. There is no test that can conclusively show that Stormy partially cut a tendon in her pastern or not. I'm willing to go on faith that she didn't."

"Okay, it's your money and time," he drawled.

"Then, you'll train us?" Hope rose in Jordana's voice. She knew McPherson was going to be a hard, demanding trainer, but she'd endured the toughest job in the world as a resident and made it. She'd make this a success, too.

"I'll take you on, Dr. Lawton. It'll cost you plenty of money. And I don't put up with anyone who's late. You show up on time or I'll send you packing."

"I'll be on time from now on," Jordana gritted, glaring up at him. His rugged features were shadowed by his tan Stetson. There was nothing forgiving about Slade McPherson. In the back of her mind, Jordana wondered what course in life had molded him into such a hard person.

"We'll see," Slade said. "Shorty, my wrangler, will show you to the training barn. You'll be writing me a check today for two thousand dollars. One thousand a month for the box stall, hay, special feed and one thousand for training you ten times a month out here at the ranch."

Two thousand dollars. Jordana blanched inwardly. Two years ago she'd settled the lawsuit against Dr. Paul Edwin. The settlement had been four hundred thousand dollars. Part of the agreement had been that she had to leave her position at the New

York City hospital. Then, the recession occurred, and she'd lost all her stock savings in the crash of the stock market. Jordana had ended up broke and out of a job when it was all over. The settlement money had bought her a home here in Jackson Hole.

Slade watched her waffle, her eyes downcast. He had doubled the cost of his services in hopes of getting rid of her. If he couldn't argue her out of it, then he'd raise his price so high she couldn't afford it. He stood there feeling badly, but he really didn't want to have to teach a woman. They were nothing but trouble.

Mind whirling, Jordana lifted her head and said, "That's fine."

Stunned, Slade kept his face carefully arranged. Two thousand dollars more a month would be a godsend. "Good." He pointed to Shorty who was walking toward them. "Go with my wrangler. He'll assign your mare to a box stall."

Jordana felt dizzy. What had she just done? Two thousand dollars was a lot of money! At what price did she want her dream? And with a man who obviously disliked the fact she was a woman and her horse a mare.

CHAPTER THREE

"This way, Miss," Shorty said, coming up and doffing his head respectfully toward Jordana.

Slade walked away. If he stayed, he'd be staring at Lawton like a lovesick puppy. Her face was arresting. And what drew him, dammit, was her fire and gutsiness. He wondered if that would translate into her endurance riding or not.

Smiling, Jordana held out her hand. "Hi, Shorty, I'm Jordana Lawton. Nice to meet you." She saw Slade walk away as soundlessly as a cougar on the prowl. Disappointed he wouldn't stay around so she could talk more to him about the training, she pulled her attention back to the bow-legged wrangler.

"Howdy, ma'am. Come with me. The Boss has one box stall left in his endurance training facility and your purty steel gray mare gets it." He turned and walked quickly to a pole barn painted the same color of red as the massive barn that sat next to it.

Excited despite the gruff manner of McPherson, Jordana felt a weight lift off from her shoulder. The trainer had tried to get rid of her. *Why?* Stormy was an excellent endurance prospect, in her opinion. Was it because he disliked mares? Or worse, women? She saw no wedding band on Slade's hand. Stormy walked at her side and Jordana decided to find out.

"Shorty, is Mr. McPherson married?"

Chortling, Shorty gave her a sly grin. "No ma'am, he's not. I'm afraid he had a run-in with a filly a while back. He's divorced four years ago and likes to keep it that way."

They walked up the slight gravel slope that led up to the pole barn. Both doors had been slid open to allow maximum air circulation throughout the building. Jordana worked to keep up with the fast walking and talking wrangler. "How long have you been working here, Shorty?"

"Too long," he laughed. Then, getting more serious, he said, "I worked for Mr. McPherson until he was killed by Red Downing, another rancher, in an auto accident. At that time, Slade and Griff, who are fraternal twins, inherited this ranch. But they were too young to take over as six-years-olds. Slade was adopted by his Uncle Paul McPherson and Griff went with Uncle Robert McPherson, who is a Wall Street broker in New York City. When Slade was ten, his adopted mother died of cancer. Then, Paul drank himself to death and he died when Slade was seventeen." Shorty halted at the concrete floor opening to the pole barn. His voice lowered. "At seventeen Slade had to take over this ranch. His brother Griff didn't want anything to do with it. So, he struggled by himself to keep it going."

"That's a lot to ask of any seventeen-year-old," Jordana murmured.

Motioning, Shorty said, "Follow me down the breezeway here. Your mare's stall is the last one on the right," and he pointed toward the other end of the long, clean barn.

Digesting the information about Slade, Jordana set it aside for later. Right now, as Stormy clip-clopped down the concrete aisle, horses on either side nickered in a friendly fashion to her. Jordana counted ten box stalls. She was the last student. Feeling lucky and happy, she followed Shorty.

Each roomy box stall had iron bars across the top half of it and sturdy oak below. Shorty slid the door open. Jordana was pleased to see that not only did the floor have thick black rubber matting to make it easy on a horse's legs, but also fresh cedar shavings were strewn over it. She brought Stormy to the opening and allowed the mare to look around, study and sniff it first. Mustangs were wild, and Jordana knew that Stormy had to check out her new surroundings before she'd ever step into the well-lit box stall. To try and force the mare into it, without giving her time to inspect it, would have been a mistake. Stormy would have balked and fought her instead.

"She's a mighty alert horse," Shorty noted, standing and assessing Stormy.

"Pure mustang," Jordana murmured.

"I can see." Shorty nodded toward her legs. "Got the zebra stripes on her legs. Good sign she's got seriously good mustang genes."

"I agree," Jordana said with a smile. "And her name is Stormy." The mustang stepped into the stall on her own. Following her mare, Jordana slid the door shut and unlatched the rope attached to the mare's red nylon halter. "You want me to leave her halter on, don't you?" she called to the wrangler.

"Yes ma'am."

Stormy moved around sniffing and checking out the shavings. She touched noses with the curious big black horse next door and then went straight for the huge water dispenser located at the front of the stall. The mustang drank deeply and then smacked her wet lips afterward. Laughing, Jordana patted her mare. "You like your new digs, girl."

Shorty slid the door open for Jordana. "She looks purty happy in there. She a beaver?" He shut the door after the owner stepped into the passageway.

A beaver in horse language was a horse that chewed on wood areas of the stall when it was bored. And that could cause wind colic or worse. Jordana knew that in those cases, they would paint the wood with a foul taste that discouraged such a chewing bad habit. "Nope, she has no stall problems."

"Well," Shorty said, "we don't have bored horses around here. The Boss works them every day, and by the time they're done, they're tuckered out and glad for a rest. On the days the students come out to ride their horses, they get a solid workout." He smiled a little and studied the rows of stalls. "Nope, none of these horses have much time to become bored."

"That's good," Jordana said. "Can you tell me the training schedule, Shorty?"

"The Boss didn't?" he asked, surprised.

Shaking her head, Jordana pulled out a small notebook from the back pocket of her jeans and opened it up. "No. And I'd like to know."

"Why, sure you do, ma'am. Let's amble down to the tack room at the other end of the pole barn. You'll be putting your saddle, bridle and tack box in there."

Jordana followed. The wrangler was so different from the owner it was stunning. Shorty was jovial, kind and open. All the things Slade McPherson was not.

"Starting tomorrow, the Boss will have me put Stormy on the hot walker for half an hour."

Mechanical walkers were a must in training. Jordana saw the machine in another nearby corral. It had four long metal arms sticking upward with a thick rope and snap on the end of each one. She knew four horses at a time would be snapped on to each rope and then the speed would be set by the operator. The circular walker looked more like a space vehicle to anyone who didn't know what it was used for. The covered motor was located in the center. The operator could make the horses walk or trot.

"He's not trotting them on it, is he?" Jordana wondered.

"Oh, no, ma'am. It's a fast walk to warm 'em up before they're worked. And he also uses it to cool 'em out after their training. Any fool who thinks they can trot a horse in that tight circle is lookin' for leg problems to develop real fast."

"Yes," she murmured, "I just wanted to make sure, was all."

Shorty slowed and opened the thick oak door. "Endurance horses have the best legs in the world. The Boss isn't interested in harming those legs, only makin' them stronger."

"Good to hear," Jordana said. The tack room was huge, roomy, spotlessly clean and smelled of leather. She loved the scent and inhaled it deeply. There was one hook for a bridle and an aluminum saddle rack suspended just below it. Shorty gestured to it.

"This will be for Stormy's gear." He pointed to a large wooden tack box below it. "Anything your horse needs insofar as brushes, combs, hoof pick and such, goes in here. I'll be puttin' Stormy's name on this box so you can identify it among all the others."

Jordana was impressed with Slade's management abilities. The box stalls had fresh shavings and were obviously cleaned daily. The waterers were automatic and filled as the horse drank it down. In the tack room, there were no cobwebs in the corners, no dust on the thick rubber mats across the floor. All the leather gear was clean, the bits shining, the saddles contained no dust anywhere upon them.

"Now," Shorty said, a bit of warning in his voice, "the Boss don't like dirt. He's a real nitpicker about it." Shorty went over to a specially made endurance saddle that had no horn on it. He lifted up a leather flap on the rear of it. "He expects you to keep your gear in tip-top shape. No dirt, crud or oil between the skirts here. And he'll be inspecting you every day you come out for training. Equally important is the cinch." Shorty picked up the white cotton girth that spanned the horse's belly and kept the saddle in place on its back. "He expects you to not only minutely look at each twisted strand of the girth for dirt or weeds, but also wash it once a week. He *hates* dirty cinches. That dirt can work into the horse's belly and create a sore and inflammation. Something this simple can take an endurance horse out of a contest. Don't disappoint him on this."

"I'm beginning to like him," Jordana said, impressed. She knew a dirty cinch was only asking for trouble. A horse had hair, but any sawing motion could pull it out and leave the horse's tender flesh open to being rubbed raw. And as a doctor, she was always aware of possible infection starting at such a site.

"Oh, he's a stickler," Shorty promised with a lopsided grin. "You'll be spending a lot of time either in here or just outside the door cleaning your gear afterward. He don't want you leaving the premises until you've bathed your horse over at the shower area and then cleaned your leather. Oh, and make *sure* your horse's hooves are clean. If he finds any mud, manure or, worse, a stone lodged in the frog area of the hoof, he'll give you one warning. The second time, he'll release you as a student."

"Got it," Jordana said.

"Crud in the hoof can make a horse lame in a heartbeat."

"Yes, it can. I'm a stickler on that, too."

"Good to hear, ma'am." Shorty scratched his chin. "Okay, let's go over to the bathing area."

Just outside the pole barn and to the left stood another enclosed area. It was painted red and made of an aluminum roof and wooden sides. Shorty led her down a thickly graveled path. He slid the door open. "Now, this is where you will bathe your horse after your training is done. It's got solid rubber matting on the floor so the horse don't slide or skid. We've got panic snaps on the cross ties that will be attached to both sides of your mare's halter."

"I like panic snaps," Jordana agreed, stepping into the shower shed. It too, was well lit. If a horse ever got scared or bolted while in the cross ties, all the owner had to do was jerk the panic snap open, and it instantly released the horse so it didn't choke itself to death in the ropes. These hardy steel snaps had saved many a horse from such an awful and completely preventable death. Yes, panic snaps cost a lot more, and some horse people didn't purchase them because of that. But what was the horse worth to them? For a little more money, they could protect their animal from such a potential fate. Jordana liked that Slade thought of all the details. It was obvious that he cared for the horse in every way possible. Would he care equally about the rider? That remained to be seen.

"Here's the showerhead and hose," Shorty told her, pointing up to the gear hanging on a hook on the right side of the shed. "The Boss doesn't believe in hitting a hot, sweaty horse with shockingly cold water. You'll find the water tepid, instead. He don't want them traumatized with a cold temperature."

"That's impressive," she murmured, deciding that Slade's earlier demeanor didn't carry through in his training philosophy. Maybe he just didn't like her? Jordana frowned and hoped not. Still, he'd been this side of testy and rude to her. Maybe he was having a bad day, she thought.

Shorty gestured for her to follow him out. "The Boss treats his horses like himself."

Jordana liked the warmth of the early July sun overhead. Having spent two winters in Jackson Hole, she had come to welcome the summer as never before. There was snow on the ground eight months out of the year. That was the part she didn't like. When spring came, however, there was no place on earth as beautiful as this valley and the dragon's teeth of the Tetons thrusting up out of the prairie.

"Now," Shorty said, walking toward the huge rectangular corral, "the Boss will be riding your mare daily in here. It's got two feet of fine sand as a base. That keeps your horse from pulling a muscle or, worse, a ligament or tendon. He's going to be seeing what her strengths and weaknesses are this next week."

"You mean he does all the riding?" Jordana was surprised. That meant ten horses a day were ridden. "I thought he had help."

"No ma'am, he does it all himself."

"No wonder he was upset with me arriving late."

Shorty grinned. "Time's money."

Nodding, Jordana now understood his frosty stance. "How long does he ride the horse?"

"Depends. At first, he's not going to push your mare. He's gonna see how she does at a walk, trot and canter. Might be on her for thirty minutes at the most, depending upon how built up she is or not."

"I've been riding Stormy ten to fifteen miles every third day. He will want to know that."

"Yep, he will. But when you come out the next time, he'll cover all that with you. The Boss can tell how in shape or not your horse is by merely examining it and watching it work."

That was true, Jordana decided. And Slade's gray eyes had missed nothing. He was handsome in a rugged kind of way. She liked his full mouth even though it had been thinned with displeasure talking to her. His nose was strong-looking and had a bump at the root of it, telling her he'd broken it some time earlier in his life. She'd liked his broad, square face, his skin burned brown by being out in the sun so much, the creases at the corners of his eyes deep. Was that from squinting in the bright, white snow or sun? Or were they laughter lines? Jordana highly doubted Slade had any humor in his bones. Not once had he cracked even a slight smile toward her. No, he wasn't Mr. Social, that was for sure.

"Oh," Shorty said, "you need to know that the Boss will *not* allow a rider to wear spurs or carry a whip."

"Not a problem. I don't do either."

"That's good because the Boss believes that if the horse and rider have a good rapport with one another, you can get all the speed out of the animal because it trusts you. Don't *ever* be seen carrying a crop. He'll kick you out of here so fast it'll make your head spin."

Laughing, Jordana held up her hands. "Not to worry. Stormy *hates* crops. In fact, when I bought her from Bud two years ago, he told me she was combative if she even *saw* a crop. He thinks the BLM cowboys used whips to get her into a corral. No, Stormy hates crops."

"The Boss will want to know that."

"Good."

Shorty walked her back to the truck. "I'll help you bring in all your gear to the tack room and then you can leave."

"Thanks for the help," she said, appreciating the wrangler. Looking around the large operation, Jordana didn't see McPherson. The robins were singing in the oak and maple trees that surrounded the one-story ranch house in the distance. There was no lawn, and it looked pretty shabby in comparison to the spotless pole barn and showering shed. Maybe being a single male was the reason. Jordana would have put in a small lawn, flower boxes on the front windows and a small white picket fence around it. A woman's touch. But this hard cowboy wasn't much for decoration. At least he cared for his endurance horses. And that was all that counted in her book.

"Now, you need to write out a check for the first month's rent and training," Shorty reminded her.

"As soon as I get the tack put away, I will," Jordana promised him, opening up the trailer door to remove the saddle and bridle.

Driving away from Tetons Ranch, Jordana felt happier than she had in two years. Hands firmly on the steering wheel of her three-quarter ton truck that hauled the empty horse trailer, she drove out just as slowly as she had come in. Maybe McPherson had a tractor stowed away somewhere and would get Shorty out here to blade it flat once more.

The sky was a bright blue. The sunlight made the Tetons mountain range west of her look tall, rugged and beautiful. By early July, the last of the snow was almost gone until September, when it would once more become a white cloak around each of the sharp, pointed peaks. Her mind ranged over the price of the training. As a physician, she made good money. Her savings was now gone. She'd spent it buying a house at the edge of town. Two thousand dollars a month for training was going to stretch her in a way she hadn't counted on. Jordana wanted to put money back into savings, but this training fee wouldn't allow it.

Grimacing, she slowed at the stop sign that would take her to the highway. Turning left, she drove back toward Jackson Hole. If she'd gone right, she'd be heading into Yellowstone National Park about forty miles away.

Between her clinic and working part-time at the hospital, Jordana made ends meet. Now, with two thousand going out a month, she was hamstrung. Yet, all her life she'd loved horses, and endurance riding had always been her outlet. Could she give that up? Was it too expensive to follow her dream of having the best trainer in the United States train her and Stormy? Jordana waffled, unsure.

Slade McPherson was challenging, to say the least to her. But he'd been gentle with Stormy. How would he treat her? A horse trainer didn't always transition well from animal to human. She'd had some bad experiences with horse trainers before. Yet, if Jordana was honest with herself, she'd been *drawn* to the iconic cowboy. That made *no* sense at all to her! Yet, she couldn't help but look at his mouth and wonder what it would be like to be kissed by this hard man who braved nature without a second thought. And as he'd run his hands lightly and gently down Stormy's legs, Jordana swore she could feel those rough, calloused hands exploring her at the same time.

"Phew!" she muttered. "This is crazy!"

Was it? What adventures waited for her two days from now when she began her first lesson on Stormy with tough Slade McPherson?

CHAPTER FOUR

Jordana tried to calm her nerves as she rode Stormy out into the huge rectangular arena where Slade McPherson stood. Her heart wouldn't settle down. It was July 3rd, the late afternoon sky filled with threatening clouds. As she looked toward the ragged-edge Tetons, she saw a massive thunderstorm over their sharp peaks. It might come their way if it was strong enough. The wind was up, and Stormy was more alert.

Today was the first day of her training with the implacable McPherson. Why had she had two dreams in a row about this hard-looking cowboy? As Jordana pressed her calf into Stormy's side to make the turn into the sandy arena, she had mixed feelings. Wasn't it enough she was working twelve hours a day either at her clinic or the hospital? Since the settling of the lawsuit, she had no desire to get entangled with a man. She was still too raw from the experience, the trauma of the move west and trying to get some sanity back into her life.

"Take her at a walk around the arena to the left," Slade ordered, his voice carrying across the distance.

Nodding, Jordana took in a deep breath and tried to relax. She knew that Slade was going to be damn tough on her. Stormy had already had two daily workouts. The mustang mare seemed completely oblivious to her anxious state, just plodding along on a loose rein.

"Quit slouching," he called. "Straighten up."

Instantly, Jordana took the bow out of her back, squared her shoulders and lifted her chin slightly. Quirking her mouth, she wondered if McPherson was going to always yell at what she did wrong, but offer no praise for what she had done right. Many trainers were like that, she'd discovered. If she didn't have confidence built up over years of being a resident, she might wither away under such an unfair training system. At two thousand dollars a month, Jordana wasn't going to let his snappish orders scare her away.

Slade eyed the pair as they walked around the arena in a relaxed fashion. He tried to keep his eyes off Jordana, but that was impossible. His job was to see how she rode, how she sat in the saddle and how she handled her horse. He'd been dreading this moment for days. Having a woman among his male students was like a thorn in his side. He didn't want her or her runt of a mare, but he needed her money. Guilt niggled at him. Jordana was sincere in contrast to his greediness. Slade didn't like that about himself. She had come to him honestly. So what did that make him?

Not looking at the answer too closely, he enjoyed watching her lower body move in sync with the horse. Wearing jeans, boots and a dark green tee, she was all woman. Curvy in all the right places, Jordana was a fit athlete. "How long you been riding in endurance events?" he asked.

"Two years," she called.

Grunting, Slade nodded. "Slow trot," he ordered.

Pressing her calves to Stormy, Jordana felt the mustang mare instantly obey. Although a small horse, Stormy had long legs. Jordana posted, which meant she lifted her butt off the saddle with every other stride of the animal. That resulted in less pounding on her mare's back. She knew it was the English way of riding a horse. The western style was to sit the trot and flow with the horse.

"Sit the trot," he called.

Grimacing, Jordana did. She hated not being able to post. After going halfway around the arena, she called, "I'd rather post. It's easier on the horse's back."

"Sit the trot."

Growling to herself, Jordana complied. It took a lot of work to keep her legs against the horse, her thighs strong and clamped solidly to the saddle and horse. If she hadn't done so, she'd be bouncing and flying all over the place. Was he testing her strength? Was that what this was all about? The wind sang through her hair. Lifting her hand, she pulled the black baseball cap a little lower over her brow. The wind would pull it off if she didn't.

"Do a series of figure eights at a sitting trot."

Jordana knew without a doubt he was seeing just how much strength and control she had over Stormy. A figure eight required her to do a circle over one half of the arena and, once they trotted down the center of it, to turn the other way and complete the second circle. This was easy stuff for her. Stormy wasn't breathing hard at all, her ears flicking back and forth. When her ears moved back, she was listening to Jordana's silent leg, weight or hand signals.

"Canter the figure eight," Slade ordered, his deep voice carrying strongly across the wide expanse. Whether he wanted to admit it or not, Jordana had a lot of good riding habits. It grated that she was using dressage, but that was only because Isabel had been a dressage rider. A well-trained horse became fine tuned with dressage training, and it wasn't a bad thing to have in an endurance horse. There would be times that Jordana would have to use her weight or legs in tight places. Why the hell was he aching to kiss this woman? Slade hadn't liked his dreams of the past two nights. Both involved kissing this doctor, who exuded quiet confidence. *No way. Just no way. Keep it impersonal,* he ordered himself.

"Go the other direction now," he called.

By the time he ordered her into the center of the arena to rest, Jordana was feeling the intense workout. She halted Stormy in front of him and dropped the reins to allow her mare to lower her head and rest, too.

Slade studied Jordana's face. He had a tough time seeing her as a physician. She just didn't look like the type. Moving to the horse, he thrust two fingers beneath the horse's cinch. It was tight but not too tight.

She was so close. He liked her long legs and the way her firm thighs curved against the horse.

"Why don't you let me post?" Jordana demanded. "It's easier on my horse's back and it also allows me to rest between beats."

Slade stared up into her narrowed blue eyes. She was tough, but then, in endurance riding, that was a good trait. "I wanted to see how your mare took to it."

Surprised, Jordana said, "Oh . . ." She hadn't thought about that.

"You can go back to posting. It's not a bad thing to do on fifty- and hundred-milers. It saves your horse's back and it also allows you to rest a bit between strides, too — like you said."

"Good," Jordana whispered, suddenly smiling with relief. She leaned forward and threaded Stormy's thick black mane through her fingers. The mare's ears flicked.

Her hands were beautiful, Slade realized as he stood near the shoulder of the horse. Jordana's rhythmic movements reminded him of water flowing gracefully in and around rocks. There was a slight sheen of perspiration across her brow as she pushed the brim of the black baseball cap upward. And her smile melted him in a way he could never have fathomed. *What* was it about this woman that made him feel like putty?

"Several things," he growled. "All mustangs came from Spaniards' horses who escaped from them when they came up here in the 1500s. The conquistador leaders had part-Arabian mounts bred with local horses in Spain. They were known as Spanish barbs and that's what your mare is." Slade studied Stormy's fine head. "She even has the slightly dished face of an Arabian."

Jordana nodded. "And she possesses that long, elastic trot of an Arab, too, but I'm sure you already saw that." After all, he'd ridden Stormy two days in a row.

Nodding, Slade found himself enjoying Jordana's knowledge. She knew her mustang well. "Yes, and that's what will make your mare a potential winner. Arabians are the only breed with the extended trot where they naturally float, all four feet off the ground." He held his hands up to demonstrate. "All other breeds have an extended trot, too, but they don't float a foot or two further with each stride when all four hooves are off the ground, like an Arab or mustang can. And it's that one to two feet of float above the ground that gives Stormy a stride advantage. She can take on horses that are fifteen and sixteen hands high and still match their stride. The taller horses have longer legs, therefore, a longer stride. Mustangs and Arabians, however, compensate with this genetic gift only they have."

"And that's why," Jordana told him, "so many Arabian and part-Arabians win the major endurance contests."

Nodding, he said, "Right."

"And Thor, your mustang stud, has the same type of stride. I've seen video on the internet of him when you've got him in the extended trot. He's magnificent."

Pleased by the sudden passion in her husky voice and the enthusiasm burning in her eyes, Slade privately arched a little over her praise. It struck him in that moment that he really had missed the soft warmth of a woman around him. There had been times when Isabel had been like that with him, but not very often. Scowling, Slade said, "Thor has won every major endurance event."

Relaxing in the saddle, Jordana brought her leg up and over the saddle. "You and Curt Downing, who owns that black Arabian stallion, are always trading for first or second. I can't tell you how many times you gave us an exciting finish."

Mouth tightening, Slade snarled, "Downing is a sonofabitch and I don't want to talk about him." He held on to his simmering

71

anger. Seeing the shock register on Jordana's face, he added, "Whether you know it or not, Downing is a cheat and up to no good out on the trail when judges and spectators don't see him."

"What do you mean?" Jordana asked, confused. She saw anger come to his narrow eyes. This time, Slade was real easy to read. She was beginning to realize when his full mouth was thinned, he was upset about something. And the way his brown brows slashed downward, it was easy to see he was furious. With her? Jordana hoped not.

"Downing has no honor out on the trail," Slade gritted out. "We've got the fifty-mile Tetons Endurance ride coming up on September 1st. He'll be there and so will I."

"What do you mean no honor?"

Studying her innocent face, Slade said, "You've been in endurance races?"

"Sure, many, but they were fifty-milers was all, and I was small stuff compared to the pros who rode their horses."

"Did you ever see anyone strike a horse and rider with a crop? Crowd them off a narrow trail?"

"Why . . . no," she admitted. "Is that what Downing does?"

Giving her a sour look, Slade said, "Oh, yeah, and worse."

"You know this from personal experience?"

"I do," he said in a clipped voice. "And so do a lot of the other pros who ride the top endurance circuit."

"If Downing is as bad as you say he is, how come he's never been caught doing these things?" she demanded. Jordana knew that the ranch next to Slade's was owned by the Downing family. Was this a local dust-up? Two arrogant endurance champions who couldn't stand one another from a competitive sense?

"Believe me, there's plenty of endurance riders just waiting to catch him in the act. Once it gets beyond the 'he said-she said' and we've got cell phone photo proof, he'll be booted out once and for all. Until that happens, it's one person's word against another and the judges can't move on that. Downing does his dirty work in areas where there are no prying eyes of spectators or judges."

Jordana felt the anger in Slade. "I never realized that went on. All the contests I've ridden on, the riders were respectful and followed the rules."

Giving her a quirked grin, Slade said, "There's *always* a bad apple in every group. Downing is it. And you might as well know it because if you're going to ride on the national circuit, you'll be meeting him at every one of those endurance events."

Shivering, Jordana ran her hand down her arm feeling the goose bumps Slade's harsh words created. "I just can't believe it."

Whipping his gaze upward, Slade met and held her innocent-looking blue eyes. "You won't have much to worry about. Your mare will never be able to keep up with his black stud or Thor."

"We'll see about that," Jordana said, keeping her voice light. She saw the steel glint in Slade's eyes. God help her, but she thought he was the most handsome man she'd ever seen. He wasn't pretty boy handsome. He was a man's man from the rugged cut of his sunburned features to the way he stood, walked and held himself. Despite his constant grumpiness toward her, Jordana allowed herself to at least appreciate him on purely a woman's level. The words "eye candy" came to mind. Despite his outer armored toughness, she'd seen him deal gently with her horse. There was good somewhere deep down in this Wyoming cowboy. And inwardly, Jordana promised herself she'd find it. Not sure how, she kept that secret to herself.

"Enough talking," Slade muttered. "Let's

repeat the gaits and figure eight in the other direction."

"May I post this time?" she asked, smiling down at him. She saw his face thaw for an instant. And just as quickly become hardened. So, a warm smile got to him? Well, that was good to know. Maybe just being friendly was all she had to do around him. Jordana wanted a less acerbic teaching relationship with Slade. She saw enough irritable and angry people in the emergency room of the hospital. She didn't need it out here, too.

"Post," he agreed, gesturing for her to get out in the arena once more.

Later, after an hour's worth of working Stormy in the arena, Jordana walked at Slade's side as she led her mare back to the stall area to be unsaddled. The sun's light was more westerly now, the thunderclouds approaching the valley beneath the slopes of the Tetons. The wind was picking up, too. "Looks like we're going to get that thunderstorm," she said, wanting to see if he would make small talk.

Grunting, Slade gave her a brisk nod.

Ouch. Undaunted, Jordana said, "When I was in residency at a New York City hospital, I always loved the storms that came during the summer. It cooled the city down for a little bit."

Staring at her, Slade almost stopped. "You're from New York City?"

She heard the stunned disbelief in his tone. Why was he looking at her suddenly as if she was an alien from another planet? "Yes, I was born and raised there. Why?"

Clamping down on an expletive, Slade said instead, "You're a city slicker."

"That sounds like a curse," Jordana teased lightly, taken aback by his scowl. Slowing up, she dropped Stormy's reins just outside the tack room. Stormy had been taught to ground tie. When the reins dropped to the ground, she was to stand and not move. Jordana eased the flap of her saddle upward to reach the cinch.

Slade stood uncertainly, his mind whirling. Isabel had been from that same damned city, a spoiled brat pouting all the time when she didn't get her way. She would throw a temper tantrum like a young horse who was saddled for the first time. And yet, as he watched Jordana release the cinch and unbuckle the breastplate around Stormy's chest, he couldn't help but stop the comparison. This woman was confident, mature and had a quick, easy smile that automatically felt as if her hands were smoothing down his irritable nature just as he'd touch a horse to calm it.

"Well?" Jordana prodded, smiling as she walked past him with the saddle in her arms, "am I a damned city slicker in your eyes?"

Bristling, Slade opened the tack room door for her. "It explains why you post. East Coast riders are taught English riding and not Western-style riding." It wasn't a lie. He just didn't want to get into the painful and private parts of his divorce with Jordana. Oddly, as Slade watched her put the saddle over the aluminum rack on the oak wall, he thought Jordana might not only understand, but be sympathetic toward him. Isabel had taken him for everything. He'd lost so much in the divorce.

Jordana would clean her gear later. Right now, Stormy was wet and sweaty and needed to bathed over at the shower barn. "Guilty on all counts," she said, walking past him.

"Were you always around horses?" he wondered, walking with her to the shower barn.

"My father is a cardiac surgeon and my mother was an Olympic dressage champion. I feel like I got the best genes from both of them," she told him, a warm feeling in her heart for her parents.

"They still live in New York City?" Slade liked talking with her a lot more than he thought he would. He saw her smile dissolve and her features become sad.

"They died in an airplane crash five years ago."

"I'm sorry," Slade muttered, meaning it.

"So am I," Jordana said quietly. She halted at the showering area. Dropping the halter lead, she slid the door open. Mustering a slight smile, she picked up the lead and asked Slade, "What about your parents? Do they live nearby? I've never seen anyone but you and Shorty here at the ranch."

As Slade watched her lead Stormy into the shower stall and put the cross ties on her mare's halter, he found himself wanting to tell her the truth. Walking around the horse and staying far enough away from getting splattered with water, he said, "Red Downing, who was Curt Downing's father, crashed into my parents' truck. They died instantly. He was drunker than a skunk."

Jordana froze when she heard his words hesitantly tear out of him. Looking over, she saw pain in Slade's face. For the first time, he'd unveiled his armor and she got to see the human in him. There was such grief in his eyes it tore at her heart.

"I'm so sorry, Slade. I really am. How

tragic . . ."

"Yeah, it was. In more ways than one," he muttered, crossing his arms. Leaning against the wall as she began to use the shower hose to wet Stormy down, he added, "Me and my fraternal twin brother, Griff, were orphaned at six years old. My parents had left us the ranch in their will, but we were too young to run it. My dad had two older brothers, Paul and Robert. Griff moved back east with Uncle Robert. I stayed out here with Uncle Paul and Aunt Patty. Together, they took over the running of our ranch."

Jordana took a plastic brush and began gently scrubbing Stormy's neck. She stood quietly, appreciating the tepid water. Looking over her back, Jordana realized that Slade was this way because of the early loss of his parents. She tried to put herself in his place. Wouldn't she toughen up, too? Would the world look scary and uncertain to Slade and his brother? *Very.* Gently, she asked, "Is your brother Griff also an endurance rider?" She had never seen him on the circuit.

Giving her a jaded look, Slade felt helpless to stop from telling her about his painful past. "No. Griff went back to New York City with Uncle Robert and his wife. He's never cared about the ranch."

"Ah, this is where city slicker comes in?" she teased softly and added a smile. Slade's face went dark, and he refused to meet her gaze. *Oops.* She'd said the wrong thing. Scrubbing Stormy's withers with a soft rubber brush where the saddle sat, Jordana made sure to get all the grit and dust washed off her because it could cause inflammation and create a saddle sore if she didn't.

Battling his sudden emotions that rose unexpectedly within him, Slade muttered, "My younger brother is a Wall Street broker. He got sent to Harvard and has an MBA. He followed in my Uncle Robert's footsteps."

"I see," Jordana said, moving the brush and the water down the center of Stormy's gray back. "Does he visit often?"

Shaking his head, Slade said, "Griff is a city slicker. He likes the east, the big money he makes, the power he has, the women who like to follow the money trail. He doesn't have time for our family's ranch."

The hurt was so evident that Jordana couldn't shield herself from his sadness. All of a sudden, she wanted to drop the brush and shower wand, run over to Slade and throw her arms around him. In that split second, he looked like the grief-stricken six-year-old who had had his family suddenly torn away from him. Privileged to see the real man, Jordana stood there unable to say or do anything. She couldn't run over and embrace him. What Slade needed was to be held, rocked, nurtured and kept safe. Now, she was seeing a little of how he saw life. It was a hard life. It took those he loved away from him. And speaking about his brother tore away a new scab that hadn't really healed at all. Moistening her lips, Jordana said, "Sometimes, life is harsh."

He snorted, allowed his arms to fall to his side and glared at her. Scared that he'd opened up to this woman, who was really a stranger to him, had him feeling uneasy. "That's right. It *always* is. I'll see you in three days."

Watching Slade leave, Jordana saw how quickly he closed up once more. His eyes, however, couldn't lie. She saw such anguish in them that it made her want to cry. And he would *never* allow her close to him. Like the hurt animal he was, he'd bite any-one's hand offering help. Sighing, she continued to scrub Stormy free of sweat and dust. The first clap of thunder rolled across the land. Looking up, she saw the churning gray and black clouds racing down upon the valley. Soon, it would pour rain in buckets. Was the sky already crying for the pain that Slade McPherson carried daily within him? No parents were here to love and guide him. No one to help him grow up safe and nurtured. No wonder he was a loner. . . .

CHAPTER FIVE

As Jordana drove into the training facility, her heart leaped with surprise. There was Slade and Thor, the most famous endurance horse in the country. She wasn't sure who was more masculine, proud and aloof: the stud or the man. Smiling with excitement, she forgot about the stress of hurrying out to Tetons Ranch to arrive on time. As a physician she had unexpected emergencies that she had to attend to before anything else. Jordana lived in continued anxiety that one day, she might be late. Slade wouldn't tolerate tardiness.

Climbing out of her truck, she grinned. "Hey, seeing Thor in person, instead of in a photo, is astounding!" Thor had a "cap" of chestnut color splotched across his head and ears. That was known as a medicine hat pattern. Native Americans considered such a horse as powerful, protective and lucky. Thor had sky blue eyes, and Jordana knew it made him even more rare and beautiful. His white hair covered part of his face along with chestnut markings down to his pink-colored muzzle and wide, flaring nostrils.

Pride flowed through Slade. His stallion snorted, his chestnut-colored ears flicking as Jordana approached. The hot July sun beat down on them. "Get Stormy saddled up," he ordered. "We're going on a fifteen-mile run."

Shocked, Jordana halted. "Really?"

Giving her a sliver of a one-sided smile, Slade said, "You brought your mare to me in top shape. Shorty said you were riding her fifteen miles twice a week. She's ready for this."

Swallowing her shock and pleasure, Jordana said, "I'll be right there!" She trotted up to the training barn, her heart soaring with joy. Stormy greeted her with a friendly nicker as she walked down to the end box stall. As she placed her mare in the cross ties to be brushed and saddled, Jordana felt hopeful. Ever since meeting Slade, her days had taken on a new brightness and hope. Not wanting to look at that aspect too closely, Jordana told herself she was drawn to the cowboy because of his rugged good looks and that was all. Clearly, Slade had no women around here.

As she hurried to the tack room and picked up the thick pad and saddle, Jordana recalled talking to one of her patients who knew Slade. Tracy Border, a thirty-year-old mother of two who was trying to lose weight, had said Slade was called The Loner. That his wreck of a divorce had all but put his ranch into teetering foreclosure with the local bank. Further, Slade had been married to a brat of a woman who had no maturity. With that information, Jordana could understand why Slade was anti-female. He had to have time to get over a divorce.

The sweet smell of alfalfa hay wafted through the barn. Inhaling the scent, Jordana often wished that some perfume company would make the fragrance. She'd wear it for sure!

Releasing Stormy from the ties, she quickly placed the hackamore on her mare, clucked to her to follow and hurried out of the facility. Slade was already mounted on the restive, powerful-looking Thor. Jordana knew that the Native Americans felt the medicine hat pattern, that was sometimes found on paint or pinto mustangs, was powerful. In fact, war chiefs often coveted such beautifully marked mustangs because they were considered the ultimate, coura-

geous warhorses. Thor was pawing the
ground, anxious to get on with the ride. He
stood fifteen hands tall, which was rare for
a mustang. Most were very small in comparison. His white body was splattered with
chestnut markings that made her think of
an artist carelessly throwing paint here and
there across his athletic body. She liked the
mixing of white and chestnut on his long,
flowing mane and tail.

"I'm ready," she called, grinning.

Warmth flowed through Slade as he sat
relaxed on his stallion. "Mount up," he told
her. For a stolen moment, Slade watched
like a starving wolf as Jordana easily vaulted
up into her specially made endurance
saddle. Today she wore a bright pink tee, a
beat-up black baseball cap and jeans. Her
curves called to him, and Slade had to tear
his gaze from her small breasts. Jordana's
cheeks were red, and he'd come to realize
when she was excited, they colored to mir-
ror her happiness.

Squeezing her calves against Stormy's
sleek gray barrel, she rode up and paralleled
Slade. "What now?"

Lifting his hand, he said, "We'll take the
path between the pastures. At the end of it,
we'll go left and then we'll be on Elkhorn
Ranch property. Iris Mason gave me permis-

sion years ago to utilize her large ranch land to train my endurance horses. I only have fifty acres, which isn't enough to toughen up an endurance prospect. On her property, there's hills, slopes of mountains as well as flat areas. We need all those to challenge the horse and get him . . . her . . . up to speed."

"What a wonderful gift Iris gave to you!"

He nodded and brought the brim of his Stetson down more securely on his head. "She's the matriarch of this valley and has a good heart. When I went to her and asked for her permission, she gave it right away. And she didn't ask for any money. That's the kind of person she is." Slade was grateful that Iris hadn't demanded money for the use of her land. She could have but knew, as every other rancher did in this valley, he was nearly penniless. Iris helped out those who had less, and he was thankful for her kindness.

"I hear Iris is marrying Professor Timothy Varden from Harvard," she said.

Nodding, Slade thought of the invite he'd just received to the event. "Yes, she's in her eighties but she fell hard for the guy." And secretly, Slade was happy for Iris. She was one of the stalwart leaders in the valley.

"One of my patients told me about her yesterday. I don't think anyone dislikes Iris."

"She's special."

"I heard that Senator Peyton was convicted and going to prison. I met Clarissa Peyton the other day over at Gwen Garner's quilt shop. After Gwen told me what had happened, I felt very sorry for the woman."

"Yeah, it's been rough on Clarissa. Matt Sinclaire was his target. This year it's been a mix of good, sad and bad news."

"I met Rachel Cantrell at a luncheon," Jordana said with a wispy smile. "She and Matt just got engaged. They're going to get married at Christmas. Matt felt that his daughter, Megan, would have the terrible memory of her mother killed in that arson fire erased by the happy one."

"Matt has gone through hell," Slade agreed, grim. The firefighter has lost Bev, his wife and almost lost his daughter Megan to Senator Peyton's attempt to kill them. "I like Rachel a lot. And Megan is speaking up a storm now. After the fire, she went mute. And it wasn't until of late she started talking again."

"I think it was due to Rachel," she confided. Slade's face had softened and he was reflective. Jordana knew that this valley's people were very close, and all had connections with one another like a larger family.

"I do, too. Megan calls her Mommy now

and I think they'll have a happy ending. Matt certainly deserves a break after all this hell he's gone through."

Nodding, she added, "I suppose you hear most of the town gossip? That Zach Mason, Iris's grandson, has been caught driving drugs to and from Cheyenne with a gang? I'll bet Iris is heartbroken."

"There's not much I don't hear," Slade drawled. "And Zach's mother, Allison Mason, was just convicted of trying to murder her stepdaughter. Good thing she didn't succeed, but her son Zach, swore vengeance."

"I heard from another patient that Zach has been in drugs for a long time."

"That's true," Slade said, running his fingers through Thor's silky white-and-chestnut mane. "I'm more worried about the sister, Reagan. She had a real career ahead of her in movie directing but she's sat tight here after the conviction. Word's out that she's going to get even with Kam, the woman her mother tried to murder."

Sighing, Jordana said, "That's what Gwen Garner said. My heart breaks for those two kids. Why didn't Allison Mason think about them before she tried this harebrained scheme to kill Kam Mason?"

Shrugging, Slade said, "People do funny

things when they're threatened." Hadn't he? After Isabel had left him, he'd turned into an angry bull, much like Diablo. Human feelings were tough to control sometimes. He lifted out of his thoughts and said, "I want you to take off in front of me. Walk Stormy to warm her up until we hit that left turn. Then, I want you to do a slow trot. At all times, I'll be behind you. I want to size up your mare on the different geological areas and see how she reacts."

"Okay," Jordana said, feeling her heart swell with a fierce affection for the taciturn cowboy. "I was doing the same type of riding in the south Jackson Hole area."

"I'm familiar with where you worked her," Slade said. "But this has more altitude, is rockier and is far more challenging. If you want Stormy to compete in the top tier, she has to not only take this type of terrain on, but excel at it. Today is a test run. We'll see how she does." He didn't say he'd also be watching how Jordana rode and negotiated the coming demands. As on every endurance ride, the rider never knew what was coming next. He'd get to see how Jordana "talked" to her mare and how the horse responded.

Nodding, Jordana smiled and said, "Okay, we're off to our first adventure with you!"

She walked Stormy past the impatient Thor. The stallion was in magnificent shape. Jordana knew that Thor was the past winner of the Tetons fifty-mile endurance ride. And he was signed up to run it in early September.

Stormy was hard-pressed to just walk. Like any well-trained athlete, she found walking boring. She pranced and danced sideways as they made their way between the two huge cattle pastures. On her right she saw a massive one-ton bull, Diablo, who was alone and looking forlornly across to the other pasture where his ladies were. In the other pasture, the calves had been separated from their mamas, and they were now fattening up on the lush Wyoming grass.

Slade liked the power of Thor as he rode. The stallion was competitive just like him, and he didn't like walking behind Stormy. Chomping at the bit, the stallion tossed his head, his long, thick mane flying like a banner in the breeze. At the corner, he watched Jordana give Stormy a leg signal to make the turn. And then, the gray mare broke into a slow trot. Thor lunged, partly reared and fought the bit.

"Easy," Slade murmured, sliding his gloved hand down the stallion's tightly arched neck. "You'll get to run here shortly."

Snorting violently, Thor pranced as he made the turn. Slade was pleased to see that Jordana was keeping Stormy at a slow trot instead of a fast one. It was so important to warm up an endurance horse the right way. Humans had to do stretches in order to limber up and get more blood into their bodies to face the demanding tasks that would be asked of them. Horses were no different. However, a highly trained and competitive endurance horse *hated* walking. They would much rather move into a ground eating trot. A horse could pull a muscle, ligament or tendon if not warmed up properly for the coming demanding distances.

Once they rode past the gate and shut it behind them, Slade told her, "See this trail? It leads up to two steep hills about five miles away. I want you to ride at an extended trot. Float her if you can. Tactics in top competition is to get your horse into any flat area where they can hit maximum stride. This is where riders can make up lost time that they'll encounter in hills or mountainous or steep areas."

Jordana rode next to the impatient Thor. "And then I'll be at those twin hills. What then?"

"There's a path up the first one. Follow it up and down to the second hill. Go up and over the second hill, then, turn left. The trail is flat for two miles. Open her up to a controlled canter. Nothing out of control. I need to see how winded she's become."

Patting Stormy's neck, Jordana said, "I think she'll sail through these challenges without a problem."

Grunting, Slade muttered, "We'll see."

Taking the gauntlet being thrown down at her, Jordana grinned. "Competition is my middle name."

Giving her a sour grin in return, Slade liked the blue fire dancing in her eyes. Her shoulder-length black hair was mussed around her face and neck. The urge to reach out and tame some of those reddish strands mixed with black ones nearly overwhelmed him. He couldn't touch Jordana. He didn't *dare.* Her winsome smile, the joy in her expression all served to make Slade happy. For the first time in so many years, he'd forgotten what that emotion felt like. What *was* it about this feisty upstart of a woman that took him on? Slade realized Jordana had never flirted with him. No, she was all business and professional. *Arm's length.* Sadness rolled through him. Maybe it was just as well, Slade acknowledged. He was in no position to think about a relationship. His whole focus was on saving his ranch from foreclosure.

Taking out a stopwatch from the leather vest he wore over his white cowboy shirt, he said, "Okay, take off. I'll be timing you."

Jordana gave him an evil grin. "Okay, we're off! Watch us fly!" and she asked Stormy to move into an immediate trot.

Slade smiled reluctantly as she moved her small mustang down the trail. In moments, Jordana had the horse in that elastic, floating trot that only Arabians could manage for miles on end. Giving his restive stallion a nudge with his heels, Slade let Thor eagerly take off in pursuit. He did not like being second to anyone and fought the bit.

Jordana moved in sync with her mare as she continued for five miles at a floating trot. It was a hard trot to ride well. Lucky for her, her thighs had been molded by fifty-mile rides for the past year, so it wasn't much of an effort for her. Just knowing Slade was behind her made her smile for no reason. Her focus was on the terrain up in front of them. When they hit the first steep, forested hill, Stormy lunged easily up the dirt path. She moved into a walk to a regular trot when the landscape allowed it. The area was strewn with fallen logs and branches from the surrounding trees. Stormy easily leaped over them. Never once did she balk, skid to a stop and refuse to jump. Jordana knew that the top endurance horses were fearless and would attempt to jump without balking. She patted Stormy's wet, gleaming neck as they trotted down and across to the next hill.

As she leaned back in the saddle as Stormy skidded down the second steep slope, Jordana laughed out loud. The warmth of the July day, the strong scent of pine in the air, the wind moving past her face all conspired to give her a sense of freedom she loved so much. At the base of the hill, she leaned forward, and Stormy immediately broke into a controlled canter. For the next two miles, they were on flat but uneven ground. Ahead of her, she saw the slope of another mountain. This one would be different. Jordana knew that trees that had been cut down, their stumps thrusting warningly aboveground, were a special hazard to a fast moving horse and rider.

She had expected Slade to stop her at the slope, but he remained behind her. *Okay, no problem.* She urged Stormy up the steep, twisting trail. Rocks were here and there, and the mustang expertly stepped over and around them. Stumps were always a special danger. Forest rangers or timber companies had come in and cut the pines down and left the stumps sticking up like spears ready to dig into her horse's fine, thin legs. Stormy was at a trot, lunging upward, always alert, but Jordana had to be, too. She couldn't just rely on her mare to see these dangerous obstacles coming up.

Giving Stormy her head, laying the reins on the horse's neck, Jordana leaned forward over the withers to keep her mustang balanced as she negotiated the ever-curving, twisting, uphill trail. Stormy was breathing hard as they moved from sixty-five hundred feet in altitude to nearly nine thousand feet.

The trail was tricky, challenging and dangerous. Jordana forgot that Slade was behind and timing her. She'd traversed this type of terrain in other rides but not often. Stormy was proving more adept at it than she was. Her legs were strong and more than anything else, Jordana wanted to stay in balance as they hit the nine thousand foot level. The trail then dipped downward at a precarious angle. Jordana clamped her legs to the horse and leaned back, giving her full head, the reins lying down on her neck.

By the time they had hit the plain once more, Jordana urged Stormy into a canter toward the two hills. This was a rugged trail and as the mustang moved along, she realized the difference between level one and two endurance competition. This was brutal stuff. It asked everything of horse and rider.

At the gate that led to Slade's ranch, Jordana pulled up. She looked around to see Thor at a gallop not far behind. The stallion was powerful, and he looked rested and as if he were just starting this competition. Slade rode like the master horseman he was. His lower body moved in perfect rhythm with the stallion while his upper body was completely quiet. Thor slowed to a trot and then a walk, snorting and tossing his head. He had beautiful light blue eyes, his forelock of mane long and covering them from time to time.

"Well? How did we do?" she asked, patting Stormy. The mare's gray hair was wet and sleek.

He held up the time. "Not bad for a first run. You made it in one hour." Giving Jordana a look of pride, he added, "And you did well, too."

Glowing beneath his unexpected praise, Jordana dismounted and opened up the gate. "That's a good time?"

Riding Thor, Slade moved through the opened gate.

"It's good for a first time."

Jordana shut and locked it. "I'm happy with it, then. That's quite a test riding range you have," she said as she remounted Stormy. They rode side by side at a walk.

"Your mare is typical mustang," Slade said as they rode. "She's used to negotiating all kinds of obstacles and doesn't bat an eye at them."

"I know," Jordana said, running her fingers through her mare's thick black mane. "She's fearless."

"So is her owner."

Jordana felt as if Slade had lightly touched her. Praise didn't come from him very often. "Thanks."

"Maybe because you're an emergency room doc? You're used to chaos and don't get rattled?"

"I like your observations, Slade. You're right, I'm a cool head when things get out of control around me."

"You took those hills like a champ. Maybe I need to revise my opinion of you and that runt of a mustang you ride." His mouth barely tipped into a smile.

Jordana laughed fully and reached out. She rested her fingers on his darkly haired arm for just an instant. When her fingers grazed his sunburned flesh, she felt his muscles leap instantly in response beneath her touch. Oh, she hadn't meant to reach out like that. But she had. Jerking her hand back, she saw surprise and then sudden darkness come to his narrowing gray eyes. Her flesh prickled with a delicious sense that he was stripping her with his intense gaze. Gulping unsteadily, Jordana knew what she'd read in those intense, large eyes of his. What had just happened? There was no room in her life for a man right now. She was working twelve to fourteen hours a day trying to make ends meet.

Slade was surprised at Jordana's warm, graceful fingers wrapping momentarily around his forearm. It had been completely unexpected. He felt helpless to remain immune to her spontaneity and childlike innocence. And that was how he saw Jordana. Oh, Slade knew she was thirty years old and life had erased the innocence from her, but somehow, she had kept some of it. He hadn't, he realized. He was so dark and glum in comparison to her light, sunny smiles she shared with him. And every time Jordana's mouth curved upward, Slade's heart pumped a little harder. Right now, he felt boiling heat building in his lower body; a sure sign of pleasure and more . . .

"A horse can trot anywhere from ten to seventeen miles per hour," he said, becoming taciturn. No way did he want Jordana to touch him again. If she did, Slade wasn't sure he could control his reaction to her the next time around. "Your mare at her float trot was doing seventeen, which is good." He picked up his timer and showed it to her. "Your canter was about twenty miles an hour and that's excellent."

"Heck," Jordana said, making sure she kept her hands on the reins, "Stormy has never been timed like this before. I know thoroughbreds can race at forty miles per hour. And quarter horses can run fifty in a quarter of a mile race."

"Yes," Slade said, "they can. But in endurance contests, you want to save up that burst of speed for the finish line. This is all about understanding the speeds of your horse and then rating her such that you have something left in her tank for the finish line." He reached down and patted Thor. "Here in the Tetons Fifty race in September, after you get off the mountains, you have a flat, five mile run to the finish."

"That's a long ways," Jordana said, sobering over that information. "I know if you let the horse run hard in the steep areas, then they will likely have little gas left for that last run to the finish. Usually, it's one or two miles, isn't it?"

"Yes," Slade said. He'd silently enjoyed when their legs had brushed against one another on the narrow trail between the pastures. It hadn't been often, but he'd liked it. Maybe a little too much. Forcing himself to stay on topic, he added, "The Tetons Fifty has one of the longest finishes in the business. If you don't rate your horse's energy in the mountain climbs, you won't have anything left on the final run."

Giving Thor an admiring look, Jordana said wistfully, "Your stallion is *such* an incredible animal! He barely looked damp from that fifteen-mile run. Look at Stormy." She ran her fingers down the mare's wet, glistening neck.

"I ride Thor fifty miles once a week," Slade told her. "So this fifteen miles is like a warm-up to him."

Shaking her head, Jordana said, "He's in magnificent condition." And so was his master. But she kept that comment to herself. Both man and animal were hard-muscled, brimming with explosive energy and power. Perhaps, Jordana surmised, that is what drew her to Slade. His masculine power. She could not remember one time when she'd *ever* met a man like him. Confidence oozed from Slade like honey she wanted to taste. Body hardened by living in

101

the harsh Wyoming climate, he exuded energy like the sun itself. She loved being drenched by that invisible sunlight that pulsed around him. It made her feel ultrafeminine. And now, she'd actually touched him. His arm was like finely honed steel, the muscles leaping to life as she'd grazed him. Her fingertips still tingled from that contact.

"So, how many times a week do I take this circuit?" she asked.

"Twice a week," Slade said. "And you'll take a stopwatch with you. I'll write down the gait and time. Then, we'll see where we need to refine and improve Stormy's performance."

"But Stormy did okay for a first time?"

Slade held her gaze. He focused on her soft, full lips. Jordana never wore makeup that he could see. Her cheeks were ruddy with health and vibrancy. She was strong, confident and truly fearless. "Yes, she did okay."

Mustering her courage, Jordana said, "Slade, if we work hard, could we be ready for the Tetons Fifty? I'd *really* like to enter her in it if you think we'd be ready for it." Jordana saw the surprise come to his eyes. His mouth thinned for a moment. Brows slashed downward. *Oops.* Had she spoken too soon? Were her dreams too high? Impossible to reach so soon? Or did he think she was talking hot air?

"She could be ready, providing the pastern with the scar on it doesn't give you trouble." He held up his gloved hand. "But don't go where I see you going, Jordana. Your mare is new to this. You'll be lucky to finish in the top fifty of the hundred riders that are coming. And if Stormy does that, it will be enough for a first time."

"Phew, I thought you were going to tear into me because I asked."

Shaking his head, Slade managed a sour smile. "You have a horse who can do it. And your riding skills are solid. There's no reason to think that you can't compete. Just don't expect to win, is all."

CHAPTER SIX

Curt Downing happened to glance up from where he was standing in the aisle of Andy's Horse Emporium. He was in here to buy some Absorbine liniment for his endurance stallion, Shah. A woman with shoulder-length black hair and incredibly beautiful turquoise blue eyes entered. The pink tee and jeans outlined her athletic body. She had the warmest smile on her face for Andy, the owner, who greeted her at the counter.

Who is she? Curious, Curt was always looking for a woman who liked horses. Setting the bottle on the shelf, he eavesdropped on their conversation.

"Andy, how are you?"

"Long time, no see, Dr. Lawton. I'm fine." Andy patted his protruding girth with his hand. "You'll probably see high cholesterol."

Chuckling, Jordana said, "Hey, I'm just here to pick up a few items, not diagnose you or your patrons."

Andy nodded his balding head. "Good to know," he said, laughing in return. "Anything I can help you with?"

Jordana looked around the large store. Andy had cowboy clothing for men and women, saddles for sale and anything else a horse person might need for themselves or their mount. "No, this is like a candy store for me. You know that. Just got to get a few items that need replacing."

"Hey, I heard through the pipeline you're in training with Slade McPherson. True?"

Sighing, Jordana leaned against the old, well-worn oak counter that Andy sat behind. "There's no secrets in this town, is there?" she said with a smile. "Let me guess . . . Gwen Garner told you?"

"Yes, she did." Andy smiled a little. "Actually, my wife, Belinda, was over buying some fabric at Gwen's store and she heard about it."

Jordana's grin widened. "Ah . . . the rest of the story. Gwen is careful with info she hands out. I'm in good hands and don't mind her spreading the word that Mr. McPherson is my teacher."

Andy nodded. "Gwen is never wrong." And then he learned forward and whispered, "You know McPherson is an ornery cuss?"

Shrugging, Jordana said, "I manage to get along with him."

"You taking that gray mustang mare you bought to him?"

"I did. He gave her a thumbs-up on her ability to be a top endurance horse and I'm jazzed."

"Nobody knows endurance horses better than Slade," Andy agreed.

Jordana was about to speak when a shadow of a man came over her. She glanced to her left. A man in his mid-thirties with short, carrot red hair and pale blue eyes studied her. It wasn't a pleasant sensation, either. His eyes were almost a colorless blue. It made his black pupils even more intense-looking. There was nothing weak about the man's face. He was dressed in a white cowboy shirt, jeans and wore a black Stetson on his head.

"I'm Curt Downing, Dr. Lawton," he said and held out his large, calloused hand toward her. "I couldn't help but overhear your conversation that you're an endurance rider."

Out of social habit, Jordana forced herself to shake the man's hand. He had copper freckles all over his face. What bothered her was his small set eyes. In fact, to Jordana, Downing's features sent further alarm through her. In the horse world, a horse with small, close-set eyes was considered mean and unpredictable. She recalled Slade had mentioned Downing in unpleasant terms. As she released his hand, she remembered that Curt's father had been drunk and killed Slade's parents.

"I'm an endurance rider in the making," she told Downing. She saw his eyes narrow speculatively upon her. Downing stood about six feet tall and probably weighed around one hundred and seventy pounds. He was lean and athletic. Maybe her negative feelings toward him were because Slade disliked him.

"How long you been here, Doctor?"

"Two years," Jordana said. She moved a few feet away from Downing. He was hovering over her like a proverbial vulture ready to clean the bones of some dead animal. Indeed, there was a fierce, hawklike look in Downing's eyes, and it unsettled her.

"And you're just starting endurance riding?"

"No, I've been competitive for ten years."

"Ah, I see," Downing murmured. He appraised her body with a sharpness honed from knowing horse conformation. Hills and valleys in all the right places, Curt liked what he saw. "Pity you went to McPherson.

Did you know I also run a championship training facility? I'm the national endurance champion." He lifted his head a little more proudly than before.

Disliking his ego, Jordana said, "Yes, I knew about you, Mr. Downing."

"Please, call me Curt," he pleaded with a smile.

"I prefer to call you Mr. Downing, if you don't mind." Jordana added a slight smile to take the sting out of her decision. She saw him frown. Downing was handsome but in a twisted way as far as Jordana was concerned. She glanced over to see Andy scowling, too. What else did Andy know about Downing? That he played dirty tricks out on the endurance rides against other riders and their horses? Jordana knew the gossip pipeline in this cow town was very, very efficient.

"Listen," Curt said, ignoring her coolness toward him, "if you get a chance and would like to see my Arabian stallion, Shah, I'd be more than happy to show him to you. No one beats my stud."

Andy coughed.

Jordana eyed Curt and held his arrogant gaze. "Oh, he's been beaten by Thor, Mr. McPherson's sunbonnet mustang stallion."

"Not often," Curt laughed. "Arabians al-

ways win the endurance contests."

Jordana admitted that was true up to a point. "Half Arabians have won them, too, and so have mustangs which have Spanish barb blood in them."

Nodding, Curt enjoyed the woman's unexpected pluck. "Right you are, Dr. Lawton." She didn't melt before him. Did she know how rich he was? When women came into his orbit, they were usually attracted by his money. But something told him that Lawton wasn't like that. He knew doctors were rich in their own right but not a millionaire like he was. A sense of power flowed through him as he absorbed her natural beauty.

"If you'll excuse me," Jordana said, starting to move away because she really didn't like talking to this arrogant man. She took a step toward the aisle.

"Hey," Downing said, grabbing her wrist.

Instantly, Jordana shook off his hand. "I'm done speaking with you, Mr. Downing," she said coldly, glaring at him for his aggressive action. Her wrist smarted where his strong fingers had wrapped around it. His grip had been hard. Controlling. Jordana was alarmed by his boldness. Suddenly, she could see the competitiveness in his eyes. And now, she understood a little better what

Slade had said about this man. She didn't like him. At all.

"Oh," Curt laughed, "sorry. I just find you fascinating. It isn't often I meet another endurance rider. We're a pretty rare breed."

Ignoring him, Jordana left the area and headed down the aisle looking for a new comb and brush for Stormy. She heard Downing talking amiably with Andy as his purchases were rung up and placed into a bag. *Good riddance!* She moved down to the endcap as far away as she could get from the rancher. Downing's ego burned into her. How unlike Slade he was! Watching warily until Downing marched out of the emporium, Jordana gave a sigh of relief. Now, she could relax and shop. This was a treat to come to Andy's place.

Andy came shuffling up to her. "Jordana, I'm awful sorry about Mr. Downing's behavior. He shouldn't have laid a hand on you."

She saw the worry in the man's eyes. "No problem, Andy. I can handle myself around men like him."

"Downing thinks every woman is for sale," Andy muttered apologetically. "I shouldn't say much more than that. I just wanted to make sure you weren't upset."

Smiling, Jordana said, "Not at all."

"You know," Andy said, a gleam in his brown eyes, "you might go over to the Quilter's Haven. The owner, Gwen Garner, knows everything about everyone here in Jackson Hole. You should get the rest of the scoop on Downing."

"I'd heard Gwen was the go-to gal for honest information on anyone in Jackson Hole," she admitted.

"Well, you might amble over there after you leave here."

Jordana nodded. "I will. Thanks, Andy."

Andy gave a relieved sigh. "Good. I'm glad you'll do that. . . ."

Jordana entered Quilter's Haven on Friday afternoon. At the counter, she asked for Gwen Garner. The clerk pointed to a section at the rear of the fabric store. For years, she had heard that Gwen, whose son, Cade Garner, was a deputy sheriff for the county, was the person who had the goods on everyone in the town. Andy's relief that she would talk with Gwen had prompted Jordana to carry through on his advice. She knew the older man who owned the emporium wasn't given to such reactions, but Downing had certainly triggered something in him.

"Gwen?" she called, seeing a gray haired

woman with a clipboard in hand. "I'm Dr. Jordana Lawton. Do you have a moment?"

Gwen looked up to see the young, confident woman walking around the end of the fabric aisle. "Sure," she said, holding out her hand to her. "Dr. Lawton. I've heard plenty of good things about you. It's finally nice to meet you in person! Are you here for fabric? Quilting patterns? Or something else?"

Jordana smiled, shook the sixty-year-old woman's hand and lowered her tone. "Actually, Andy from the Horse Emporium, suggested I come over here to talk with you."

Gwen put her pen on the clipboard. "Oh?"

Jordana told her what had happened at the store. She saw Gwen's face pinch and her eyes go hard. When she got done telling her the experience, Gwen moved a little closer and lowered her voice.

"Red Downing owned the Lazy D Ranch that butts up against the McPherson ranch. He was an alcoholic. Sally Downing, his wife, was constantly abused by her husband. And so was the son, Curt. When Red plowed into Bob and Dolly McPherson's car and killed them, he died, too. That left the ranch to Sally, who had the battered wife's syndrome. Fellow ranchers gathered around her and her young son to help her. Red had controlled everything and Sally was useless, but she was a victim of violence. Eventually, Sally got the ranch on better financial ground. In the meantime, Curt fell in love with endurance riding and it was his only passion. When Sally died of a heart attack in 1996, Curt was willed the ranch."

Gwen looked up to ensure no one was nearby to eavesdrop. The store was pretty much empty, and the few patrons who were shopping were at the front of her store. "Curt Downing won a lot of races, bought a good stallion named Shah and, through smart marketing, made millions. His ranch is now solvent, he owns an endurance training facility and he also breeds his Arabian stallion to other endurance mares from around the country."

"That sounds like a rags-to-riches story," Jordana said. "As a physician I've seen plenty of abused women and children in my E.R. back in New York City, so I know what abuse does to people."

Gwen moved to the corner of the store. "Abuse is wrong. But it's *how* the person handles it that counts. And that's why Andy got protective of you today. Curt Downing is known to play rough and dirty on endurance contests. No one has caught him at it — yet. He will do *anything* to win. When he

113

whips a rider or their horse, or pushes them off a trail and endangers them, these people file complaints to the judges. But without a third witness as proof, or a camera photo, they can't do anything. So, he continues to get away with it."

Nodding, Jordana said in a low tone, "I'm in training with Slade McPherson. He said the same thing about Downing."

"Yes, I know you are." Gwen smiled a little. "We hear everything that goes on in this town."

Smiling faintly, Jordana said, "I feel like Downing is stalking me. It's my gut feeling. When he put his hand on me like that, I wanted to run away."

"And run you should," Gwen said. "He goes through women like water from a faucet. And he carries on his abuse. He's beat up his other women and they've all left sooner or later. And he made a move on you at the Horse Emporium. My advice is stay clear of this guy. He's no good. Further, there's plenty of his students come in here and talk how he uses the whip and spurs on the endurance horses they own. They don't like it. He might have a state-of-the-art facility, but he continually loses students who don't abide using those instruments to make their horses run faster to win a race."

"He sounds amoral," Jordana said. Sighing, she said, "Slade doesn't like him. Now I see why."

"Oh," Gwen said, "it goes a lot deeper than that. Slade hates Curt Downing for Red killing his parents. It wasn't Curt's fault, but he's done nothing to heal that wound between them, either. These men are the top two champions in the U.S. when it comes to endurance riding. Curt wants to win to pat his ego. Slade has to win to keep his ranch from falling into foreclosure."

Eyes narrowing, Jordana said, "I didn't know that."

"Slade's a proud man. He busts his butt to make ends meet. The bank isn't working with him." She shook her head. "The banker, Frank Halbert, is in bed with Curt Downing. Slade went several times to get his loan readjusted, but Halbert, I think, has been paid off by Downing not to do it."

"Why?"

"Five years ago, when Slade was making his mark as an endurance champion, Curt was threatened. He offered Slade ten million for his ranch. The way Curt figured it, if he could get the Tetons Ranch, then he'd have a much larger ranch and he could expand his training facility. Of course, Slade turned him down and that's when everything went to hell in a handbasket. Curt has made sure the bank won't remortgage Slade's ranch."

"But can't Slade go to another bank?"

"No. Money is so tight now and they won't loan hardly anyone anything. We're in a Depression, pure and simple. Everyone is belt tightening. Slade teeters between foreclosure and keeping his family ranch every month. It's that bad."

Jordana sighed. "I didn't know that, Gwen. That's *awful.* He's such a good person. And he's a wonderful trainer for me and Stormy."

"The man's got a heart of gold, but few can see it. He's a loner. He sticks to himself. And he's got just as much pride as any Wyoming rancher. All he does is buckle down and work harder and longer hours to make ends meet."

Jordana said, "I hurt for him. He's wonderful with horses."

"Oh," Gwen said, "no question there. Slade is known as the horse whisperer here in the valley. And Curt hates him for that. Plus, Slade beats him in the endurance contests."

"Bad blood," Jordana agreed. "I knew some of the past history between them."

Wagging her finger at Jordana, Gwen

warned, "You watch Downing. Chances are he already knew you were a student of Slade's. I wouldn't put it past him to squeeze information out of you about Slade and his ranch. If he tries, clam up."

"Not to worry," Jordana promised, "I disliked Downing the moment I saw him. He has small, close-set eyes. That was enough to put me on guard."

Chuckling, Gwen nodded. "And he's just like a small-eyed horse — meaner than the dickens. You'd do well to stay as far away from him as you can. My sense tells me he's up to no good. No one will talk about Slade to him. He's angry at everyone because we protect Slade from him."

"He must think the town is against him."

Laughing softly, Gwen said, "We are. Downing has no morals or values. We know he plays dirty tricks on other endurance riders. And the locals around here who sign up to ride the Tetons endurance contest know him too well. The judges might not have the proof that he's using his whip on another rider or horse or that he's shoved a rider off a horse, but we know he's done it."

Shaking her head, Jordana said, "Slade's a hero, then."

"Oh, he is. And ranchers stick together like fleas on a dog. They help one another out. And Slade has done the same for others. He's a good man in a bad position. He's got to win the Tetons ride this September. There's a ten thousand dollar award for the winner. With that win, Slade can give the mortgage a breather."

"If he doesn't win it?" Jordana asked, feeling worry for Slade.

Shrugging, Gwen said, "Then he's probably going to lose his ranch sooner rather than later. And that would be a pity."

"Curt is riding in the same race?"

"Yep. And you can bet those two will go at it like they always do . . . out of sight of the judges. Curt has had his crown taken away from him by Slade. And truth be told, Slade is a far better endurance rider and has a better horse under him. But Downing is competitive and he'll be out to win that race by hook or crook. It will turn dangerous for Slade and Thor. We all worry about them and there's nothing we can do."

Feeling helpless, Jordana quirked her lips. "I'm glad I'm contributing to Slade's ranch, then."

"He never advertises his training facility. Sometimes, he's as dumb as a box of rocks."

Laughing, Jordana said, "He's an anachronistic kind of man. He has a cell phone and a computer, but he says he hates both of them." the nineteenth century instead of a modern-day man. Most ranchers use ATVs to round up their cattle, but Slade still uses his horses. Old-fashioned, but he also has those old values, too. He's a man of integrity. His word is his bond. If he shakes your hand, he means it and will carry through with whatever was agreed upon."

"Why isn't he married?" The words popped out of Jordana's mouth, unbidden.

"Oh, he was married for four years to an immature New York City socialite. Isabel was a pre-Olympic dressage champion. She came out here on a vacation, met Slade and in a week, they were married. Stupidest thing I've ever seen that man do," she muttered, shaking her head. "It was hell for Slade. Isabel had millions and he was a pauper in comparison. She had temper tantrums and pouted and sulked when she didn't get her way. Eventually, Slade divorced her, but it's left a real bad taste in his mouth for women ever since."

"I see," Jordana said. "It explains why he feels armored up and unreachable to me."

"Slade can be a knight on his horse, but no one can reach him and how he really feels. You just have to accept him as is. I'm hoping that over time, he'll drop his walls and be more friendly and social. He's ashamed of his whirlwind marriage to Isabel and the divorce. Slade hides as much as he can."

Smiling a little, Jordana said, "You nailed him, Gwen. Truly, he's boarded up and no one can get to his soft parts except the horses he cares for and trains."

"Well, if I were you, I'd hold out hope that one day, he would become human and join the rest of the world again," Gwen murmured with a smile.

Jordana agreed. Her heart opened wider now as she had a much more clear picture of Slade and why he was a loner. Life had been hard on him, and it hadn't let up. "Thanks for the info, Gwen. I really appreciate your help and warning about Downing."

Picking up her pen from the clipboard, Gwen nodded. "Anytime, Jordana. If you got questions, bring them to me. I'll probably be able to give you some truth and background to 'em."

As Jordana left the shop to drive out to Slade's ranch, she reran his sad, hard life through her mind. He was a good man in a bad place. And she knew a ranch was often handed down to the next generation. He was battling to keep the memory of his beloved parents alive. Because it was his life, too, with or without them around. As she drove her Ford truck through the town, Jordana wondered if life was going to finally give him a reward instead of more punishment.

CHAPTER SEVEN

"Is something bothering you?" Slade asked as Jordana walked Stormy back to the barn. She'd arrived and rode the fifteen-mile circuit and hadn't said much. Which wasn't like her. The July sun was hot, and it felt good to him. Slade knew he wasn't the most sensitive person on earth, but even he could see a murkiness in Jordana's glorious blue eyes.

"Oh, it's nothing," she protested as he walked with Stormy to the cross ties located in the center of the barn. Jordana didn't want to tell him about meeting Downing. She knew there was bad blood between them now, thanks to Gwen Garner's information, and she didn't want to stir the pot. What bothered her was Slade had seen she was upset. Slipping off the hackamore from Stormy, she pulled on the nylon halter and then put her horse between the cross ties. Slade had taken off Stormy's saddle and took it into the tack room. Jordana had seen him become less icy and unavailable the past week. Maybe he was getting used to having her around?

When Slade returned from the tack room, there was a nice breeze through the center passageway of the barn. It felt good against the eighty-degree heat. Jordana was busy brushing Stormy down. Slade liked to watch her move around the mustang. There was such natural grace to Jordana. As he leaned against the wall of a box stall, his arms across his chest, Slade absorbed the pleasurable moment. Every time he saw Jordana, he wanted to be around her even more. Slade fought the inexplicable desire. Acidly, he told himself he was a pauper and getting tangled up with another woman just wasn't in his cards.

"Stormy seemed upset today, too," he drawled, watching her expression.

"She has her days like I do," Jordana joked, hoping her smile would stop him from digging any further. It was unlike Slade to be concerned about her. Why now? Did he have a sixth sense for smelling trouble? Or for Downing, in particular? Brushing Stormy, she worked to get out the sweat and dirt along her back. They were now doing fifteen-mile rides three times a week. She'd changed her schedule to compensate for this new training demand. Next week, Slade was going to up her to thirty miles in preparation for the fifty-mile Tetons contest.

Compressing his lips, Slade murmured, "You're unhappy."

Straightening, Jordana looked across her mare's back at him. His hat was tipped down, shading his gray eyes that felt like X-rays moving through her. He was incredibly handsome, shaped by the elements. She broke down and told him about the incident at the Horse Emporium. Jordana knew instantly by Slade standing, his arms coming to his sides, that he had hate for Downing. When she finished, she didn't tell him that she'd went to Gwen Garner. More than anything, as he stood there bristling with rage, his eyes hard and gleaming, Jordana simply wanted to throw her arms around Slade and hold him. He'd been without love and nurturing for so long. In her imagination, she saw him as a lonely, grieving six year old boy who had just had his parent torn from him.

"You can't trust him. *Ever,*" Slade gritted. His fist curved. For the longest time, he'd wanted to punch the arrogant and rich bastard in the face. Red Downing had taken everything from his family. Curt had grown up to be hard and mean and did anything he had to do in order to win, just as his father had.

"I know that," Jordana said in a soothing tone. Now, Slade was upset. His entire tall, powerful body was tense, fists knotted at his sides. "I handled it and there won't be another confrontation. Trust me, Downing got the message."

Pacing, Slade wasn't so sure. "You've lived here two years and never ran into him. Gossip in the town is everywhere. He knew you'd come here to train with me."

"It's jealousy on his part," Jordana said, using an aluminum blade to shed the excess sweat off Stormy's body. "Nothing more."

"Damn him," he ground out to no one in particular.

"Frankly, I'm more worried for you, Slade." She held his startled look. "You're competing against him in the Tetons ride."

"Nothing new there. Don't worry about me. I've handled him before and I know his tricks." Still, Slade felt his chest expand with an unfamiliar emotion. Jordana's eyes were warm and anxious-looking. She cared for him. She really did. Slade hadn't been born yesterday. He knew that look. And it made him go soft inside for a moment. What would it be like to relax and be himself around Jordana? Something told Slade she was utterly trustworthy, unlike Isabel. Still, the past screamed at him, and he tucked that warmth away like a stolen moment within his heart.

Sighing, Jordana said, "Getting to meet Curt face-to-face makes me worry *more,* Slade." Unhooking the panic snaps on both sides of Stormy's halter, she led her tired mare down the concourse to be washed. She heard a man's voice boom from the other end of the barn.

"Slade! I'm back!"

Turning, Jordana saw a man who was almost as tall as Slade standing at the opened door. He wore a dark brown suit, tie and white shirt. Blinking, she thought he looked an awful like Slade. And then it hit her. Could this be Griff McPherson? Slade's younger fraternal twin brother? If it was, Slade had not said anything about his visit. Glancing toward Slade, she saw him freeze for a moment. And then, his face darkened with an unknown emotion. Sudden tension crackled in the barn. Confused, Jordana stayed where she was as this meeting played out.

"Slade, good to see you again," Griff said, striding forward, his hand outstretched toward his older brother.

"What the hell are you doing here?" Slade growled, refusing to shake his brother's hand.

"I've come home for good," he told Slade.

"You're a city slicker. An easterner. And you have a job on Wall Street. Since when have you said this ranch was your home?" Old anger stirred through Slade. Griff had black hair and green eyes, like his mother. His younger brother was an inch shorter than him, more slightly built than he was. Griff looked painfully out of the norm by wearing his Wall Street suit. Few people wore suits around here.

Griff grimaced and held his ground. "Hey, brother, I own half this ranch. And I was born here in Jackson Hole." Giving him a grin, he added, "Besides, I'm done with Wall Street. I wanted to come home."

"Damn nice of you to let me know you were coming," Slade said, glaring at Griff. His younger twin had always been spontaneous and gave no second thought to how his decisions might affect others. He was very immature compared to Slade.

"Sorry, but I wanted to surprise you. I thought you'd be happy to see me."

Snorting, Slade growled, "What? You visit once every five years? Stay for a day and can't stand being out in the middle of nowhere? Pining away for your exciting, nonstop life back in New York City? Give me a break."

Unfazed by his older brother's snarling disposition, Griff said in a lower tone, "Look, I've lost everything, Slade. My company went belly up and I don't have a job. I've tried getting another one, but no one is hiring." Opening his hands, he added, "I was in stock derivatives. I lost *everything,* Slade. I lost twenty million dollars in a blink of an eye. I should have diversified my portfolio, but I didn't."

Staring into Griff's tormented green eyes, Slade snarled, "And so you come crawling home to the ranch I've kept going without *any* help from you?"

"I have half ownership of this ranch," Griff reminded him more strongly. "The will decreed we'd each own half."

"Not that you've *ever* dropped a dime to help keep it afloat. Hell, you wouldn't even give me a loan six years ago when I asked for it."

Grimacing, Griff fearlessly met him on this comment. "In my opinion as a Wall Street banker, you were a bad risk, Slade. I wasn't going to throw my money away. When you loan money, you expect interest and payback. I just didn't feel at that time you could do that."

Glaring at him, Slade barely tolerated his sibling. "I'll never forget that day. I'll go to my grave remembering you wouldn't loan your brother money." Snorting, Slade added, "And now, you're broke. Well, if you think you can come back here and leech off me, you have another think coming." He held up his hands. "I *work* for a living. Not like you living in some posh skyscraper playing with computers and enjoying the good life."

Wincing, Griff said, "I'm staying here. I'll take one of the spare bedrooms in the main house. My old bedroom."

Helpless to stop him, Slade said, "You're worthless to me and this ranch, Griff. You don't know how to ride, brand a calf, put up fence posts or string barbed wire."

Mouth tightening, Griff held his brother's rage. "I'll learn."

"This is insane," Slade growled. "And how long before you leave and go back to your precious Wall Street? When the first person offers you a job, you'll be out of here in a heartbeat. You won't care a tinker's dam about this ranch once more." Slade wanted to add, *or me,* but didn't.

"I can work hard," Griff said stubbornly.

"You show me what has to be done and I'll do it. I'm not lazy."

Shaking his head, Slade muttered, "You're useless as tits on a bull, Griff. Look at your hands." He jabbed his index finger down at them. "They're white, soft and pretty." He thrust his hand into his brother's face. "Look at *mine.*"

Griff didn't blink. He saw the sunburned quality of Slade's large hand. It had small white scars here and there, plus thick calluses on each palm showing the hard physical work performed daily. "We're brothers," he reminded him in a tight tone. "And I'm not unlike you. I can't help it if we got split up after our parents were killed. I had no choice when the court decided to send me to Uncle Robert's part of the world any more than you did when you got to stay here."

Bristling, Slade hated to be reminded of that painful time in the past. In his opinion, Griff was like a butterfly compared to his anvil hammer. They didn't see each other very often at all, the brotherly ties broken a long time ago. "Drop the excuses. There's no way I'm taking you on as an employee. I don't have the money to pay you a dime."

Shrugging, Griff said, "I'm not an employee, Slade. I'm half owner. And I expect to work. I have a lot of good ideas for the ranch —"

"Another time," Slade growled. He saw two bags of luggage at the opening of the barn. "You know the layout of the house."

"Good," Griff murmured, giving his upset older brother a smile. "I'll make myself at home." He turned and walked with his shoulders back, head tipped at a proud angle.

Slade put his hands on his hips, glaring after Griff. Spinning emotionally from his unexpected arrival, he hung his head and wrestled with the snakes writhing violently in his gut.

"Slade?" Jordana walked down the passageway with her horse. She hesitantly put her hand on his broad shoulder. "Are you okay?"

Her softened words were like ice water to his boiling anger and shock. Lifting his head, he absorbed her tentative touch like the starving animal he was. "Yeah . . . yeah, I'm fine."

Removing her hand, Jordana stood there seeing a host of emotions pass across his face. This was the first time she'd seen Slade without that hardened expression. Seeing desperation, grief and anger in his eyes, she said gently, "No, you're not fine. Who was that?"

Taking off his Stetson, he wiped his brow with the back of his hand and then settled it back on his head. Slade had no intention of spilling out the painful past but somehow, Jordana was able to wring it out of him. He told her about his past and how he and his brother were split up at age six. His voice turned steely as he said, "And Griff took to Wall Street and New York City like ticks on a dog. He was filthy rich. I once asked him for a loan, but he turned me down. He didn't care if I lost the ranch to the bank. Even though he supposedly owns half of it by our parent's will, he didn't give me a dime."

The bitterness in Slade's tone tore at Jordana. She stood quietly. He was obviously in shock. And sometimes, when a person was able to just talk out the trauma, it blunted the shock and they felt more emotionally stable. Her job was to ask questions. "What will Griff do now that he's penniless? I know a number of big-name stock brokerage firms went under."

"I don't know," Slade admitted, some of the venom dissolving in his tone. Jordana's quiet, calming presence was what he needed, he realized. She had a soft touch and asked the right questions to defuse him. "He's a city slicker just like my ex-wife, Isabel. She was lazy. She screamed if she got some dirt under her painted fingernails. And she refused to clean out box stalls with me. She said it was a man's work."

Catching his gaze, Jordana smiled a little. "Box stalls are gender neutral."

"Yes," Slade sighed. He looked up and then around the quiet barn. "Griff is going to be a burr under my saddle. He's useless. He doesn't know the first thing about running a ranch." And then he gave her an apologetic look. "I shouldn't be washing my family's dirty laundry in front of you."

Reaching out, she slid her fingers along his slumped shoulder. Each muscle leaped where she'd grazed his dark blue cowboy shirt. "It's all right, Slade. I consider you not only my trainer, but a friend as well. I want to be here for you."

More than Isabel ever was for him, he thought. His skin felt as if it was on fire where she'd grazed his shoulder. Jordana's touch was calming. Slade felt his anger beginning to recede. "You not only have a quieting touch with a horse, but with me, too," he said wryly, giving her a quizzical look. Drowning in her warm blue gaze, Slade suddenly wanted to pull her roughly into his arms and kiss that soft, haunting mouth of hers. That jolted him. He couldn't ignore the building ache in his lower body, either. The whole thing was loco!

Jordana felt a shift within Slade. Suddenly, she saw raw hunger burning in his eyes — for her. It was so unexpected, she took a step back. Blinking, she managed, "Blame it on my doctor's demeanor."

It was much more than that, Slade realized, feeling suddenly dizzy beneath her gaze. *Much more.* For the first time in four years he ached for a woman. But not just any woman. Jordana made him feel alive as never before. And Slade knew her touch was meant to calm and soothe, not incite flaming desire within him. But it had. Feeling nakedly vulnerable, he said gruffly, "You've got to get Stormy washed. I'll see you in two days. We'll start Stormy on a thirty-mile route at that time." Turning, he left her standing in the middle of the barn.

Jordana swallowed hard. It was a good thing Slade had abruptly left or she wasn't sure what she'd have done next. The man was unpredictable! Yet, so were her yearning emotions, too. Something had happened between them, and she couldn't think clearly enough to understand what had gone down. She watched his long, striding form as he headed back to his ranch house. Feeling suddenly alone without his masculine presence, Jordana sighed.

Leading Stormy out of the barn, Jordana headed for the shower facility. Afterward, she would go to the tack room and clean all the leather. The fragrance of oiled leather was always a perfume to be inhaled deeply. Her mind raced as she sat there with the oil and a cloth, the saddle nearby. What was Slade going to do now that Griff had dropped into his life? She had no idea what the siblings were like together. Maybe talking to Gwen Garner might give her a clearer picture of Griff. He certainly looked a lot like Slade, but there were differences, too. And he was just as handsome as Slade. Yet, his face was not deeply lined, but pale because in his job as a Wall Street broker, he didn't see the sun that often, never mind braving the elements.

The day had been one of lightning bolts, Jordana thought, as she scrubbed down Stormy in the bathing facility. First, Curt Downing was stalking her like a cougar would follow his intended prey. But she was no prey. Jordana could see why Slade disliked Downing. She felt as if some invisible stickiness was left behind after he'd grabbed her wrist. Wanting to take a hot shower to feel clean once more, Jordana moved the rubber brush across Stormy's gleaming back. As if Slade didn't have enough to worry about with Downing in the coming race, he was now saddled with his twin brother.

Feeling sorry for Slade, Jordana wished she could do more. But what? He'd finally broke through his armored barriers and shared with her. Those moments were sweet and Jordana began to realize their relationship had changed because of that. Slade was no longer iconic and distant. When he'd dumped his frustration out about his brother to her, he'd been vulnerable and emotional. Was it possible not to love a sibling? Jordana had seen this happen in other families. Hadn't Slade been dealt a hard enough hand without Griff barging in unannounced? Clearly, Slade didn't want him here.

Finishing up Stormy's bath, Jordana led her back to the box stall. Next, she had to clean her gear. She saw Shorty on his paint mustang herding in a group of growing calves. They would have to be vaccinated and branded. She raised her hand in hello to the wrangler, and he did the same. Looking around, Jordana did not see Slade or Griff. What was going on inside that house?

Were they arguing? Coming to physical blows? Frowning, she thought it wasn't her business. She was a student here, not Slade's lover.

Later, all her chores completed, Jordana drove slowly out of the parking area. She tried to appreciate the clear blue sky, the high cirrus clouds that reminded her of a horse's mane blowing in the wind. Her heart was still back there at the ranch as she drove the two miles to the highway that would take her back into town. In the distance, the Tetons, now nearly bare of any snow, showed their deep, rugged blue granite slopes. Their flanks were covered with thick green forest of pine below the ten thousand foot level. And one day soon, she and Stormy would be hidden beneath those pines on a rocky trail competing in her first big endurance ride.

Her excitement was cooled by her worry for Slade. Driving down the highway, the valley lushly green and the mountains silhouetted against the sky, Jordana wanted to turn around and go back. But what good would that do? Slade had trusted her enough to open up and speak about something deeply personal with her. Jordana knew she had to wait it out. Slade was so distrustful of women because of his bad marriage to Isabel. Further, she knew he didn't like city slickers from New York City. There were so many hurdles to jump!

Somber, Jordana paid attention to her driving as she sped down a long, gently sloped hill that would take her into downtown Jackson Hole. And why was she so anxious to have some kind of personal relationship with Slade? Right now, Jordana knew she couldn't afford to get into anything like that. She was working long, hard hours. And every penny had to be accounted for. Until she was past her endurance training, she had no savings, and that bothered her. Her parents had drilled into her that savings were always important. Symbolically, she felt rich in a personal way, but in reality, she wasn't financially. That was okay for now. She'd weathered storms in her life before, and she'd get through this one.

As she slowly moved through downtown traffic, tourist season in high gear, Jordana appreciated the plaza of the main part of town. Elk horns were bundled together to form a massive arch that was twenty feet high. Tourists stood, marveled and took photos of it. Her heart lifted. Every time she pictured Slade's hard, weathered features, she felt her insides becoming as soft as a marshmallow. No man had ever had that effect on her.

Turning off to a side street that would take her to the southern end of town where her home was located, Jordana wondered what the next two days would be like for Slade and his unwelcome brother.

CHAPTER EIGHT

Slade held on to his shock and rage as he strode into his ranch house. Inside was a brother he'd rarely seen since they had been separated. Griff had conveniently forgotten about him and the ranch. There was the occasional Christmas card, but that was it. And Slade could count on one hand how many times Griff had bothered to come out for a visit.

"Dammit," he seethed under his breath, jerking open the screen door and stepping inside. Halting in the mudroom, he took off his hat and hung it on a nearby elk antler hook. His boots thunked hollowly down the pine hall. Heading for Griff's old bedroom, he heard a noise to his left in the kitchen. Turning on his heel, he strode into it. Griff was making coffee and he had changed out of his suit for a pair of jeans and a white long-sleeved shirt. He *almost* looked like a cowboy.

"We need to talk," Slade told him gruffly without preamble.

Griff glanced over at his older twin. "Sure." He smiled a little. "I think I should have warned you I was coming home. I'm sorry I didn't."

Resting his hands on his hips, Slade said, "Yes, you should have, but then, that's your way, isn't it? Did you learn that on Wall Street? Just traipse in and think people are going to be okay with that kind of city slicker attitude and rudeness?"

Switching on the coffeemaker, Griff turned and rested his hips against the kitchen counter. The anger was leaping in Slade's narrowed eyes. "I don't see it that way," he countered strongly. Looking around, Griff murmured, "Not much has changed here, has it?" The light over the table was the same one he recalled as a young child. Their mother had loved yellow, and the kitchen was still painted that bright color.

Slade walked over and brought two cups down from the cabinet. "*Nothing* has changed. Our parents struggled every month to pay the mortgage on this place. And now, so do I."

Griff frowned. "You still aren't solvent?"

Stung, Slade snarled, "No, thanks to you.

I came to you years back for a loan. If you'd have loaned me the money, it would have gone toward stabilizing the mortgage. But you couldn't see your way clear to do that for whatever your stupid reasons."

"You weren't a good loan applicant," Griff said coolly. "And if you're still in deep trouble with the mortgage, that proves my original assumption that you weren't a trustworthy loan applicant."

Cursing to himself, Slade wanted to strangle his younger twin. Griff looked smug and self-assured. Oh, he might be wearing Western clothing, but the look on his face told a different story. "And that's why I don't want you here. You've paid nothing into this place except to write it off."

Shrugging, Griff said lightly, "Legally speaking, I'm half owner. I'm not going anywhere." He grinned. "Besides, I have a host of ideas that can turn this ranch around so we can get it onto solid financial footing."

"Bull," Slade muttered, "you don't have a clue as to how to keep a ranch solvent." The coffee was done, and he poured himself a cup and put a splash of cream into it. Sitting down at the pine table with chairs hewn from the same wood, he watched Griff pour his own coffee. His twin wandered over, far less tense-looking than he felt.

Sitting down, Griff sipped his black coffee and said, "Before you throw the baby out with the bathwater, Slade, I *do* have some good ideas for our ranch."

The word "our" grated across Slade like a file rasp running across his exposed flesh. It wasn't morally right that Griff suddenly dropped in out of the blue to claim his half of the ranch. "You've done *nothing* to earn half this ranch." Slade glared at his unperturbed brother. Griff's black hair was military short. He hadn't been toughened up by the harsh elements of Wyoming.

"I know that, but now," Griff said lightly, "but now, I intend to rectify the situation."

"Only because you can't find another job on Wall Street," Slade acidly pointed out. "And I'll bet my last, bottom dollar that as soon as someone you know in your network has a job offer, you'll leave this place in a heartbeat and fly East again. Out of sight, out of mind with you, Griff."

"I do miss my job. I miss the money I made. And had," he admitted. "Right now, we're in a depression and there's no doubt about it. A lot of people are going back to their parents' homes right now because they've lost their jobs. I'm coming back here because I have a legal right to do so. I know

143

you're not happy about it, but I'm staying."

"Until things improve on Wall Street."

Nodding, Griff said, "Most likely that is so." He swept his hand around the kitchen. "You can't make money ranching. You've proven that. And frankly, I like *big* money. I like living in a three-million-dollar penthouse in the upper east side of Manhattan. I like being able to buy the best of wines, throwing big parties for the rich and famous."

Shaking his head, Slade stared down at his coffee cup. "Your heart isn't here in Wyoming, Griff. It never was."

"I don't know that," he countered strongly. "We were *born* here, Slade. Until our family was killed by Red Downing, we were happy."

"Yeah, well, life is hard," Slade uttered, sipping his coffee and nearly scalding his tongue. Setting the mug down he added, "And your heart and soul are in Wall Street, making millions and not sharing it with anyone else in the family."

"You're my only family," Griff said. "And you're a bad loan risk. I can't help that."

Slade jadedly eyed him. "You're an eastern city slicker." He jabbed a finger at Griff's hands that were enclosed around the coffee mug. "Your hands are lily-white and soft like a little girl's would be. You're out of shape. You could no more sink a fence-post hole than a ten-year-old girl. You don't ride. You don't know how to herd cattle, vaccinate or care for them. And you don't get to stay where it's warm when there's a blizzard going on. You have to care for ten horses, clean out box stalls and get to the feed store for hay, feed and other supplies."

"I've got skill sets in engine mechanics and construction. When I was at Harvard, I had a part-time job with a major construction company. I know how to use tools, and I'll apply my knowledge to the ranch," Griff said grimly, holding his twin's hard stare. "I had a gym membership in New York City, and I worked out regularly." He held out one of his hands. "It's true, I don't have sunburned skin and thick calluses on my hands, but that doesn't mean I can't use them to work with. That's what leather gloves are for."

"You know *nothing* about endurance riding."

"No," Griff said steadily, trying to hold on to his rising temper, "you're right. I don't know a thing. But I don't think I have to remind you, I'm the one with a Harvard MBA, not you. I'm a fast learner."

Stung, Slade knew he had only a high school education compared to his brother.

"No, I don't have a diploma from an uppity Eastern school. Uncle Paul died just as I graduated from high school and I had no chance for college. If I hadn't decided to stay and fight to keep this ranch going, I could have walked away from it. I had planned to go to college, but it just didn't happen."

Nodding, Griff said, "So you're a hero, Slade, and I'm not. My MBA opens doors you could never open."

Grinning sourly, Slade muttered, "Seems like all those golden doors are closed to you from what I can see. That's why you came slinking home with your tail between your legs. No one *wants you,* Griff. And I don't, either."

"You don't have a choice," Griff said, anger in his deep voice. "Legally, I own *half* of this ranch. You can't kick me out."

"You're right about that. And I'll guarantee you, Griff, if you stay, you're going to work your butt off just like Shorty and I do." He held up a finger and wagged it in Griff's face. "And I'm the *boss* here, not you. In my eyes, you're a green wrangler learning the trade. Nothing more."

"And do I get paid?"

Snorting, Slade said, "Hell, no! My budget allows me to pay one wrangler and that's it.

You work to keep a roof over your head and eat, that's all."

"Why not get rid of Shorty? That way you can pay me?"

"In a pig's eye," Slade growled, rising. "You're worthless, Griff. We work twelve hours a day around here during the summer. I don't have *time* to break you into our business without a solid, reliable wrangler like Shorty around to pick up your slack. You're wasting my valuable time trying to train you. All you get out of this gig is room and board. You don't like that, you go into town and hire a lawyer and we'll duke it out in court." Turning, Slade walked out of the kitchen. He was this close to hitting his stubborn brother. Griff didn't have an ounce of common sense, which ranchers had to have in order to survive. He was worthless!

Griff sat there feeling his burning anger toward Slade. The kitchen was quiet. He heard Slade slam the front screen door. He was gone. Looking around, he felt frustrated. In his former life as a Wall Street broker, he moved billions of dollars a day. Now, Slade was telling him he got room and board. That was it. No money for the work he'd be doing.

Mulling over the situation, Griff knew it

would be useless to sue Slade. First, he had no money to do it. And he knew Slade probably didn't either. It was a standoff. Right now, Griff needed a place to land. He lamented their parents had been killed. His father would have welcomed him back to the ranch, and he knew it. But Slade wanted no part of him. How to fit in? Or could he?

Studying his left hand, Griff knew he was soft in comparison to Slade. He made his money with his brain, not his physical body like his older twin. Grudgingly, Griff felt his heart break a little. There was no love lost between them. He'd had idealistic expectations that Slade would welcome him with open arms, but he hadn't. Instead, Griff was sure Slade saw him as an interloper who was nothing more than a pain in the ass who had to be babysat.

Rubbing his chin, Griff looked around the kitchen. He dimly recalled sitting at this very table with Slade and his parents. He had few memories from that time. After all, he'd been only six years old. Smiling fondly, he recalled his father had always sat at the head of the table and his mother at the other end. He and Slade had sat opposite one another. There had always been a radio playing in the background. His mother had loved what was now termed elevator music.

His father had loved Nashville music. Griff could recall both types of music being played as they sat at this dinner table. Running his hand along the varnished grain of the reddish-gold surface, he felt a sense of returning home.

Getting up, Griff walked over to the kitchen sink and rinsed out his mug. Setting it in the dish drainer, he looked around. No dishwasher, either. Well, that meant he'd be washing dishes, too. What a comedown! The sky had fallen open and disgorged him from his place in the stock brokerage firm where he'd been was a banker. In one week, he'd lost everything. Being in derivatives, he'd amassed nearly twenty million dollars. And in the blink of an eye, it had disappeared in a poof. And the next day, he'd found out his firm was going under. Everyone had scrambled to call other brokerage firms for a new job, but no one was hiring.

Looking out the yellow curtained windows, Griff saw Slade walking toward the big red barn. He saw Shorty, his only wrangler, coming up and speaking to him. Ego smarting over Slade's harsh judgment of him, Griff had to figure out a way to show he was an important part of this ranch. One way or another . . .

■ ■ ■ ■

Slade's day went from bad to worse. He was at Andy's Horse Emporium that afternoon to pick up some skid boots. And as he walked down one of the aisles, he saw Curt Downing come in. Instantly, he went on internal guard. Downing saw him and grinned like a wolf ready to bite him. Slade knew he would.

"Hey, Slade, good to see you," Curt hailed, raising his hand.

Glaring, Slade said nothing. As he walked up to the cash register, he saw Andy grow nervous.

Curt continued to grin as he stood at the opposite end of the counter. Slade was dark and angry-looking. Prodding him, he said, "You looking forward to meeting me on the field of battle on September first?"

Pulling his wallet out of the back pocket, Slade muttered, "To you, every endurance contest is a war, Downing."

Laughing heartily, Curt said, "Isn't it?"

"No," Slade snapped at him. "But you don't get that, do you?" He itched to put his fist into Downing's arrogant face.

"Oh," Curt drawled, relaxing, "it *is* war. Every endurance race is a war against all the other horses and riders. That's the way it is."

Andy's hand shook as he took the bills from Slade's hand. He didn't want a fight breaking out in his store.

Smiling tightly, Slade murmured, "I hear you're losing your students, Downing. Could it be because of your war mentality?"

Scowling, Curt retorted, "I am not! Is Gwen Garner spreading lies around?"

Slade knew how much Downing bragged all over town about how many students he had. His grin turned sour as he held Downing's angry stare. "I don't have to go to Gwen. All I have to do is read the newspaper where you have ads in every week trying to snare some students." Snickering to himself, Slade saw Downing's smiling mouth turn down into a snarl. "Besides," he added, putting salt into Downing's wound, "most people don't like the idea of hitting other riders with a whip or shoving them off the trail."

Andy rolled his eyes and said nothing.

Curt stared hard at Slade. "Those are all lies! Just because Shah and I are damn good at what we do, there's no reason to believe a bunch of whiners who are sore losers!"

Taking the change from Andy, Slade said, "In my experience, Downing, endurance riders are somewhat like knights of old: *most* of them have high morals and values, except for a few, like you. They aren't whiners. They're in those rides because they've put in a lot of hours and days of training with their horses."

Downing could feel his face flushing. His anger flared, and he wanted to strike Slade. "Are you accusing me of *not* being moral out on the trail? I've *never* stopped anyone from going around me."

A grin leaked from Slade's tightened mouth as he pocketed his change and thanked Andy, who was sweating profusely. "Oh? Seems that just last year when me and my stud caught up to pass you, you had that whip of yours ready." Slade had seen him pull it out to strike Thor. Slade had lifted his boot out of the stirrup and slammed it into Downing's body. He'd shot off his startled mount like a bullet. And Slade had passed him safely and gone on to win the race. Downing had eventually caught his mount and come in fourth in the race. He'd never spoken a word about the incident to anyone. And Slade knew why. The judges might not take action on riders in general, but he had national standing. If he'd turned Downing in for his dirty tricks, the judges would have listened, and there would have been a convening of all involved. Slade knew no one liked Downing and would have sided with him on this charge. Downing's career would have taken a big hit. Without proof, nothing could be done, but Slade's word would have destroyed him in the endurance riding world. And Downing knew it.

Curt glared at McPherson. "We'll settle this out there on the trail in September," he ground out.

Slade halted at the door, turned and rasped, "You can *count* on it, Downing."

Jerking the door open, Slade left. The late-afternoon sunlight was delicious compared to the air-conditioning within the Emporium. Anger lapped at him. How badly he wanted to expose Downing. This year, he was riding with a small camera around his neck. No one would see it until he brought it out from beneath the shirt he wore. Once and for all, Slade intended to prove the bastard was committing fouls out of sight of the judges. He smiled a little as he sauntered down the weathered wooden steps to his green Chevrolet pickup.

For a moment, he had a spontaneous urge to go see Jordana, whom he knew would be on duty at the E.R. of the hospital. She worked twelve hours at night so she could ride and get Stormy in shape during the day.

Would she be surprised if he showed up? Pleased? Or not? Slade didn't know as he opened the door to his truck. Getting in and pulling the seat belt across his body, he waffled over the idea. It was unlike him to be spontaneous. He'd had such a hellish day he ached to be with Jordana. Starting the engine, he decided to hell with it. He'd surprise her.

Jordana's mouth fell open. She was just coming out of a cubical where she'd attended a new patient when she saw Slade walking into the E.R. What was he doing here? Worried, she gave the nurse her orders and then pushed the door open to the entrance area.

"Slade?" she called.

Turning, Slade saw Jordana. He'd never seen her in her hospital clothing. She wore dark green scrubs with a white coat over them. The stethoscope hung around her slender neck and her name was sewn onto the lab coat. This time, her hair was tied up on her head, a far different look than he'd seen before. His heart pounded briefly as he managed a twisted smile.

"I was just passing by and I thought I'd come and see the world you live in."

How tall, handsome and powerful he was

he stood in the waiting room. All around her, there were sick and suffering people waiting to receive help. Slade was like magnificent sunlight in the room. Grinning, she said, "What a nice surprise. Listen, I have about ten minutes' worth of paperwork to finish before I get my dinner."

Slade looked at his watch. "It's only four p.m."

Laughing a little because she suddenly felt like a giddy teenager, Jordana said, "I have the midnight shift. Dinner comes early. Can you meet me in the cafeteria? I'll be there shortly."

Tipping his hat, Slade said, "Like a cup of coffee waiting for you?" She always had a coffee thermos with her at his ranch.

Giving his arm a squeeze, she said, "Absolutely. See you in a few. . . ."

The coffee was waiting for her when Jordana hurried into the quiet cafeteria later. She waved to Slade, who had chosen a large table near the window. Grabbing a tray, she went through the line choosing dinner items. After paying the cashier, she walked over to the table. Slade had laid his hat down on the chair next to him. Her cup of coffee sat opposite him. A sense of happiness threaded through her. Slade stood as she approached and pulled the chair out for her. She thanked him and sat down.

"That's quite a tray of food," Slade observed as he sat.

Chuckling, Jordana said, "It's a full moon tonight. I know we're going to get super busy. I tank up and top off for these times with a lot of protein." She picked it up the coffee and lifted up to him in a toast. "Thank you for the surprise visit."

"My pleasure," Slade murmured. Just sitting here in her calming presence made the whole miserable day dissolve. How was that possible? What was happening? Slade didn't know. He folded his large hands in front of him. "What happens when it gets busy for you around here?"

"I go into super doc mode," she laughed. Cutting her beef steak, she gave him a shy look. Slade's face was utterly relaxed for the first time. She was actually seeing the man, not his armor. It was an amazing gift for Jordana and her heart opened wide because he smiled just a little bit. It made Slade look even more handsome in her eyes.

"Super Doc. Is that what they call you around here?"

"You hit the nail on the head. I'm the manager calling the shots to my team of nurses."

"I'll bet you don't yell."

She salted her spinach and squeezed some lemon juice across it. "Yelling gets you nowhere."

"You never lift your voice to Stormy. I've found that people who treat animals well usually treat humans pretty good, too."

His observations were simple and yet profound. "I like the way you look at the world, Slade." Jordana ate and simply absorbed his demeanor. Slade might be sitting quietly at the table, but there was such strength and sunlight exuding off him, it made Jordana feel dizzied by his utter maleness.

"How has your day gone?" she asked.

"You don't want to know."

Hearing the sudden heaviness in his voice and a darkness come to his eyes, Jordana realized she was watching him shift into a more protective mode. Would he ever open up and remain that way with her? She found herself desperately wanting that. "Is that why you dropped by?"

The softness of her voice opened him up. "Yeah, it was a bad day and when I see you, it doesn't seem so bad after all. . . ."

CHAPTER NINE

The coolness of the early morning was dissipating as the sun rose higher in the sky. Slade took a deep breath and got ready to enter the corral where Diablo, the shorthorn bull, was standing.

"Boss, be real careful. He's been pissy since the sun rose," Shorty called, standing outside the pipe corral.

Grunting, Slade nodded. Yesterday Shorty had seen the bull limping out in his pasture. Now he'd herded the testy one-ton animal into the small corral where they could get a closer look at his left rear leg. After coming home yesterday, it had been one more thing that had gone wrong. The only thing good about it was having the impromptu visit with Jordana at her hospital. That had lifted his troubled spirits.

Diablo tossed his head, his short, thick horns sticking out of the top of his massive brown-and-white head. His dark eyes were ringed with white; a sign that the bull was highly unpredictable. As Slade opened the gate and quietly stepped into the small, rectangular corral, the bull's ears twitched. Not a good sign. Closing the gate and locking it, Slade never took his attention off Diablo.

Shorty moved opposite of where Slade was, his face filled with tension. The bull snapped his attention to the wrangler.

Perfect. Slade moved closer, within five feet of the massive animal so he could get a good look at that bloody rear leg. Shorty was keeping the bull's attention. Diablo would never allow a human this close under ordinary circumstances. Leaning down, Slade had trouble seeing the leg clearly. He saw dried blood on the inside of bull's pastern. The flesh had been peeled back.

"Look out!" Shorty yelled.

Too late!

Diablo whirled around, throwing his massive one-ton body straight at Slade, who was caught in a crouched position.

One second, Slade was leaping to his full height, and the next, he felt the bull's powerful impact against his body. White-hot heat and pain roared through his right thigh. In seconds, the bull had hooked him with his deadly horns and tossed him upward in the air like a puppet.

Slade heard the bellowing of the enraged bull. He landed close to the gate, crashing into the ground with an oomph!

Shorty was screaming to get the bull's attention. For a second, Diablo broke his charge and whipped toward the frantic wrangler.

Those seconds enabled Slade to scramble to his feet and lunge for the gate.

Diablo whirled around and charged, his bellowing echoing around the area.

Slade slammed and locked the iron gate. The bull hit it full force, sending him flying backward several feet into the dirt.

Safe! He was safe! Dazed, Slade sat up, breathing hard. Diablo eyed him through the pipe rails, huffing and snorting. He angrily pawed the dirt and lowered his head once more, wanting to get to Slade. But he couldn't. That iron-railed gate had withstood his massive charge. It would hold.

"Boss! Boss!" Shorty scrambled around the corral and ran toward him.

Slade shook his head. He'd screwed up. *Damn it!* As he tried to get up, his right leg collapsed beneath him. Slade fell to the ground.

Shorty breathed in gulps as he knelt down next to where he sat. "Boss, you're hurt.

Oh, my God, you're bleeding bad!"

In shock, Slade looked down at his right thigh. Diablo's horn had ripped his Levi's open and gored him. Blood was pumping and purling quickly out of a very deep wound. Mind numb and wrestling with the shock of the attack, Slade pressed his hand hard against the heavily bleeding wound.

"Get Jordana on the phone," he rasped.

Shorty's hands were shaking as he pulled his cell phone out of his back pocket. He dialed.

Slade sat there, knowing he shouldn't move. He wasn't a medic, but he knew there was a huge artery in his leg, and it appeared to him that Diablo had struck it. That accounted for the heavy bleeding. Cursing softly, he saw Shorty's face grow hopeful as he connected with Jordana.

"Give it to me," Slade ordered, holding up his other hand.

Shorty did as he was told.

"Jordana," Slade grunted.

"Hi, Slade. What's up?"

"I just got gored by my bull. It's my right thigh. Where are you at?" He knew on three days a week she had her clinic in town.

"You're gored?"

"Yes. I need your help."

"It is bleeding badly?"

"Yes." He heard her suck in a breath.

"Listen, I'm just next door to you. I've just finished a house call with Iris Mason. I'll be right over. Whatever you do, keep pressure on that wound."

"I will, thanks," Slade said. Blood was oozing through his fingers no matter how hard he pressed down on the wound.

Handing the cell back to Shorty, he said, "Give me your belt."

Without blinking, Shorty quickly pulled off his well-worn leather belt. He knew what Slade was doing. In ranching, knowing first aid was a must. "Okay, Boss, you just keep pressure on it. I'll slide the belt around your leg above it and we'll see if we can't slow the bleeding."

Slade was glad his brother was asleep in the house. He'd be useless in this kind of emergency, anyway. Pain was beginning to drift up his leg and into his torso. Diablo had nailed him but good. Shorty quickly slid the leather belt around his thick thigh, and then he hauled hard on it to tighten it. Grunting with pain, Slade clamped down, gritting his teeth.

"It's working, Boss," Shorty said, out of breath. He pulled again and locked the belt down. The bleeding was slowing.

"Good," Slade said, his voice sounding far

away to him. He'd lost a lot of blood. Maybe too much.

"You want me to help you stand?"

"No. Just leave me here. Jordana will be here any minute. Get some towels, a bucket of water and bring it to me."

Shorty leaped to his feet and ran for the ranch house. Slade sighed. Damn, this was bad luck. He felt that the world was caving in on him. First Griff showed up. Now this. Even worse, Slade knew it would be impossible for him to ride Thor in the endurance race. A deep puncture wound like this would take a minimum of six to eight weeks to heal up properly. And if he tried to ride a horse while it was healing, it would simply tear it open and make things worse.

As Shorty came running out with the pail of water in one hand and a bunch of towels in another, Jordana drove in. She slammed on the brakes, dust rising all around the truck. In her hand she had her black physician's bag. Running toward Slade, her face set with concern, she met up with Shorty as she got to Slade.

"Slade?" Jordana asked, kneeling next to him. "Tell me what happened?" She quickly donned protective gloves and pulled his bloodied hand away from the wound site.

"Damn bull hooked me," he muttered.

163

Getting out a pair of scissors, Jordana quickly cut away the material to get a better look at the wound. She gently probed the area. She felt Slade tense. "Okay, this is serious, Slade. Call 911. You need to get to the hospital right away. I can't fix this out here."

"I'm *not* going to the hospital," he growled. He felt faint and fought it.

"You've lost a lot of blood," Jordana whispered. "That bull has hit a major artery in your leg, Slade. That belt is stopping most of the flow, but you need immediate surgery to repair this. What blood type are you?"

"Sonofabitch," Slade whispered. "I'm O positive." Of all things, he was going to have to go to the hospital. He glared up at her. Jordana was incredibly calm and centered. She saw things like this all the time, he reminded himself. "Are you sure? I don't want to go to the hospital."

Shaking her head, Jordana quickly wrapped it with a dressing. "You're going, Slade."

"I don't want a damned ambulance out here."

He was so stubborn! Compressing her lips, Jordana finished protecting the wound. "All right, then I'll take you in myself." She twisted a look up at the wrangler. "Shorty, get the passenger-side door of my truck open and come back and help me get Slade to his feet. He's lost a lot of blood and he's going to be weak."

"How can you tell?" Slade wondered, watching the red blood quickly soak through the thick dressing she'd placed over the injury.

"You're white as a sheet, Slade," she said tensely, closing her bag and standing nearby. 'You're going to need a transfusion. Has Diablo had all his shots?"

"Yeah," Slade said. "So have I."

"Tetanus?"

"Yes, two months ago. I'm fine."

He wasn't fine. Jordana saw how murky his eyes were looking. He was frighteningly pale, which told her he needed a blood transfusion pronto. Worse, he'd torn that major artery. If it wasn't repaired quickly, he could bleed to death. She didn't want to tell him the details. Pulling out her cell phone, she connected with the E.R. of the hospital, telling them to be ready to receive Slade. She ordered two pints of O positive blood to be on standby for him. Dr. Jonas Powers was the surgeon who was on duty. She ordered them to prepare the O.R. to accept Slade as soon as she could get him there. Everything was in motion.

Shorty came running back, his face filled with anxiety.

Jordana hooked her arm beneath Slade and Shorty took the other side. Together, they hoisted Slade to his feet. He was none too steady and walked with a heavy limp toward her truck.

"I hate hospitals," Slade growled unhappily as Jordana strapped him in and got inside the truck.

Shorty closed the passenger door after putting the seat belt across him.

Starting the truck, Jordana said, "It can't be helped, Slade. That's not a puncture wound you want to argue with. If we don't get that artery repaired pronto, you'll bleed out. I don't think you want to die." She gunned the engine as she turned the truck around. Luckily, Slade had had the road bladed by now, and it was smooth, graveled and flat. Forcing herself to pay attention to her driving, Jordana would occasionally glance over at Slade. His dusty cowboy hat was in his lap, his bloodied hand holding it in place. He had leaned back, eyes closed, his face pasty-looking. Heart pounding, Jordana knew the seriousness of his injury. He didn't seem to, but she knew he was in shock and going deeper.

"Are you in pain?" she demanded, turning the truck onto the highway and speeding toward the town.

"Not much," Slade muttered. It felt good to close his eyes. Suddenly, he felt sapped of all his mighty strength. He didn't like it. Feeling the movement of the truck, hearing the engine roaring, he asked, "How fast are you going?"

"Fast enough for the police to give me a ticket," she answered grimly. Both hands on the wheel, Jordana sorted out options of the quickest way to get to the E.R. Back roads were best because this was high tourist season with heavy traffic on major streets. Worriedly, she looked at his thigh. Blood was now leaking down his hairy leg below the wound. Even with the belt closing off a lot of the blood supply to that leg, it wasn't enough pressure.

By the time Jordana pulled her truck into E.R., Slade was slipping in and out of consciousness. Two young, strong orderlies helped him out of the truck and placed him on a gurney. Together, they quickly wheeled him inside while Jordana parked the truck.

Running into E.R., Jordana was pleased to see Jonas was already attending to Slade. There were seven nurses and orderlies waiting for his next orders. Breathing hard, Jordana saw they'd put an oxygen mask on

Slade. His eyes were closed. She quickly looked up at the monitors they'd hooked him up to. His blood pressure was down. Way down. Too far because he'd lost so much blood.

"Let's prep him," Jonas ordered his team. "He's going into O.R. 1."

Jordana saw that he'd probed the wound. It was still glistening with bright red blood, indicative of an arterial bleed. Slade lifted his hand and gripped her fingers.

"I don't want surgery. I don't want to be knocked out."

His eyes were dark and confused. Jordana leaned over him and whispered, "Everything's going to be okay, Slade. I'll be in the operating room with Dr. Powers. He's the best. He'll get that bleed stopped."

It was the last words Slade heard. He felt himself spiraling down, down, down. The only shred of consciousness he could retain was Jordana's warm, strong fingers gripping his. He felt movement. It must have been the gurney moving. Voices were all around him, but he could no longer make out what they were saying. He didn't want to be in the hospital. And he never wanted to be in here for surgery. Unable to open his lids, he homed in on Jordana's comforting hand gripping his. In a moment of need, she had been there for him. It was the only good thing to happen in this whole sordid mess. His whole world crashed down upon him at that moment, and Slade lost consciousness.

Voices. Slade heard voices. But one he recognized as he slowly emerged from the anesthesia. It was Jordana's calm, husky voice. It took every bit of strength he had to just crack open his lids enough to see where he was. Jordana was at his side wearing green scrubs. There was a man next to her. His mind wouldn't work. His mouth felt like cotton balls were stuffed inside it. There was a dull ache in his right thigh.

"He's coming around," Jordana said. She leaned over Slade and laid her hand on his gowned shoulder. "You're in the Jackson Hole hospital, Slade. Dr. Powers just repaired that artery tear. How are you feeling?"

She was so close. Slade clung to her warm blue gaze and hungrily absorbed her hand on his shoulder. "Like hell . . ." he managed to say thickly, words not easy.

She smiled a little. Slade was no longer pasty-looking. His deep tan was back once more. "Are you in pain?"

"A little," he managed. "No big deal. Just give me . . . some aspirin."

Jonas grinned. "Mr. McPherson, I'm your surgeon, Jonas Powers. We'll put a pain med in your IV. We repaired that artery. That bull of yours did a good job and ripped it open."

The information was too much for Slade to digest. He continued to drown in Jordana's blue eyes that were warm with an emotion he couldn't decipher. It was her hand on his shoulder that helped him orient back to the here and now. "Dr. Powers did a good job on you, Slade. Are you thirsty?"

Nodding, Slade closed his eyes. The anesthesia was wearing off but it was hell trying to think two words, much less put a sentence together.

Powers ordered the nurse to bring in another IV that would help manage his post-surgery pain. He then patted Jordana's shoulder and said, "I think you can handle it from here on out."

"Yes," she said, giving Jonas a quick smile. "Thanks for all your help."

"He'll live despite himself," Jonas added with a grin. "Tougher than nails."

Jordana agreed. The nurse moved with quiet, quick efficiency, and in no time, she had the pain medication flowing into the main IV. Jordana could see almost an instant relief on Slade's face. She thanked the nurse. Now they were alone in the private room.

Picking up the glass of water, Jordana put a straw into it. "I'm going to raise your bed, Slade. You'll hear a whirring sound. I have to get your bed up enough so you can sip this water out of a straw." Jordana knew that people were groggy and confused as they came out of anesthesia. Pressing the button, Slade's bed moved up so that he was placed in a partial sitting position.

Opening his eyes, he saw Jordana holding the water glass. She slid the straw between his cracked, dry lips.

"Drink all you want. Most people are thirsty after surgery."

The water was cold and delicious. Slade found himself gulping the water like a thirsty horse after a fifty-mile endurance ride. The fluid served to wake him up more. After he finished the glass, she pulled the straw from between his lips. Everything about Jordana was gentle. He looked forward to every contact with her.

Pouring a second glass, Jordana watched Slade finish it off in short order. "Your eyes are looking a little less dark. Are you feeling more here than there?" she asked with a teasing smile. It was sheer delight to touch Slade, to help him. And he seemed to respond powerfully to her voice and touch. Yes, there was something between them, no doubt. Jordana hadn't had time to think about it.

Swallowing the last of the water, Slade held up his hand and whispered, "Thanks, that's all I want . . ." The truth be known, Slade wanted *her.* Each time Jordana touched him, his heart pounded. It made him feel better. Truly, she was a healer.

"Anything else?" she wanted to know, standing beside him, her hands on the bed.

Looking around, Slade slowly absorbed his surroundings. Feeling more like himself, he asked, "What happened?"

"You were in surgery for two hours. Dr. Powers opened up the wound and repaired the artery. I was there beside you all the time, Slade." She smiled a little, lifted her hand and pushed several dark strands of his hair off his wrinkled brow. There was such pleasure in getting to touch this hard, tough cowboy. Even now, lying in a bed and wearing a white cotton gown, he couldn't hide his powerful masculinity. There was nothing weak about Slade.

Scowling, Slade muttered, "Did you call Shorty and let him know I survived?"

Nodding, Jordana smiled and said, "Yes, I did." She'd asked Shorty to tell Griff because she knew his brother would be worried. She didn't tell Slade that, however.

"And how long will I be laid up?"

"At least six to eight weeks," she told him. Seeing his brows slash down, Jordana understood his reaction. "You won't be able to ride at *all*, Slade. That artery must heal completely before you can throw your leg over a horse."

His mind whirled with anger and frustration. "The Tetons ride is coming up."

Placing her hand gently on his upper arm, Jordana said, "I know . . . I'm sorry." She didn't let on what Gwen Garner had told her earlier, that Slade was counting on that ten-thousand-dollar prize to push away the bank foreclosure that was looming over his family ranch. "I wish . . . I wish this hadn't happened," she added softly. How badly she wanted to touch Slade. His face was drawn in a different kind of pain. All Jordana wanted to do was hold him tight and protect him against harsh reality. Moving her fingers up and down his upper arm, she had nothing else to say because it couldn't change the facts.

Her fingers created warmth throughout his arm. Slade lay there, eyes closed, simply soaking in her grazing touch. Terror overrode it, however. Terror of losing his ranch.

If he couldn't ride Thor in the race, he couldn't get an opportunity to win that ten thousand dollars. And he knew Frank Halbert at the bank was just waiting like a vulture to swoop down and take his family ranch away from him once and for all. Up to this moment, Slade had managed to stave off the bank. Now . . . oh, hell, he was going to lose his ranch. A ranch his father and grandfather had carved out of the wilderness and made bloom. He tasted the ashes of defeat in his mouth. Slade knew no bank would loan him money. His credit was worthless. Struggling with the enormity of what his injury had just done, Slade felt hot tears jamming into his closed eyes. Fighting them, he refused to give into his emotions.

"Excuse me, Dr. Lawton, but Mr. McPherson's brother Griff is downstairs and asking to see him," a nurse called from the door.

Jordana saw Slade's eyes snap open. She saw tears mingled with anger. Automatically, her hand tightened a bit more on Slade's shoulder.

"I don't want to see him," Slade ground out, lifting his head and glaring at the blonde nurse.

"Yes, sir, Mr. McPherson," she murmured, "I'll let him know."

The door closed.

Slade's gut felt like a nest of writhing, angry snakes. Only Jordana's quiet presence helped him calm down enough to think clearly. He looked over at her.

"Get me out of here, Jordana. I don't want to stay."

"But," she said, stunned, "you have to, Slade. You need to be here at least two days."

Forcing himself up into a sitting position, the blue blanket falling away, he growled, "No. Either you help me leave or I'll do it on my own."

Jordana saw he meant it. "Okay, hold on, Slade." She lifted her hands to stop him from climbing out of bed. "Let's compromise."

Scowling, he said, "What do you mean?"

"I know you want out of here. And it won't do you a bit of good to be around your brother at your ranch right now. You need some quiet and rest, not agitation." Jordana lowered her voice and said urgently, "You can't move around much. That artery was just sewn up. What if I took you over to my house? I have a second bedroom. And I have the next two days at my clinic, so I could come home and check on you from time to time."

Startled by the idea, Slade nodded. "I appreciate this, Jordana. I'll go home with you."

CHAPTER TEN

Just as Jordana was wheeling Slade out in a wheelchair to the front door of the hospital, his brother Griff met them. He was obviously concerned, and she saw anxiety in is green eyes.

Slade glared up at him. "I told you I didn't want to see you," he growled.

"I wanted to see if you were okay." Griff nodded respectfully toward Jordana. "Doctor, thank you for saving his life."

"You're welcome," Jordana murmured as she pushed the wheelchair down a wide hall. "You are Griff? His twin brother?" She saw how agitated Slade was becoming. It had taken her fifteen minutes to persuade him to sit down in a wheelchair. If he'd tried to walk, it would have torn the artery open again. He'd angrily sat in the wheelchair. Pride was evident even now in his ashen face. And his eyes were black with rage that his twin had come for a visit.

"Yes, I am. May I push the wheelchair for you?"

"No," Slade snarled at him. "Go back where you came from, Griff. You have *no* business out here."

For a moment, Griff was hurt by his brother's angry behavior. Shoring himself up from the unexpected attack, he said, "Are you coming home?"

"No, thank God, I'm not," Slade said bitterly.

Giving Jordana a searching look, Griff stumbled. "Then . . . where?"

"My home," she explained. Jordana didn't want to get into any more of a discussion. Slade was enraged, and, she was sure, embarrassed that his brother had seen him in a wheelchair, of all things. Giving Griff a sad look, she said, "I'm taking him to my home for the next few days. If you can have Shorty, his wrangler, bring him some clean clothes, I'd appreciate it." Giving Griff something to do would help Griff deal with this situation. She saw his face lighten.

"I can do that," Griff said, managing a slight smile. He looked down at Slade. "I hope you get better. If there's anything I can do —"

"There isn't," Slade snapped flatly. He saw hurt come to Griff's eyes and tried to protect himself from his twin's reaction.

Jordana knew how helpless Griff felt. Slade was going to have it his way or no way. And she knew he was not going back to the ranch because he didn't want to rely on his brother to help him out in such a tight spot. "We'll see you later," she murmured, giving Griff an understanding look. Griff perked up beneath her softened tone. Nodding, he turned and strode out of the sliding glass doors.

"Good riddance," Slade muttered. Feeling ashamed and weak in the wheelchair, Slade wished to hell this was all over. His leg was aching. So was his heart. He hadn't expected Griff to show up. "I wonder how long he's been waiting around outside my room?"

Keeping her voice light and without judgment, Jordana slowed the wheelchair and waited for the huge glass doors to automatically slide open. "I don't know. It's not important right now, Slade. You're looking very pale, and we need to get you to my house. How is your leg feeling?"

It had taken every ounce of Slade's energy to dress himself. He'd refused Jordana's help. And he'd told the nurse to leave. The struggle had drained him. "A little ache, but it's not bleeding."

Nodding, Jordana pulled a huge breath of fresh air into her lungs as she pushed Slade down the wide sidewalk. "If you'd let me help you dress, you probably wouldn't be feeling so exhausted," she said. There was no sense in making Slade feel more angry and upset than he already was. He looked shaken by Griff's unexpected appearance. Slade was having to deal with a lot right now, and she touched his shoulder gently. "Things will work out, Slade. I just have that feeling."

Shaking his head, his Stetson on his lap, he muttered, "They can't get any worse."

Wheeling him out to the asphalt parking lot, she laughed. "Well," she said wryly, leaning down and catching his stormy gaze, "yes, they could. You could be dead."

Grunting, Slade said nothing. He saw Jordana's pickup. A sense of freedom flowed through him. "Thanks for letting me stay with you a couple of days. I realize this isn't what you need, either. You work all the time. You're riding thirty miles twice a week. . . ."

"Hush, Slade," she murmured, parking and braking the wheelchair beside her truck. "Don't you try and carry my loads for me, too." Jordana patted his shoulder to try and give him solace. "Right now, I know things look dark to you. We all have those times in our life." She unlocked the truck and opened the passenger side door. "But we get through them because other people support and care for us. Life is never lived in a vacuum."

Nodding, some of Slade's anger dissolved. Being around Jordana was heavenly, but he couldn't tell her that. Even the ache in his leg receded when she grazed his shoulder. She was a healer, he realized. And inwardly, right now, he was starved for every smile, every touch, she would bestow on the likes of him.

"Okay, cowboy," Jordana murmured, holding out her hand, "let's get you into my truck."

Slade didn't refuse her hand this time. Being stubborn or prideful could get his leg artery torn open again and he bitterly swallowed his pride. Reaching out, he grasped her opened hand. Her skin was cool and soft. Slade could feel the strength in it and her as she helped to bring him to his feet.

"Dizzy?" Jordana asked, concerned as she gripped Slade's elbow. He'd put out his other hand on the truck to steady himself. Often after transfusions, there could be some dizziness when suddenly standing after being in a sitting position for a long time.

"Yeah," he admitted hesitantly. One step at a time, he made it to the truck and carefully eased himself into the passenger side seat.

"It's because of the loss of blood," Jordana murmured. Leaning across him, she pulled the seat belt in place. He was a powerful man even though he was injured. His barrel chest was well sprung. There was nothing to dislike about Slade as a man. Jordana felt herself trembling inwardly as she worked so closely to Slade for those few moments. Her dreams had become more and more sensual regarding Slade. And she was so close to his face and that wonderful mouth of his, that she could have turned and kissed him.

Shaken by her own neediness that was growing for Slade, Jordana eased away and shut the door. The sunshine was warming, and she looked up to appreciate the deep blue sky. A hawk was flying high above the area, its rust-colored redtail bright for a moment as it turned. She took the wheelchair, closed it up and placed it in the back of the truck. Struggling to contain her own emotions because being around Slade automatically stirred her up, Jordana opened the truck door and climbed in.

On the way through traffic to her home on the outskirts of Jackson Hole, Jordana kept an eye on Slade. He'd leaned his head back and rested it against the seat, eyes closed. His pallor was unchanged. She knew the confrontation with Griff had take anything he'd had left out of him. How badly Jordana wanted to simply put her arms around this prideful man and give him a moment's ease from his world that had just crashed down upon him. Understanding that Slade felt safe enough to be with her made her heart sing with unexpected joy.

"When we get home," Jordana told him softly, so as not to speak too loud and disturb him, "I'll take you through the garage to the inner door. I have a second bedroom nearby. And there's a ramp so it will be easy to push your wheelchair up and into my house."

Slade barely opened his eyes. It felt good to just be alone with Jordana. "Sounds good," he murmured. "I need to thank you for doing this. I know it's putting a hell of a burden on you."

She smiled a little, reached over and touched his hand that rested over his Stetson in his lap. "I'm happy to do it."

"I can't go back to my ranch," he uttered tiredly. "Not right now. I have to get strong enough to do the work around there. I don't want Griff in the way. He knows *nothing* about ranching."

"You're injured, Slade. You need to be somewhere safe so you can heal up. Maybe being here for a few days will help you sort everything out and you'll come up with a plan."

"Are you always this hopeful?" he wondered, feeling a desperate need to sleep. The surgery and anesthesia had taken even his powerful energy and sucked it out of him.

"Always," Jordana said with a soft laugh. Slowing down, she said, "We're here."

Opening his eyes and sitting up, Slade saw a white single-story ranch house with dark brown trim. The lawn was small and rectangular. The bushes were trimmed, and flowers were on either side of the concrete walk leading up to the front door. "Nice place," he said, meaning it. Jordana pressed the garage door opener. Easing the truck up and into it, Jordana turned off the engine. She gave him a gentle look. Slade looked exhausted. "I'll bet you're ready for a nap."

"How did you know?"

"Your eyes are dark-looking, Slade. And you can barely keep them open," she said with a full smile. "What you need is a bed and some good, uninterrupted sleep. Come on, let's get you inside. . . ."

■ ■ ■ ■

Slade groaned as he lay down on top of the queen-size bed in Jordana's guest bedroom. If he hadn't been so exhausted, he'd have appreciated all her efforts to make the room look as if it came straight out of the nineteenth century. Instead, as she guided him to lie down, all he could do was slur, "I need to sleep. . . ." and that was the last thing Slade remembered.

Jordana saw Slade's pale face relax. His beard needed to be shaved and it gave him a dangerous look. The house was cooled by central air-conditioning, and she took a blanket from the closet and put it over him. He was too tired to get undressed and slip beneath the covers. Tucking him in, she saw for the first time the real Slade as he sank into a deep, untroubled sleep. Standing there, Jordana felt guilty for looking upon him without his knowledge.

Slade's face was utterly free of strain. She saw the fullness of his mouth for the first time. The wrinkles that were always on his brow had dissolved. The slash marks on either side of his mouth lessened. As she stood there, Jordana tried to imagine what Slade would be like without the awful weight of his ranch balancing on the edge of foreclosure. Or the fact he couldn't take part in the Tetons endurance ride to save his ranch from the bank. Jordana knew from personal experience that financial woes were the most stressful of all.

Moving quietly, Jordana pulled the dark burgundy curtains closed. Slade would probably sleep for six to eight hours. She knew what the stress of surgery did to people. Forcing herself to leave, Jordana quietly shut the door. Slade felt safe enough to sleep, and that made her feel good. Looking at her watch, she saw it was nearly five o'clock in the evening. Her stomach growled. She had taken a few hours off from her shift to help Slade. Luckily, another doctor had agreed to come in and take her place so she could take Slade home.

Humming softly, Jordana walked into the kitchen. It was painted a soft yellow with white curtains on either side of the long rectangular windows across the twin sinks. From where she lived, she couldn't see the Tetons. Instead large hills loomed out of the valley floor. Tinkering with the coffeepot, she was grateful to have the next twelve hours off. That meant she could stay with Slade and be here as a nurse of sorts. The phone on the wall rang.

"Hello?"

"Jordana, this is Shorty, out at the ranch."

"Hi, Shorty."

"Is the Boss okay? His brother, Griff, came back here and was lookin' worried."

"He's fine," Jordana soothed, hearing the anxiety in the wrangler's tone. "Right now, he's in the guest bedroom sleeping off the stress of the surgery and the anesthesia."

"And his leg? I tried to ask Griff about it, but he didn't know nothing."

"Slade refused to see him, that's why," Jordana explained.

"Oh, there's plenty of bad blood between those two," Shorty agreed heavily. "But what about the Boss? Is he gonna be okay?"

Jordana gave Shorty all the information.

"When can he come back to the ranch?"

"Probably in two or three days," she told him. "Right now, he needs no distractions, Shorty. That artery has to heal up so when he puts weight on that leg, it doesn't tear it open again."

"I see, I see," he murmured. "Well, you tell the Boss to get well. Tell him he has no worries. I can manage here by myself."

"What about Griff?" she wondered. "Can't he pitch in?"

Shorty laughed a little. "Him? Oh, Dr. Lawton, he don't know the right end from the sharp end of a pitchfork. You know how they are?"

"Indeed I do. But it looked like Griff *wanted* to be of help. Maybe if you could assign him some easy jobs around the ranch?" She was hoping Shorty wouldn't be as hard on Griff as Slade was. All he needed, she thought, was a chance. And he'd looked as if he'd wanted to be of help to Slade but really hadn't known how.

"That's an idea," Shorty said. "He's following me around like a lost calf. I think I'll hand him the tools to go start cleaning out the box stalls. That should keep him outta my hair."

Laughing softly, Jordana said, "Don't be too hard on him, Shorty. He loves Slade and he wants to help. Griff may not know how exactly, but my bet is you'll come up with chores he can do around the ranch."

"Yes, ma'am, I know I can. Are you coming out here tomorrow morning to ride Stormy thirty miles? Tomorrow is your day to ride. Or are you staying there with the Boss?"

"I'll be out," she promised. Jordana didn't want to say anything right now, but she thought they might have a chance to try for the big money of the Tetons endurance ride. Oh, it was true she was a greenhorn when it came to the top level of competition, but she wanted to win the money for Slade and his ranch. But that was her secret. She wasn't sure she could pull it off, but she was going to give it one heck of a try.

"See you at seven a.m., then," Shorty said, his voice lighter and sounding almost happy.

"See you then," Jordana promised. Hanging up the phone, she stood there for a moment digesting her newly hatched plan. There was no doubt in her mind that her sturdy, small mustang mare could win that race. The only real question was her. She lacked the competitive knowledge of a ride like this. And she recalled that Slade was very worried about Curt Downing. Shrugging, Jordana compartmentalized the daunting idea and put it aside. What she would do was cook Slade dinner. She was sure when he awakened, he'd be a starving cow brute.

Slade had just sat up, leaning against the headboard, when the bedroom door opened. He wiped the sleep from his eyes. Jordana looked beautiful wearing a red-checked apron around her waist. He saw a smudge of white flour on her left cheek. "What time is it?" he asked in a sleep-thickened voice. He didn't have his watch back, and he missed it.

"Eight p.m. You slept three hours," Jordana murmured, walking over to the bed and peering down at him. Only the light from the hall was spilling into the room. Jordana thought he looked stronger. "How are you feeling?" she asked, picking up his thick, hairy wrist to take his pulse.

"Like I'll live," he told her. Her touch was electrifying to him. Slade almost lifted his other arm to pull her down beside him. Jordana no longer looked like a doctor. She had changed out of her scrubs and white lab coat into a soft orange tee with three-quarter sleeves and a set of figure-revealing jeans. Her fingers were cool and soft. Another ache began in him, and this time it wasn't at his injury site. He wanted to reach up and thread his fingers through her mussed hair. Jordana looked vulnerable.

"Good, your pulse is normal," she said with a smile. Reluctantly, Jordana released his wrist. "And you look less pale. Ready for a light on in the room?"

"I'm ready to get up," Slade said. He threw off the blue blanket.

"Not so fast," she cautioned, going to the wall and flipping on the overhead light. "You need to move around with that wheelchair for at least forty-eight hours."

Groaning, Slade said, "I hate that thing."

Laughing, Jordana brought the wheelchair beside his bed. "I know you do, but it can help you heal faster."

Slade was strong enough to bring his legs over the bed and sit up. It felt good to simply move. "I don't want anyone seeing me in that contraption."

"Cowboy pride," she laughed softly, leaning down to put the brakes on the wheels so it wouldn't move when he stood up.

"I guess so," Slade admitted, frowning. Jordana stood back and allowed him to stand on his own.

"Dizzy?"

Shaking his head, Slade moved carefully into the wheelchair. "Not so far."

"Good, your body is adjusting. Bathroom?"

"Yes," he said. In moments, Jordana was pushing him down the pine-floored hall to a huge bathroom that had plenty of room for his wheelchair.

"I'll leave you here," she said lightly. "When you're ready to come out, just open the door."

Slade nodded. "I'll be out in a bit."

A few minutes later, Slade sat at a large, rectangular pine table in the dining room, the home filled with delicious odors. He wasn't prepared for the meal that Jordana had made for him. It struck him that she'd gone to a lot of trouble. There were fresh rolls, and now he understood where that bit of flour on her cheek had come from. A small beef roast surrounded with potatoes, carrots and celery sat in front of him. And best of all, thick, dark brown gravy was in a bowl next to it. *Homemade gravy.* How long had it been since he'd tasted good gravy? Slade could remember his mother making the best gravy in the world.

"Are you hungry?" she teased, smiling as she untied the apron and placed it on the counter.

"I am," Slade admitted. As she sat down near his left elbow, he added, "This is a mighty fine-looking meal, Jordana. You shouldn't have gone to all this trouble." Slade didn't want to add that at his ranch, he ate a lot of frozen dinners, pizza or canned goods. This meal was a feast, and his mouth watered in anticipation.

"It's nothing," she assured him, placing a dark blue linen napkin across her lap. She picked up a large spoon and said, "Give me your plate. I'll put what you want on it."

Slade was starving. By the time Jordana handed the plate to him, it was piled high with food. He saw a slight, sparkling smile in her eyes, but she said nothing about the amount of food.

"I feel like an interloper," Slade confided, spooning the gravy over his beef and potatoes.

"Oh?" Jordana took the gravy boat from him. When their fingers touched, she inwardly sighed. Any reason to touch Slade was a good one. Did he know how much she loved these moments? Jordana didn't think so.

"Yeah," Slade said, digging hungrily into the food. "My mother used to make the best gravy in the world. And yours tastes just as good."

It hurt Jordana to see him wolfing down the food as if he'd never had a home-cooked meal in his life. As she sat there eating with Slade, she realized that he probably cooked for himself. "You don't make gravy?" she wondered.

Embarrassed, Slade murmured, "No. I don't know how."

Grieving for Slade, for the loss of his mother at such an early age, she saw how much he appreciated the gravy she'd made. "It's something that's easy to make," she assured him. "If you're interested, I can show you how some time."

"I'd like that," Slade said, meaning it.

How beautiful Jordana looked in that moment. Her cheeks were pink, her blue eyes sparkling with joy. As Slade's gaze slid down to her mouth he felt his lower body suddenly go hot with longing. For her. There was such grace in every movement she made, whether it was spooning out gravy on his potatoes or the simple act of eating her food.

Uncomfortable with his neediness of her, Slade found himself helpless in the wake of his epiphany. Her shoulder-length hair had been tamed into a ponytail at the nape of her neck. A few long, black strands of hair dipped across her unmarred brow. Slade fought the need to slide his fingers across those strands and tame them back into place behind her delicate ear. Why hadn't he seen her beauty before this? Had the surgery and anesthesia done it? Shaking himself internally, Slade felt confused. His whole world had been upended with Diablo goring his thigh.

"How soon can I get back to the ranch?"

"Probably in two or three days."

"Not any earlier?"

"No. That artery has to heal up to a certain point."

Slade scowled. He continued to eat as if he were starved. Really, he hadn't realized how he'd hungered for a good home-cooked meal. "Are you going out tomorrow to ride Stormy?"

"Yes," she said. "Thirty miles. Why?"

"I was just thinking I could hitch a ride back with you, was all."

Giving him a merry look, Jordana said, "Bed rest means exactly that, Slade. You don't get to go home right now. You need complete rest."

The look he gave her melted her heart. Despite his condition, Slade was a powerful, masculine cowboy. Jordana thought that he was the perfect iconic cowboy of the nineteenth century. Strong, silent and enduring. *The last cowboy.* She saw the worry in his gray eyes, the anxiety about his ranch on the brink of foreclosure. It was easy to read Slade's face right now. Jordana was grateful that his armored mask wasn't in place. It probably had to do with his surgery. Trauma and surgery were a powerful combination to strip anyone of their normal personality traits.

"Well," he murmured, a catch in his deep voice, "this feels like home to me."

CHAPTER ELEVEN

Home! The word held such power for Jordana. After dinner Slade had reluctantly agreed to sit in his hated wheelchair and watch some TV in the living room. She placed the dishes in the dishwasher. Afterward, she went to her office at the other end of her home and answered calls from her patients. She was never without her pager, and although her clinic was involved only in a Functional Medicine specialty, her patients had questions that needed to be answered. That took an hour of her time.

Slade heard Jordana's phone ring just as she walked through the living room and into the kitchen. She was a model of efficiency, and he reminded himself she was a physician. In some ways, her life wasn't her own; it belonged to her patients. And he was intensely jealous of them right now. Inwardly, he wanted that time with her. Watching television was something Slade rarely did. He was simply too busy out at the ranch with things that were far more important and that needed to be handled on a daily, ongoing basis.

Trying not to eavesdrop on the phone call, he realized it was something serious. Jordana hung up.

She popped into the living room. "Slade, I've got to go to the hospital."

"Okay," he said, frowning. "Do you ever get any time off?"

Jordana smiled a little and picked up her purse from a table in the corner. "I'm out riding Stormy every time you said I needed to, don't I?" She saw he was looking weary. "Do you want to go back to bed? I could wheel you in there before I leave."

Shaking his head, Slade said, "No, I'll stay up. Will you be back soon?"

"I don't know," she said, lifting her hand to tell him goodbye as she headed for the front door.

The door closed with finality. Slade felt suddenly and inexplicably abandoned. He knew it was silly to feel that way. For so long he'd wanted quality time with Jordana. And now, this. Running his fingers through his short hair, Slade realized he was emotionally raw from the surgery. Jordana had warned him about that. Looking around the warm apricot-colored living room that had several living plants sitting here and there, he realized just how much he missed having a woman in his life.

It wasn't a pretty picture, Slade decided. This injury had set him back in uncounted ways. And being here in Jordana's home simply reminded him of something else he didn't have. Unwillingly, he continued to absorb the room from where he sat. There were dark green drapes at the huge picture window. The evening sunlight was making the sky a paler blue. The overstuffed velveteen green and brown chairs made the golden pine floor prominent. There wasn't a bit of dirt or dust anywhere. If he didn't know better, he would have thought he was in a nineteenth-century home.

The furniture was made of blond oak, and it was old and stained from probably a hundred years of use or more, Slade guessed. The stained-glass floor lamp and table lamps reminded him of Tiffany's work. On one wall was a series of photos, and he pushed his wheelchair in that direction to get a better look at them. They were all family photos. He saw a baby photo and thought it might be Jordana. Next to that, she was six years old, her parents on either side of her as she sat on a black-and-white pinto

Shetland pony. At six, Jordana had a cute little red cowboy hat, a leather vest and red bandanna around her neck. A smile cracked his tense veneer.

For the next fifteen minutes, Slade hungrily absorbed Jordana's life. He saw photos of her riding in dressage classes, in another, holding a trophy and smiling with relief that she'd won. There was always a horse in her life, Slade realized. He'd taken her for little more than a greenhorn who rode English and did a little bit of dressage. But these photos told a whole different story. An impressive one.

As he moved down a few feet and observed her college years, she was still riding in dressage and endurance contests. And he saw her in a white lab coat during her residency years. Another photo showed her holding up her stethoscope and smiling triumphantly. Slade guessed that's when her seven-year residency was over and she was now free to be an E.R. physician. Moving his wheelchair back to the center of the room, his mind spun. The television was on, but he didn't hear it.

By the time Jordana arrived home, it was dark. Slade had had plenty of time to digest her life and how badly he'd erred regarding it and her. When the door opened, his heart leaped. As Jordana walked into the living room, she smiled a little tiredly over at him.

"How are you doing? Bored to death?" she teased. Slade looked thoughtful, not tense as before. His mouth softened and was no longer a thinned line. "The pain meds must be working. You look relaxed."

Slade watched her progress to the table and said, "Do you ever take care of yourself?"

Startled, Jordana suddenly laughed. "Of course I do, Slade." She came up to him and peered down at his recently washed jeans. Barely touching the area where the dressing over the wound was, she murmured, "This looks good. I don't see any seepage." Looking up, mere inches from his face, she asked, "No pain?" Jordana was sorely tempted to lean just a little bit forward and kiss that masculine mouth of his! Shaken by that need, she straightened and removed her hand from his thigh.

"I'm fine," Slade said. His whole leg burned white-hot from her unexpected touch. Oh, he knew it was a doctor's touch, a medical examination, nothing more, but his body didn't know that. And neither did his galloping heart. She stood there smiling down at him and taking off her bright red, yellow and orange scarf from around her slender neck. Her hair was softly mussed, and Slade ached to slide his fingers through it.

"Good. I'm ready for a cup of coffee. How about you?"

Nodding, his spirits soared as he was now beneath the spotlight of her warmth and care. She wheeled him into the brightly lit kitchen and placed him at the pine table so he could see what she was doing at the counter. Suddenly, Slade realized he felt a strange, new emotion. It was happiness. Shocked by it, he watched Jordana move around the spotless kitchen as she made them a pot of fresh coffee.

"What happened at the hospital?" he asked. Her hands were long, her fingers beautifully tapered. Hands that performed surgery on people who had gotten into traumatic accidents. Hands that healed. Hands that he wanted touching him everywhere.

"A rollover truck accident," she said over her shoulder as she put the coffee grounds into the coffeemaker. "The kid was sixteen, going too fast and the sheriff's deputy found him at the bottom of a hill."

"Did the kid live?"

Jordana turned after she finished getting the coffee ready to perk. "Yes."

"Did you perform surgery on him?"

"Yep, I did. But I had another specialist in there with me. He was an orthopedist. This kid shattered his left leg. He wasn't wearing a seat belt, and as he was thrown from the cab, his left leg smashed through the front windshield and struck the side of the cab as he flew out of it." Shaking her head, Jordana added more softly, "I don't think he's going to keep that leg. It's too shattered. The bone surgeon did all he could, but he's doubtful, too."

"Sixteen," Slade muttered, his brows falling. "Messing up your life that young by losing a leg? That's bitter medicine."

Sighing, Jordana felt her sadness lift as she sat down opposite Slade at the table. "I know. The parents are taking it hard."

"Whose the kid?"

"Randy Bateman."

Cursing softly, Slade said, "I know them. They're a local cattle ranching family south of Jackson Hole. That's a real shame."

She settled her elbows on the table and absorbed Slade's quiet, strong presence. Even if he was crippled for a while, he was still so powerful that it rocked her emotionally as a woman. "That's the hard part of my job, Slade. I love being a surgeon and I love helping people mend. What I don't like

—" and she clasped her hands in front of her "— is days like this. Randy is only sixteen. One stupid mistake of driving too fast around a curve is going to change his whole life, forever."

Frowning, Slade touched his injured leg. "I guess I have nothing to bitch about, do I? I might be laid up and crippled for a little while, but that kid might lose his leg."

"Right," Jordana said, giving him a soft smile. "Hey," she said teasingly, "I like this sensitive side to you, Slade. How come I never see it when I'm out at your ranch?"

Giving her a shy grin, he melted beneath her sunny smile. "I'm your teacher out there. You're my student. It's a different relationship than what we share here."

Chuckling, Jordana stood up and went to the counter. "That's true, but I like seeing this other side to you. It's a pleasant surprise."

"Don't get used to it," Slade teased back with a slight chuckle. His heart opened powerfully as he sat there watching her take down two orange ceramic mugs and pour the coffee into them. How slender and firm she looked in her jeans and tee. Her hips were flared, her legs long and coltish looking. The tee outlined her small breasts and waist. She wasn't voluptuous, but that didn't matter to Slade.

Sitting down after she'd delivered the coffee, Jordana said, "I'll need to open that dressing before you go to bed tonight. It has to be changed twice daily."

The thought of her hands on him like that made Slade almost burn his tongue as he sipped the dark brew. She'd said it matter-of-factly, not like a woman who wanted to intimately touch him. Slade warned himself to be careful with how he was overreacting to Jordana in such close, intimate quarters. "I appreciate it. Thank you."

"After forty-eight hours, you will be able to do it for yourself."

"After forty-eight hours I'm going to be back at my ranch," he warned her. Although Slade wistfully found himself wishing he could stay here with Jordana instead. When she walked in that door, the whole place lit up with sunlight. When she was gone, it felt cold and lifeless. Slade didn't know a woman could affect him so powerfully in such a positive way. He'd never experienced this with Isabel. And really, all Jordana had done was a generous offer to keep him here because he hated hospitals.

Chuckling, Jordana said, "Yes, as your physician, I'll write a script for you to go home." She grinned over at him, and she liked his boyish reactions. This was a side to Slade that she'd never encountered. And she liked it maybe a little too much.

"That's big of you," he said. Seeing the merriment sparkle in her blue eyes, Slade liked the fact he could make her smile. Teasing wasn't something he did a lot, but with her, it came naturally, and it was playful and harmless. It made her laugh, and that sent a keening ache through him. Isabel had never made him laugh. Her contact was nothing like Jordana's hand upon him. Their touches were so different, it made Slade realize how bad a choice he'd made when he'd impulsively married Isabel. His wife had been flirty, always grazing his hand or shoulder and giving him that sultry, come-on look. Jordana was the exact opposite. There was so much Slade wanted time to sort out. But time wasn't on his side.

"Uh-oh," Jordana said, giving him a slight smile, "what were you just thinking? You went from being open to closing up like an iron book."

Startled, Slade realized he had allowed her to see his emotions. "Uh," he stammered, "just thinking about the past was all." He didn't want to lie to Jordana. She was too kind and loving to have that done to her. And Slade wasn't the type to lie, anyway. His blunt, unvarnished truth usually got him into more trouble than not. Lies weren't a part of his makeup.

Jordana had to tread carefully. She knew Slade's financial house was in ruins, but he'd never let on about it to her. She surmised he was worried about not being able to ride Thor and winning the Tetons endurance race. "I don't know about you, but my past put me in a financial hole the size of the Arizona meteor crater," she said lightly. When Slade's demeanor changed, and he looked interested, she added, "When I was at a New York City hospital earning my spurs as a resident, my boss made it impossible for me to continue working there. I sued him for sexual harassment. And when it was all over, I was just about penniless."

Frowning, Slade recalled the photos on the living room wall. "You lost the suit?"

"No, I won it, but as that happened, the stock market plunged and I lost my entire savings. I won the suit, left my job at that hospital and came out here. For the last two years, everything has been stressful for me insofar as finances went. I had to start all over. I didn't want to put my money back into the stock market ever again."

Stunned, Slade digested her story. "I guess

I never thought doctors were poor."

She smiled a little, her hands sliding around the mug. "Normally, you're right. But I had to pay hundreds of thousands of dollars to my attorney. When we settled the case, there was four hundred thousand dollars given to me. I bought this house with it."

"I'm sorry to hear this. I didn't know. . . ." And he didn't. Conscience eating at him, Slade said, "I want to reduce your monthly training bill to one thousand dollars."

Shocked, Jordana sat up. She had paid him two thousand dollars. "What? Are you serious?"

As badly as Slade needed that money, he could not go on with his scheme to milk her for extra money. Even though it could hold off the wolves from the bank, he couldn't do this to Jordana. She was the soul of kindness, and he'd rooked her because he hadn't wanted to train a woman. "I'm very serious. I'll write you a check when I get back to the ranch for that extra thousand. You need it worse than I do."

Alarmed, Jordana didn't think so. "But Gwen Garner said you were on the brink of foreclosure, Slade."

Oops! She didn't mean to blurt it out! Slade had already told her, too. She knew the topic was painful for him. Pressing her hand against her mouth, her eyes went huge, and Jordana saw the impact the words had on Slade. His gaze narrowed and his gray eyes darkened with pain.

"Yeah, that's right," he said, his voice suddenly dull and bitter. The cat was out of the bag, so Slade didn't tell Jordana that he'd tried to milk her out of an extra thousand a month because he'd thought she was a filthy rich doctor.

She reached across the table and gripped his hand. "You've had such a hard life, Slade. Everyone who knows you tells me that you're one of the hardest working ranchers in the valley." She saw his eyes widen for a moment as she touched his hand that was curled in a fist upon the table. It felt so good to touch him. She could feel the latent power in that hairy hand. A hand she wanted exploring her. Surprised over her thoughts, Jordana quickly pulled her fingers away.

"You need that extra money from me, then," she said stubbornly. "I *want* to pay you that two grand a month, Slade."

"You can't afford it, either, Jordana."

Hearing the frustration in his tone, she shook her head. "If I don't put a thousand dollars into my savings a month, I'm not losing this house." She gestured around the kitchen. "You, on the other hand, can use it to stop bank foreclosure."

Giving her a look of impatience, Slade growled, "You don't understand, dammit. I charged you *twice* the amount of my other students because I didn't want to have to train a woman for endurance!" There, the truth was out.

Jordana's brows flew up. "Oh," was all she could choke out.

Slade reached over and placed his hand over hers. "Listen, I was wrong about you, Jordana. Dead wrong. My own past with my ex-wife, who was from New York City, made me do this. I'm sorry. I really am. And I want to make things right between us because you don't deserve this kind of trickery." And she didn't. Slade moved his fingers across her hand and watched her eyes turn soft and hungry. It was then he realized that not only was he attracted to her, but she was to him, too. Slade removed his hand. He'd hurt Jordana. Basically, he'd defrauded her. And Slade was ready to accept her censure, even if it meant she'd leave him and go train with Curt Downing.

Sitting there, Jordana felt the wild tingles moving up from her hand, arm and encircling her pounding heart. Oh! Slade was dangerous-looking, his beard darkening his face, emphasizing his high cheekbones and those icy gray eyes of his. Her gaze kept returning to his mouth. A mouth she wanted to cherish and kiss and then make hot, untrammeled love to this man. Swallowing hard, Jordana whispered tautly, "Slade, you had good reasons for your choices. I can forgive you for them."

Staring at her, Slade shook his head. "If I were you, I'd be damned angry."

Shrugging, Jordana finished her coffee. "You told me the truth, Slade. You're willing to give me the money back. We all make mistakes. It's what we learn from them that's important."

How different Jordana was from Isabel! Her maturity was like a warm blanket surrounding him. "I'm learning to stop comparing you to my ex-wife, Isabel. It's not fair to you. You're nothing like her."

"After hearing your story about her," Jordana said with a pained smiled, "you're right about that." She got up, feeling suddenly exhausted. It had been an intense one-hour discussion. "I don't know about you, but I'm ready for bed. I need to change your dressing, but would you like to get a shower first?"

Slade nodded. He saw the dark circles

starting to appear beneath her eyes. "Is the dressing waterproof?" he wondered.

"Yep, sure is. Come on, I'll take you to the master bathroom because it's very large and easy for you to maneuver around in."

"I can stand and take a shower on this leg?"

"Yes," she assured him, wheeling him out of the kitchen. Her master bedroom was on the opposite side of the house from the guest bedroom. "Do you need help undressing?"

The thought was hot and provocative. Slade put a lid on it. "No, I'll be fine. Just get me my hospital robe and I'll call you when I'm done?"

Nodding, Jordana wheeled him into the tan tiled bathroom. It had a shower at one end and a Jacuzzi-style bathtub at the other. "I can do that." Putting the parking brakes on the wheelchair, she called, "I'll be right back with your robe."

Slade sat there appreciating the huge master bathroom. The tile floor allowed easy movement of his wheelchair. There were metal handholds outside the shower and inside as well, so he could hold on to something if he felt dizzy or weak. Hearing her footsteps down the pine hall, he twisted his head. Jordana smiled and placed his bathrobe across one of the two basins.

"Holler if you need help, okay?"

"I'll be fine. You just take care of yourself," he told her gruffly. When she smiled a little, his heart raced. How could he ever have deceived this woman? Jordana was kind and generous. Reeling from how he'd treated her initially, Slade swore he'd right that wrong.

Jordana closed the door. Her heart felt like singing. Almost giddy from the intimate and personal talk with Slade, she felt as if she were floating down the hall toward the kitchen. Although Slade had pride, he could swallow it when the chips were down. As she puttered in the kitchen cleaning up for the night, Jordana knew he didn't have to tell her about the thousand dollars extra he'd hit her up for. She understood on a deeper level that Slade needed it to keep the bank at bay.

Where was their relationship going? Jordana wasn't sure. Had it been a mistake to bring Slade over here for two nights? She knew if he'd gone to his ranch, the rancor and bitterness he held against his twin, Griff, would have interfered with his healing process. Jordana knew this instinctively and breathed a sigh of relief for Slade. This was the first patient of hers that she'd ever allowed in her home. So what *else* was going on? As she stood at the sink staring out the curtained windows into the night, her heart whispered to her. She was powerfully drawn to Slade. But what were the consequences?

CHAPTER TWELVE

The morning was clear and cool as Jordana trotted Stormy down between the cow pastures. The sun was barely tipping above the Rocky Mountains to the east of her. Stormy was prancing and dancing beneath her hand, eager to get on with the thirty-mile training ride. Happiness thrummed through Jordana. Just having Slade in her home was working miracles for both of them, she realized. The intimacy was powerful, like an aphrodisiac. She hadn't made love to a man in over two years. Now, she wanted to.

Stormy snorted and tossed her head, her black mane flying. Laughing softly, Jordana leaned down and whispered, "Easy, girl. You have to warm up before we start."

Another snort and Stormy danced sideways.

Jordana laughed out loud and pressed her left calf against the barrel of the horse.

Stormy righted immediately and was impatient at being kept to such a slow trot. Jordana knew that if her horse was not properly warmed up, she could pull a tendon and that would take her out of the competition for a year. Tendon pulls or tears were an endurance rider's worst nightmare. It could easily sideline a horse for six months. And sometimes, if the tendon didn't heal properly, they could never resume that level of athletic challenge again.

Up ahead, Jordana saw that Diablo, the Hereford bull who had gored Slade, was tossing his head. He, too, felt the coolness and was frisky. She knew he was being taken over to the cows for breeding, and it was obvious he was ready to take on that role today. Shorty would be coming out in an hour to herd the feisty bull over to a smaller pasture where his girls awaited him. She saw the white jets of steam shooting out of his large nostrils.

Joy filtered through Jordana. Yes, the day was young. Full of promise. She felt the movement of Stormy between her strong legs and smiled. Riding a horse was like being rocked in a cradle by a mother, she thought. It was a rhythm and movement she couldn't live without.

Suddenly, Diablo bellowed. Startled,

Jordana saw the bull charging toward them! Stormy reacted first. As the bull hit the pipe railing with all his weight, the mustang leaped away to avoid the oncoming attack. Jordana followed through with her mare's defensive movement. Diablo had never charged them before! She watched the metal pipe railing tremble beneath the bull's unexpected charge. He bellowed again. Leaping forward, his eyes rolling and spittle drooling out of his opened mouth, he charged.

Jordana was about to ask Stormy to gallop in order to get away from the angry bull. Just as she pressed her calves into the horse, she felt Stormy falter. *Oh, no!* In seconds, the mare, who was trying to avoid the next assault by the angry bull, had slipped into a newly made gopher hole at the edge of the trail. Jordana threw the reins away to give Stormy her head in order to try and regain her balance. Stormy grunted. Jordana felt her left rear leg suddenly crumple beneath her. They were going down! Instinctively, Jordana jerked her feet out of the stirrups and lifted them upward. It felt as if she were in slow motion as the stalwart mare tumbled sideways and fell toward the ground.

Pushing off the saddle with her right foot, Jordana sailed out of the saddle. Stormy hit the grassy ditch next to the cow pasture with a grunt. Jordana hit the ground on her back, and she curled into a ball to absorb the fall. Air whooshed out of her lungs. Jordana rolled several feet before coming to a stop. Anxiously, she leaped to her feet, alarmed for Stormy. Jordana ignored the bruises to herself. Diablo galloped down the fence line away from them.

Stormy clawed with her four legs momentarily up in the air after she rolled into the ditch. The mustang righted herself and tucked her legs beneath her body. Jordana ran to her and Stormy lurched to her feet.

"Oh, no . . ." Jordana whispered, more alarmed as the mare stood, holding up her left rear hoof off the ground.

Speaking softly to her, she pulled the reins over Stormy's head. On the other side, Diablo bawled and continued to run down the fence line away from them. Jordana knew the fence would hold the angry bull and devoted her full attention to Stormy. The mare's nostrils were flared, and she was breathing hard.

"Easy, girl, easy," Jordana crooned as she slid her hand over the mare's steel gray rump and ran her hand down the lifted rear leg. Jordana's fears ballooned as she felt the lower leg where the tendon was located. It was mushy feeling, and already she could see swelling. Moaning to herself, Jordana realized Stormy had fallen into a gopher hole, twisted her rear leg and either tore or sprained the tendon as a result.

Grief avalanched Jordana as she gently felt the entire length of that tendon. Stormy stood quietly, her ears flicking back and forth. Jordana could tell the mare was in pain. Straightening, she looked toward the ranch area. She had to get hold of Shorty and pulled out her cell phone. With shaking fingers, she punched in the numbers. When he answered, relief shot through her.

"Shorty, call the vet. I think Stormy has pulled a tendon. And then, drive out here and bring me some elastic wraps. I've got to wrap her leg and walk her slowly back to the barn."

Slade heard the front door open. He'd just finished taking a shower, shaving and getting into his jeans and shirt when he heard the door. Moving out of the master bathroom, he pushed the wheelchair down the hall. Jordana appeared out of the foyer looking grim. Instantly, his heart accelerated. He saw her face was smudged with dirt, her hair loose and messy. As he looked closer, he saw mud on the left side of her jeans.

"What's wrong?" he demanded, meeting her in the kitchen.

Tearing up, Jordana halted and said in a choked tone, "Slade, I have awful news. I was trotting Stormy between the pastures when Diablo charged us." She sniffed and wiped the tears from her eyes. "Stormy jumped sideways, her left rear hoof falling down into a gopher hole at the side of the path. We went down. She's got a torn tendon."

"No . . ." Slade rasped. Of all things! He saw the tears continuing to stream from her eyes. He knew how much Jordana had wanted to race in the Tetons ride. "How bad is it?"

Sniffing, Jordana said, "The vet said it was a small tear but that Stormy was going to have to rest for a minimum of six months." She tried to shrug her shoulders, the bruising pain flowing through her shoulder and back where she'd hit the ground. "That ends my endurance career for a year."

Reaching out, Slade cursed his own weakness. If he'd been whole, he'd have pulled Jordana into his arms and held her and let her cry. He gripped her dirty hand. "Are you all right?"

"I — I'm fine," she rattled. "I'm sorry for crying . . ."

"Don't be," Slade rasped. Her hand was cool in his. How badly he wanted to console her, but he couldn't. She continued to wipe the tears from her face. "You're okay, that's all that counts."

Managing a grimace, Jordana whispered brokenly, "I wish I had the torn tendon and not Stormy. This is bad, Slade."

He watched the dream she had for Stormy die in her blue eyes. His heart contracted with anguish for her. Jordana didn't deserve this. She just didn't. Slade squeezed her hand gently. "Stormy is a mustang. They're as tough as they come, honey. So don't give up on her. Mustangs have an unbreakable spirit. They overcome odds other horses can't. It's in their genes, their breeding."

Nodding, Jordana couldn't be consoled. "For years, I've dreamed of this, Slade. Years . . . And when I found Stormy, I knew she was the one that could carry me on these endurance rides. She was my outlet, my dreams. . . ." and she choked back a sob. Embarrassed, Jordana whispered, "I've got to get cleaned up. I'll see you in a little bit. . . ."

Slade nodded and grimly watched her move into the master bathroom. The door shut. He felt pain over the incident. Wheeling toward the counter, he made coffee.

Jordana was probably crying in earnest now, and he couldn't be there to hold her. That hurt him more than anything else. Feeling weakened and angry, Slade hated his breeding bull for a moment. There was nothing he could do about it. Coffee and talk after her shower were in order. But Slade wasn't so sure he could do anything to lift her crushed spirits. Shaking his head, Slade cursed softly under his breath. He hated when dreams died.

Jordana took in a deep breath and opened the door to her bedroom. Her hair was washed and combed, and she had changed into a fresh pair of jeans and a yellow tee and put on her leather shoes instead of her cowboy boots. Running her fingers through her damp hair, she reluctantly headed to the kitchen. The scent of freshly perked coffee filled the air, and she managed a wobbly smile of thanks as Slade sat at the pine table, two cups of freshly brewed coffee sitting on it.

"That's nice," Jordana whispered, holding his dark stare. "Thank you."

"I imagine you want something stronger than coffee right now," Slade offered in a rasp. He watched as she sat down next to him, her long fingers curving around the orange ceramic mug.

"Yes," Jordana admitted sheepishly, lifting the cup to her lips, "if I were a drinker, I'd be drinking now."

Watching how the damp hair framed her face, Slade ached to kiss her. Normally, Jordana's cheeks were flushed with good health and vibrance. Right now, she was pale, and her blue eyes looked liked wounded holes of grief. Reaching out, he squeezed her hand gently and said, "It's a bad break for you, but it doesn't mean Stormy can't come back for next year's ride."

Gripping his strong, callused fingers, she set the mug aside. "Thanks for being optimistic." Jordana could see the burning care in his dark gray eyes, the way his mouth was thinned. Slade cared, she realized dully. He cared for *her*. And her fingers tingled after he released her hand. Giving him a slight smile, she added hoarsely, "I cried my eyes out in the shower. I guess I never realized how important this was to me, Slade. I'd just come out of a nightmare lawsuit, left a job I loved and moved out here on blind faith to start all over. I always wanted to compete at the top level of endurance riding. And when Stormy suddenly dropped into my life when I bought this house, I couldn't believe my good luck."

Nodding, Slade knew to just let her talk it out. Women were like that, he'd discovered. Talk was like opening an infected wound and letting it discharge the toxic stuff. Talk was healing for them. He sipped his coffee and simply listened. Jordana's face was always readable. There was never any hiding how she felt, at least around him. He knew in the hospital, however, she had to mask her real feelings in order to help the traumatized patient under her care. He stared down at her fingers. They were long and graceful. Hands that healed the wounds of others. Did she know that she was healing him?

"I'm a very competitive person," Jordana continued in a whisper. "I like to win. I've devoted my life to being the best at everything I ever undertook. Even with the doctor who I worked under in New York, I made the decision that I wasn't going to let him stop me from being a damned good trauma surgeon. And I didn't." Jordana frowned and sipped her coffee. "I paid a price for it, Slade, but I won. I won back my integrity after he shredded it, and I graduated at the top of my class at that hospital despite him."

He nodded and pursed his lips. "You're

the kind of competition rider that someone like me dreams about having. You have heart, guts and a can-do spirit."

"Well," she said bitterly, giving him a sad look, "it's all for naught. I don't have a horse to ride, Slade. I'm grounded. And we both know it takes a year of working with the right horse to get him or her up to that point where you can potentially win an endurance competition."

"I'm sorry, Jordana." And he was. "I'd do anything to make this right," he told her in a deep tone. *Anything.* Slade wanted to hold her because that's what she needed right now. Her proud shoulders were slumped, and her eyes held nothing but grief. It hurt him to sit here and not be able to fix this situation.

"Wait!" Jordana came out of her seat. She stared down at Slade. "I got it!"

Sitting up, he said, "Got what?" He saw her face come alive, her cheeks flush with sudden excitement. The grief in her eyes disappeared in a heartbeat and was replaced with unparalleled excitement.

"Slade, let me ride Thor in the competition! I know I can do it! He's the right horse. I'm not you, but I know I could potentially ride him and win the money you need to save your ranch!" She leaped for joy and clapped her hands. "Slade, I can do this!"

His eyes widened. She stood before him, hands clasped, her eyes suddenly filled with hope. He sat back, stunned over the idea.

"Slade," Jordana whispered, leaning over and gripping his shoulder, "I can *do this!* I know I can! If you'll just trust me with Thor, I know we have a chance to win this competition! Think about this. I would give you any money we earned. All I want is my dream to ride in a level one competition. I don't want the money. If you could just see your way clear to let me try? Please?" Never had Jordana wanted something as much as this. She knew Thor was the optimum endurance mount. He was mustang, he was tall, his stride long, and he had a built-in toughness that always put him in top position to win. But would Slade entrust his valuable mount to her? That was the real question.

Feeling her hand gripping his shoulder, seeing the hope suddenly glinting in her eyes, Slade was at a loss for words. He saw the excitement dancing in her blue eyes, the soft parting of her lips begging him to say yes. Mind spinning, he remembered those photos in her living room. He'd underestimated Jordana's riding ability, her experience over the years with horses. Yes it had been in dressage and lower level endurance riding competitions, but she'd been a winner at both. And more than anything, Slade wanted to make Jordana happy. He didn't know why, and that didn't matter. All he did know is he couldn't stand to see her crying and so sad. And there was something he could do about it.

He lifted her hand off his shoulder. "Sit down," he told her.

Jordana sat, her heart beating so hard she could hear it in her ears. Slade looked thoughtful, and she knew he was mulling over her impromptu idea. Squirming, she forced herself to remain silent as Slade chewed over the idea. Would he entrust Thor to her? That was the crux of the request. Plus, Jordana knew how desperately he needed the money to put his ranch between foreclosure with the bank and surviving. Biting down on her lower lip, Jordana silently prayed that Slade would trust her enough to give her permission.

Giving her a hard look, Slade demanded, "Have you ever ridden a stallion?"

Some of her hope died. "No, I haven't," Jordana admitted. "But I can. I know I can!"

Mouth quirking, Slade kept her gaze. "Studs are different. You get a mare in heat on that endurance ride, and he's going to want to breed. Studs are powerful, Jordana. They aren't your sedate gelding or mare. They're testosterone on legs times ten."

"I *know* I can manage Thor," she told him strongly. "I've had all kinds of horses throughout my life, Slade. I know how to handle a horse that wants to run away or do something I don't want it to do." She held up her hands. "I might look weak, but I'm not."

"You've never been weak," Slade agreed. "But a stallion is a whole other proposition. They're headstrong, and they think they know what's best. When a stallion is passing another horse, he's in the heat of competition and he wants to win. A stallion can bite another horse so damn fast that you have to know it's coming. In endurance riding, a stud can't kick or bite another competitor's horse. It's against the rules. Stallions see every horse as competition to beat. He doesn't think about being nice when he wants to win. He'll do things instinctively to do that. And biting is one of them."

"I won't let Thor bite or kick at anyone," Jordana promised breathlessly. "I won't. I'm strong and I can handle him."

Slade wasn't so sure. "It's one thing to be around horses all your life, Jordana, and it's a helluva another to ride a stud. All that's on his mind is breeding and winning. That's it."

"You need the money, Slade. What if I could ride Thor well enough to win that ten thousand dollars? The money means nothing to me. All I'd like to do is have a chance at riding at this level."

She wanted to fulfill a dream. He desperately needed the cash to stave off foreclosure. The look in her eyes, the pleading, tore at him. "What if you can't control Thor? I'm risking my stud, his breeding fees and his good name. You could fall off, be knocked off by a low hanging branch, or be unable to control him."

Nodding, Jordana sat down, her voice urgent. "I know all that, Slade. I would do everything in my power to keep Thor safe and sound."

He wasn't convinced.

Jordana saw him open his mouth. "Wait!" she pleaded, holding up her hands. "What if we go out to your ranch and you let me ride Thor in the corral? You could then see if I have what it takes to handle him." Anxiously, she drilled her gaze into his. Slade closed his mouth and scowled.

Feeling the shift in energy, Jordana leaned forward, gripped his hand and whispered,

"Let me *try,* Slade! Just give me *one* chance?"

Slade knew Thor hadn't been ridden for two days now. Ordinarily he took the stallion out on a thirty-mile training run every three days. Thor would be so full of himself that he'd be tearing through his bit to run. The stallion loved to compete. Slade really didn't think Jordana could control his mustang. And by putting her on him in a corral, there was little chance that Thor would hurt himself. On the other hand, Jordana could easily be bucked off by the vital stallion and hurt herself.

"If you can't control him, Jordana, you could be thrown off and injured."

Shrugging, she released his hand and sat up. "Slade, I've lost count of how many times I've been thrown or fell off a horse. That doesn't scare me."

"You'll wear a helmet," he warned, not wanting her hurt.

"Of course. I'll wear one." Excitement roared through Jordana. She could see Slade considering the idea. "Slade, if I could win . . ."

"You'll *never* win it, Jordana."

"But I've got the horse!"

"You've *never* competed at this level," he said heavily. "And even if I let you ride

Thor, that's no promise you'll finish. Horses break down on these rides. Quirky, unexpected things happen."

"We'll be okay," she promised him. She wanted to sound confident because she could see the worry in Slade's gray eyes. "Let me *try,* Slade. Tomorrow I'll take you back to your ranch. That forty-eight-hour period for your surgery will be over. You can call Shorty and ask him to have Thor saddled and ready to go. I can ride him in the large arena. You can use your cane and walk out there and watch us. Please?"

Her voice was husky with joy. How could he tell her no? Slade lowered his gaze and stared at the table for a moment. Did Jordana know how much he was coming to like her? Even with Isabel in the back of his mind screaming at him not to trust her, he was beginning to do just that. Mouth thinning, he muttered, "All right, we'll *try* it." He lifted his gaze to hers. Happiness was written all over Jordana's expression. Best of all, he saw the soft mouth of hers lift, and it sent his heart racing with need of her.

"Great!" Jordana whooped, clapping her hands together. "I *know* this can work, Slade! I just know it!"

"I don't," he warned her in a worried

tone. "And don't go getting your hopes too high, Jordana. Thor's a handful even for me. You'll be like a fly on his back to him."

"My weight is much less than yours," she agreed excitedly. "And that should help Thor even more in the race!"

Slade grunted. That was true, and he hadn't thought of that angle. He weighed over two hundred pounds, and she was barely one hundred and thirty-five pounds. Thor could conserve his energy even more with a flyweight like her riding him. "We'll see," was all he'd agree to. "We'll see. . . ."

CHAPTER THIRTEEN

Jordana had to hide her excitement. As Slade eased out of the passenger side of her truck, Griff came out the back door of the ranch house. He looked concerned as he walked toward them. Inwardly tensing, Jordana knew Slade wanted nothing to do with his twin brother. Compressing her lips, she lifted her hand in greeting to Griff as he approached. He smiled a little and nodded in her direction.

"Hey, I'm glad to see you home," Griff said to his brother as he rounded the front of the truck.

Glaring at Griff, Slade leaned heavily on the aluminum cane. He hated looking weak. "I'm fine. Now why don't you leave me alone?" He saw his twin's eyes widen with shock. Right now, Slade did not want his brother around.

Halting, Griff said, "I've been working with Shorty while you've been in the hospital."

Limping toward the barn, Slade said, "It's about time."

Jordana came up. "Good morning, Griff."

"Hi, Doctor Lawson," he said, tipping his hat to her.

She looked into his eyes and saw pain in them. Slade had rebuffed him without a second thought. "We're going to try me out on Thor over in that corral," she said, pointing toward it.

"Oh?" Griff said, falling in step with her.

"With Slade's wound, he can't ride his stallion in the competition," she explained. Slowing down to let Slade keep the lead up to the training barn, Jordana added, "And Stormy pulled a tendon yesterday and I can't ride her."

"I heard from Shorty about that. I'm really sorry," Griff murmured.

She could see that New York City Wall Street broker Griff didn't really grasp the enormity of the situation. Jordana said gently, "It's more than that, Griff. Slade needed that ten-thousand-dollar first-place prize in this coming competition to stave off bank foreclosure of your ranch. Did you realize that?"

"Why," Griff said, halting and stunned, "no . . . no, I didn't. Slade said nothing about that. I knew the ranch was precarious, but not in *that* much in trouble." His brows fell and he looked at his older twin and then back to Jordana. "He doesn't share much with me," he added quickly under his breath.

Nodding, Jordana said, "Don't feel bad. He doesn't share much with anyone." She reached out and squeezed his upper arm. "Give him time and space, Griff. If you prove yourself worthy in his eyes by hard work around here, he'll soften toward you over time."

Griff nodded, grateful. "Thanks, Dr. Lawson, I'll keep that in mind. I appreciate you taking the time to talk with me. Is Slade going to be okay?"

Releasing his arm, Jordana said, "Yes, in the long run. Slade isn't going to be able to ride for six weeks, well past the time to get in shape for the endurance competition. He'll need to use that cane for the next week and then he can get on with getting back to ranching a little more. He won't be able to lift heavy stuff, either, so you might be there to help him in that way."

Relieved, Griff murmured, "I can do that."

Nodding, Jordana gestured toward the training barn where Slade had just arrived. "Let's go see Thor." Keeping her voice businesslike, Jordana didn't want Griff to know just how badly she wanted to show Slade that she could handle Thor. They walked together up to the training facility.

Slade was needled by Griff's presence. He noted that Griff had a pair of leather gloves tucked into his belt. Maybe he really was listening to Shorty and working odd jobs around here. Still, Slade felt as if his twin was imposing himself on them, and he didn't like it at all.

"Thor's ready," he told Jordana, hooking a thumb over his shoulder.

Shorty waved hello to Jordana as she walked down the airy passageway. She returned the wave. In the cross ties stood tall, powerful Thor. Her heart pounded because she'd seen the stallion when Slade had ridden him. But now, it was different. She could feel the heat of Slade's gaze in her back as she approached the saddled stallion.

Thor's small, fine ears twitched back and forth as Jordana approached. His large nostrils opened to pull in her scent as she halted at his left side.

"He's rarin' to go," Shorty chuckled, getting the saddle stirrups changed for her leg length. "Too many days of not being exercised."

Jordana held out her hand for Thor to smell. "Yes, he is." Smiling over at the wrangler, she added, "But so am I." She knew a stallion who wasn't well mannered would sometimes bite the hand, and so she was on guard.

Thor's nostrils flared, showing red deep inside as he took in her womanly scent. His blue eyes were pinned on her. Jordana kept her hand outstretched while he picked up on her scent. She knew how important it was the for the stallion to know her long before she threw a leg over him. "That's it," she crooned to the stud, "this is a handshake, isn't it, fella?"

Ears moving forward to pick up the sound of her soothing, husky tone, Thor shook his head, the cross ties jingling.

Laughing softly, Jordana allowed her fingers to slide firmly along Thor's massive jaw. His white-and-chestnut coat gleamed. He felt like smooth velvet beneath her touch. The stallion pawed his right hoof against the concrete.

"He's ready to go," Slade agreed, coming up alongside her. He nodded to Shorty who was coming around the front of the stud.

"Does he always paw like this?" she asked.

"Always. He's born to run."

Nodding, she asked, "Do you walk him

out of here?"

"Yes." Slade saw his twin standing well off to the side. It was obvious Griff was unsettled by the powerful stallion. "I take the reins and walk on the right side of him."

"Okay," Jordana said, "I can do that."

"No," Slade said, waving for Shorty to come over. "Go to the arena. We'll meet you there."

Trying to hide her disappointment, Jordana nodded and turned away. Slade didn't trust her to even walk his stallion to the corral! Heart sinking, Jordana realized that Slade probably wasn't going to let her ride Thor in the competition. A fifteen-hand-high horse was tall, and she was diminutive against Thor. Or, was he just taking extra precautions? Walking out of the training barn, Griff hurried to her side.

"What now?" he asked.

"Slade is going to test ride me on Thor down in the arena," was all she said.

"Can you ride that stud?"

Nodding, Jordana saw Griff's expression told her different — he didn't believe her. "Yes, I can."

"He's a big horse."

"*Every* horse is, Griff. Not just Thor."

"He's mean," Griff muttered, turning to see Shorty leading the dancing, prancing stallion out of the barn.

Jordana heard the growl in his tone. "What do you mean?"

"Shorty was having me feed the horses in the training barn two days ago. When I tried to slide open Thor's box stall door, he attacked me."

"What?" Surprised, she almost stopped.

"Yes," Griff said, unhappy. "He bared his teeth and charged me as I started to open the door."

"That's not good," Jordana murmured.

"It scared the hell out of me. I've never been around horses at all, and he was the last horse on that side of the barn to be fed. The other horses whinnied or nickered and welcomed me into their box stall when I brought in the hay. Not him." He turned and glared at the medicine hat stallion who was prancing and tossing his head.

Jordana got to the arena and pulled open the long pipe rail gate. Griff followed her in, and they stood holding it open for Shorty. Thor danced into the large arena, snorting and continuing to impatiently toss his head. Slade limped in at a slower pace, a scowl locked into his expression. Jordana waited until he moved into the corral before pushing the gate shut and locking it. Climbing between the pipe rails, she walked

238

out to where Slade stood next to his stud. Griff remained outside the corral, hands on the fence and watching from a safe distance.

"I'm ready," she told Slade as she halted beside him. Shorty was walking the stud around the arena. The sand flew beneath his small, sharp hooves as he danced from side to side. Shorty was calm and quiet and just maintained a steady walk.

Slade looked down at her. "Are you *sure* about this? He's full of himself today. More than usual."

"More than ready," she said with a grin. "Just because he's full of himself doesn't mean he's intractable."

Grunting, Slade said, "Come on. . . ."

Following him, Jordana took a deep breath to quell her excitement. She wasn't afraid of the stallion. She knew Slade was afraid for her. He obviously didn't believe she could even mount Thor, much less handle him.

"Shorty, give her the reins and step away."

"Sure, Boss," he murmured, smiling at Jordana as she opened her hands to receive the reins. He stepped over to Slade's side.

Now for the test. Jordana saw the stallion's eyes flick toward her. His ears were pointed in her direction. Good, he was listening.

Talking softly to him as she did to any horse she was going to ride, she slowly moved the reins over Thor's head. The stallion snorted and started to step away.

"Whoa," Jordana murmured in a firm tone. "Stand."

Instantly, the stallion stopped moving. A well-trained horse knew "whoa," "stand" and a whole bunch of other English words. Pleased that Thor obeyed her, she kept her full attention on the stallion. He whipped his chestnut-and-white tail, which was long and flowing, from side to side. That was okay. If the stud had moved his tail up and down, it was a sign of anger. Thor was curious about her. And that's exactly where Jordana wanted the stallion to be.

Gathering the reins in her hand, she gripped a piece of his long mane and inserted her left boot into the stirrup. Thor was tall, so Jordana had to draw on all her strength to pull upward and lift her right leg over the horse's back. She had a good pull on the horse's mouth so he couldn't step forward while she was mounting.

Like a gentleman, Thor stood quietly as she mounted. Slipping her boot into the right stirrup and settling down in the specially made saddle, Jordana quickly gripped the horse's barrel. Thor's ears were flicking restlessly. Snorting, he tossed his head.

Jordana didn't look toward Slade or Shorty. She clucked and squeezed Thor's barrel. Instantly, the stud jumped forward. Not surprised, Jordana flowed forward with him. She used both hands on the reins. The stallion wanted to run. She wanted him to walk. The battle was joined.

Slade stood there, eyes narrowed speculatively, as he watched the featherweight deal with over a thousand pounds of raw stallion energy. At first, Thor tried to take over, but Slade saw Jordana sit the saddle and play with the reins so that Thor had to curve his long neck and bring his head perpendicular to the ground. He knew enough about dressage to realize that Jordana's legs and hands were asking the stallion to collect himself in a highly balanced way. Thor wasn't used to dressage, so Slade wondered what his stud was going to do about it. Would he fight Jordana? Or submit? Slade wasn't sure as she got the horse to do a dancing walk around the corral.

Tension thrummed through Jordana. She kept her shoulders squared, her spine supple and legs taunt and firm against Thor. The power of this animal was exciting to her. He was ten years old and in excellent shape for an endurance horse. His white-and-chestnut coat gleamed in the sunlight, his mane fine and feathery as it moved like ripples of water across his deeply arched neck. She felt as if she were sitting on top of a keg of dynamite that was ready to explode at any second. Yet as she asked Thor to flex his neck and collect himself, he did just that. Exhilaration swept through Jordana. She knew this horse had not been trained for dressage, yet, with her light, constant touch on his bit to keep it from sawing on his mouth, Jordana had secured the horse's surrender.

"I'll be darned, Boss," Shorty whispered, impressed. "Lookie at that stud. He's mighty tame under her direction."

Grunting, Slade didn't say anything. As Jordana worked with her strong legs and light hands, she was getting his stud to do things he'd never seen him do before. Looking like a tiny jockey on the massive stallion, Jordana impressed Slade. But he kept those thoughts to himself.

Jordana felt the stallion respond quickly to her leg pressure. She had him moving diagonally across the arena, neck flexed, his body in balance. When she arrived at the other side, she moved him the other way in the arena with a simple pressure of her other calf against his barrel. Her joy soared. Not only was Thor listening, but he was trying to please her! Allowing the reins to ease, she asked a slow trot of Thor.

Thor wanted to run. He snorted and lunged forward, wanting to gallop. Instantly, Jordana countered and pulled on the reins just enough to let him know he couldn't do what he wanted. He had to do what she asked of him, and that was all. Headstrong, Thor snorted violently, humped his back and tried to throw her off. Instantly, Jordana gripped his barrel hard with her legs and rode out the two hopscotching jumps.

Shorty snickered. "Hey, Boss, she's got his number!"

Grinning a little, Slade nodded. It wasn't unusual for Thor to do what they termed "crow hopping." It was a series of bucks and jumps designed to throw off an incompetent rider. But Jordana had stuck like proverbial glue to the stallion's back when he'd tried those antics with her. "Yes, I think she might," he admitted in a gravelly tone.

Jordana worked with Thor. It was important the stallion do exactly as she wanted, when she wanted. He was chomping on his bit, foam gathering on the sides of his opened mouth. She could feel the power of each of his long strides as she kept him at a sedate trot. Literally, she could feel the stallion puffing up and trying his best to run, but she kept him under control. With every stride, he grunted and snorted, as if to scare her. But she wasn't scared. Riding Thor was like riding a lightning bolt.

When she finally allowed him into what was called an extended trot, she felt Thor begin to release some of that stored power. Amazed at the speed and stride of the stud, she posted in the saddle. Jordana was sure that Slade never posted in the saddle, and the horse seemed confused by the motion on his back. Talking soothingly to Thor, his ears flicking, Jordana understood the stud's sudden wariness. His long legs struck out, and as she continued to keep a firm, guiding hand on him, Thor eventually adjusted to her posting.

Now, Jordana wanted to see if Thor had the floating trot of Stormy. She knew not all mustangs possessed this very Arabian trait. Did he? Squeezing her legs more, and yet holding the reins where they were, she asked that of Thor.

"I'll be darned, Boss. Look it!" Shorty crowed.

Eyes slitted, Slade watched his powerful stallion move into a strong, flowing trot. Thor's tall legs snapped out with military precision as he moved into that distance-eating floating trot. He knew to ride that kind of a trot was the hardest on the rider. Yet, Jordana was flowing like a ribbon in the wind as he moved with effortless ease around the arena. Some of his anxiety abated.

"She's doin' it!" Shorty said, smiling.

"So far . . ." Slade muttered. "Let's wait and see what happens when he gallops." Slade knew from long experience that the stud's favorite gait was an all-out gallop. He lived to run. It was bred into his blood and bone. Jordana might think she had control over Thor, but until she had ridden him at that all-out gallop, she wouldn't realize his raw, competitive power.

Jordana slowed Thor back down to a sedate trot and then asked him to stop. The stallion fought her, moving his head and trying to take control of the reins. *No way!* Jordana glanced for the first time toward the center of the arena. Was Slade unhappy with her? Or did he trust her? She saw his face dark and unreadable and those gray eyes narrowed like those of a predator.

"Okay," she told Thor, "he still doesn't think we can get along."

Thor snorted and finally halted. He switched his tail from side to side, his ears back and mouth opened and closing. All signs that he didn't like what was being asked of him.

Jordana knew enough about the stallion to now ask him to canter. The canter was a slow, controlled run. In a gallop, the horse was asked for all his speed and stride. They were very different gaits. She collected Thor with her hands and legs. And then, she gave the stallion the signal to canter.

Thor exploded beneath her, nearly unseating Jordana. Caught off guard by the powerful leap forward, she quickly seated herself and got him back beneath her control. Thor fought the bit, shaking his head from side to side. He was grunting and snorting with every cantering stride. How badly he wanted to run! Jordana felt the unequaled power of the stallion she was riding. Never had she felt this kind of massive energy in any horse. Now, as she flew around the arena fighting Thor with every stride to get him to canter, Jordana saw why he was the top endurance champion. The wind tore past her even at a canter. Jordana's whole focus was on being ahead of this feisty stallion and guiding him where she wanted him to go. Her hands ached and sweated on the slick leather reins. She couldn't afford to let Thor get the best of her now. Would he buck and crow hop at this gait? She didn't know, and she wasn't about to be caught off guard again.

After warming Thor up in the arena at a canter, she glanced over at Slade.

"Let him run!" he called out.

Okay, a full gallop. Sucking in a breath, Jordana got ready for the ride of her life. Thor heard his master and lunged. For a split second, Jordana was behind the horse's change of gait. Settling down, she released the reins. Thor dug into the deep sand, grunted and stuck out his long neck. His hooves plunged into the soil, the sand flying in veils all around him as he sailed forward at high speed. His tail lifted up like a flag, a very Arabian characteristic. Jordana's attention narrowed to the quick striding stallion who was finally off the leash and running as hard as he could. They flew around the arena in a blur. For a bit, Jordana simply let the stallion get it out of his system. She was a mere jockey on the hard-running stud. But at a certain point, she needed to re-establish control.

When she pulled in on the reins, Thor snorted and fought her hard. The reins slipped through her fingers. He lunged forward, ears pinned against his neck. It was his way or no way! Quickly gathering the reins through her aching fingers, Jordana leaned forward and hauled him in. Again, Thor fought her. Again, she reestablished her superiority. The stallion reluctantly slowed down, his legs high and long.

Slade watched the battle between woman and stallion. Jordana's face was intense, her mouth thinned, her eyes ahead of the horse to ensure he was going where she wanted him to go. An unwilling sliver of a smile tipped the corners of his mouth.

"I'll be darned," Shorty crowed, "she's handling him, Boss! How about *that*? I never thought another man except yourself could handle Thor." Taking off his hat and shaking his head, Shorty added, "Much less a *woman* to ride that machine!"

And Thor was a machine, Slade knew. There had been times when he'd had trouble handling the competitive stallion. He watched as Jordana worked and wrestled with Thor. The stallion didn't want to surrender his will over to her. But he didn't like surrendering over to Slade, either. It was always a fight, a part of his makeup as a stallion. But handle Thor, she did. Pride for her flowed through Slade. He found himself watching Jordana move the stud around and move him in the other direction. Thor hated giving over his freedom to any rider. He constantly tossed his head, chomped aggressively down on the bit and flattened his ears against his neck. Yet, Jordana was controlling him. His heart opened to this woman who looked as light as a postage stamp on the back of his stallion. She was small but mighty.

Jordana took Thor in the other direction, forcing him to canter for several minutes before she opened him up again. This time, she was ready for that explosion. And explosion it was! Thor grunted, crow hopped twice and leaped forward. Jordana moved with him this time. She didn't allow him to run full speed. Instead, she kept him between a canter and a gallop. The stallion had to do as she wanted every moment or this wouldn't work at all, and Jordana knew it.

Pleased, Slade watched his stallion succumb to Jordana's more stubborn spirit than his. Shorty was cackling and pointing at them and constantly making remarks about Jordana's amazing riding skills. Yes, she had guts and savvy to ride that beast of his. Thor had never known another rider but him, and for this small woman to come and ride Thor and force him to obey her was simply stunning to Slade. It made him want Jordana even more than before. He saw the muscles of her arms leaping as the stallion constantly challenged her. The set look on her face, her eyes narrowed and mouth thinned, told him she was fighting him every second. Yet, she was winning.

"Okay," Slade called, "bring him in."

Thor snorted and squealed as Jordana brought him down to a trot. The stud crow hopped some more, but she stayed with him and remained quiet in the saddle, her hands firm and guiding. Giving up for a moment, the stallion broke down into a trot. And as she guided him to the center, she asked him to walk. Tossing his head in protest, Thor settled into a prancing, dancing walk.

Finally, Thor stood still. Jordana smiled down at Slade. She was breathing hard, sweat running off her. "Well? What do you think?"

"I think he damned near tossed you off."

Shorty came up and gripped the reins. Jordana eased them and laid the reins against Thor's neck. She grinned and patted the stallion's sweaty neck. "Yes, he's a horse that wants to run. Hates walking and trotting."

Nodding, Slade came up alongside her. Jordana's face was flushed, her eyes sparkling with joy and those lips, he found he couldn't stop staring at, in a wide, joyous smile. As Slade patted Thor's neck, he wondered what it would be like to see her smiling like that as they made love to one another. The thought slammed into him, and it took Slade's breath away for a moment. Stunned, he stood there speechless until he felt Jordana's hand coming to rest on his shoulder.

"Slade, he's marvelous! I've never had such a ride in my life! Thor is incredible!"

Just her hand on his shoulder for that brief moment made Slade start aching from his heart down to his lower body. He turned and looked up at her. Jordana's hair, once in a ponytail, had been mussed by the wind and the wild ride on Thor. Her eyes were sparkling, and he felt heat flow through him, lifting his dour look on life. "He is incredible."

"I mean," Jordana said, sighing, "I knew he has been a great breeding stallion and passed on his endurance traits to others, but getting to ride him . . ." She rolled her eyes and laughter flowed out of her. "Thor is amazing, Slade." She leaned forward and patted the stud's neck once more. "Just amazing."

"He is," Slade agreed. "Dismount."

Doing as he ordered, Jordana walked to Thor's head and spoke quietly to him. Rubbing his face, which was beaded with sweat, she smiled at him. "You're one hell of a horse, Thor. But I think you and I can get along. Don't you, boy?"

Snorting, Thor's ears twitched. He nuzzled into her hand and tried to rub his sweaty head against her shoulder.

Laughing softly, Jordana stepped back, keeping her hand on Thor's jaw. "I'll give you a bath, but you're not using me as your towel to wipe off that sweat," she told him with a grin.

"Shorty, take Thor to the bath," Slade ordered.

"Yes, Boss."

Jordana stepped out of the way as Shorty took the reins and led the stallion toward the gate. Griff was there and opened it for them. She looked up at Slade's set face. "Well? What do you think?"

"I think you rode a wild stallion that likes his way or no way," he told her. He stopped himself from reaching out and taming those strands of hair around her face.

"He's a handful," she agreed. Searching his light-colored gray eyes, Jordana said, "but I controlled him."

Nodding, Slade turned and began to limp back toward the opened gate. He saw Griff accompanying Shorty at a healthy distance from the dancing stallion. His twin was

252

afraid of horses, no question. He felt Jordana come to his side as they walked down the center of the arena. "You weren't afraid of Thor," he said.

Shaking her head, Jordana grinned. "Like I said before, Slade, I've been tossed and bucked off by horses much worse than Thor. He was crow hopping because he wanted to run." She met his gaze and thought he saw respect for her in them. "The other horses were trying to get rid of me because they didn't want to be ridden. That's a huge difference."

"Yes," Slade murmured, pleased with her insight, "it is."

"So," Jordana said as she turned and stood in front of him. "Will you let me ride Thor in the endurance competition?" She held her breath, never wanting anything more. Would Slade say yes? Or no?

CHAPTER FOURTEEN

Slade limped into his ranch home. Griff was sitting at the kitchen table having a cup of coffee. For a moment, he felt sorry for his younger brother. But not for long.

"Take your coffee and go out and help Shorty," he muttered, gesturing toward the front door.

Griff stood. He took the mug and nodded deferentially to Jordana as they passed one another in the foyer.

Slade felt his leg throbbing. He needed to sit down.

"Can I make us some coffee?" Jordana asked as she walked into the kitchen, noticing the pot was now empty. She saw Slade's face had turned pasty; it was a sign of pain.

"Yes," he said, scowling. Looking around at the kitchen, it was a mess. Dirty dishes abounded. Nothing was cleaned up, nor was it neat. He saw the red tile floor was dirty, too. "Damn brother of mine doesn't know how to use a vacuum cleaner, dust, mop or wash dishes."

"Mmm," Jordana agreed. "It's not like I've seen your place before," she said getting down two mugs. Griff had used the coffee-maker but had neglected to turn it off when it was empty. She quickly shut it off and rinsed out the glass container with hot water so it wouldn't suddenly crack from the drastic temperature change. The bottom was black with boiled coffee, indicating Griff had done this many times before.

Slade sighed. "I'm gone two days and he lets this place go. What the *hell* did his uncle and aunt teach him? All he has eyes for is making millions in the stock market. He probably had a maid he hired to keep his million-dollar penthouse clean."

Hearing the bitterness in Slade's gravelly tone, Jordana scrubbed out the container and then set to work making fresh coffee for them. She desperately wanted to know if Slade would allow her to ride Thor in the coming endurance event but knew this was the wrong time to broach it again. He was very upset over the dirtiness of his normally clean ranch home. She didn't blame him but didn't know enough details of his relationship with Griff to make comments one way or another.

Slade absently rubbed his thigh where the operation had taken place.

"Are you in pain?" she wanted to know, coming over and standing near him.

"Yeah," Slade admitted sourly.

"You stood on it too long out there."

"I had no choice."

Smiling a little, Jordana placed her hand on his shoulder for a moment. "You're a big mama hen in disguise, Slade."

The warmth of her hand on his shoulder neutralized the ache in his leg. It was an amazing experience for Slade. How could her hand *stop* the throbbing of his leg wound? Twisting a look up at her, his heart briefly pounded. Her black hair was now hanging around her shoulders and framed her flushed oval face. She was beautiful, Slade realized, in such a natural way. Jordana rarely wore makeup. Hungrily absorbing her lingering touch on his shoulder, he managed a lopsided smile. "Maybe a rooster, but never a hen."

Laughing, Jordana wanted to lean down and kiss those lips of his. But it would be impossible to do. He might take such an act as manipulation. And she knew enough about his ex-wife, Isabel, to know she was a premier manipulator. Jordana had no desire to be compared to this woman. "Okay, you can be Big Daddy Rooster." Lifting her hand, she walked back to the counter where the coffee was gurgling away. Looking out the window, she saw Griff walking up toward the training barn. Thor had been unsaddled and washed, and Shorty was taking him back to his stall in the barn.

Slade enjoyed absorbing her curvy figure as she stood at the drain board, hands resting on the tiled surface of the sink. The room just seemed to light up with sunshine when she was present. What was so different about Jordana? Was it because she was a professional woman? Unlike spoiled, rich Isabel? He made a mental comparison of the two and had more questions than answers.

Jordana poured two mugs of coffee and brought them over to the table. There had been crumbs on the pine surface, and Slade had absently corralled all of them into one group near one corner. She took a dishcloth hanging across the spigot and wiped the table clean. It gleamed once more with golden and reddish colors across its surface. Griff was definitely not housebroken, she decided.

"Thanks," Slade murmured, appreciative of her sensitivity to him not liking dust and dirt around.

Coming back, Jordana smiled and sat down at his elbow. "I can't stand a dirty place, either," she confided.

"My brother is lost. He's lost his job, lost all his millions, lost his self-esteem, and now he's here on my doorstep telling me he owns half this ranch."

Sipping the coffee, Jordana nodded. She could see the anger and frustration in Slade's look.

"Now he's trying his hand at ranching. And he's no good at it."

"Maybe with time he might be?" Jordana said. She saw Slade's thick brown brows move downward.

"He came back here because he had nowhere else to go. All his 'friends' wanted nothing to do with him after he lost his money. Some friends they were. . . ."

"What did he want from you, Slade?"

"He wanted me to take care of him until he could get back on his feet." His laugh was short and harsh. "Money! Hell, I'm scrambling every month to find enough just to pay the ranch mortgage. He didn't believe me that I didn't have the money. He said I was holding a grudge against him because he'd refused to loan me money about six years ago."

Surprised, Jordana set down the mug, her

hands around it. "He refused you a loan?" And he had millions? Inwardly, she thought that was crazy.

"Yeah, my little brother decided I was a 'bad risk' for a loan and that's why he refused." Looking around the quiet kitchen, he muttered, "Can you imagine? Me? A bad loan risk? Hell, I've worked twelve to fourteen hours a day, seven days a week, to keep this ranch going. That hurt."

Nodding, Jordana reached over and touched his hand that had drawn into a fist as he'd spoken about the loan experience. "I'm so sorry, Slade. I didn't know."

Shaking his head, he rasped, "He's a spoiled greenhorn. And when his world collapsed, he came crawling back here to try to figure out what his next entrepreneurial idea would be." Snorting, Slade met her eyes as she withdrew her hand from his. "Griff doesn't get what hard work and earning your way in this world is really all about. He was sent to Uncle Robert who was a Wall Street broker. Griff learned about money, how to make it, and his world was about millions of greenbacks."

She saw Slade's face go grim, his mouth thinning. "A lot of people have been hit hard in this recession," she agreed in a soft tone. Jordana didn't see Griff as bad; merely

259

out of touch with the reality of the middle class that was the backbone of this country. He'd had it easy for too long and didn't know how to settle into the reality of having to earn a daily living.

Sighing roughly, Slade slid her a glance. "You're always gentle with people. How did you get that way?" And when he saw her soft mouth curve upward, Slade instantly wanted her. In every possible way. His hands tightened around the mug in front of him. He was finding that just sharing time and space with her was like a delicious and unexpected dessert.

Shrugging, Jordana said, "It's just me, Slade. When I was in residency in New York City, I saw too many of my friends and the doctors who were our bosses be short, hard and disconnected from a suffering patient. I didn't want that kind of connection with sick people. I know a smile and a touch can give someone a world of hope to cling to. I've seen my way of working with a person work miracles. I took what I've learned from that arena and applied it everywhere."

Slade held her sparkling blue gaze. "And why do you think Thor responded to you?"

Her heart beat hard, once. Losing her smile, she said in a low tone, "Slade, I know horses. It's true I've never ridden a stallion before this, but they all have personalities. I've handled some spoiled and wounded horses when I was younger. I treat them like people, and ask myself how would I respond best? It's a mind game with each horse to feel him or her out. What will make the horse *want* to work with me instead of working against me?"

Nodding, Slade said with some admiration in his tone, "Well, you sure as hell got Thor's number."

Chuckling a little, Jordana leaned back in the chair and held his stare. "I believe I did, but that's for you to ultimately decide." Would Slade allow her to ride Thor? How badly she wanted to know his answer!

"He's never had another rider but me," Slade said, staring down at his nearly empty coffee mug. "I broke him gently and we grew up together. I know his every quirk and eccentricity. You didn't. And you handled him firmly but gently. Because of that, he responded to you."

"Well," Jordana insisted with a grin, "Thor responded when he *wanted* to, not when I wanted him to."

"Yes, I saw him fighting you from time to time, but that's his nature." He swallowed more of the coffee and set the mug aside. Giving her a look, Slade said in a low tone,

"I believe that the more you ride him, the more he'll fall in line and respect you. Thor likes to get away with his antics, but you stopped him every time he tried one of them."

Nodding, Jordana wondered if Slade was going to let her ride Thor. "Every horse has quirks, Slade. We both know that."

"What I didn't know until I was over at your home was how extensive your riding credentials really were. You told me your mother had been a dressage rider but you said little about your own accomplishments. I was out in your living room one time and saw all the photos, the trophies and newspaper clippings you had hanging on your wall. You never let on that you've been riding since you were six, or that you were a pre-Olympic rider in dressage." He held her startled gaze. "I may be a Westerner and pooh-pooh English saddles in lieu of western gear, but I do understand dressage. And when you were out there riding Thor, you were using your knowledge of dressage to haul him into line. And he responded."

"Dressage is a riding art form that *any* horse will respond to," Jordana told him in a serious voice. "Thor is an exceptionally intelligent horse, Slade, but I don't think I need to tell you that."

"He's smart and clever," Slade agreed. "But he isn't going to agree to work *with* you unless you're damn good at what you do. Mustangs originally came from Arabian stock. And Arabians are the most intelligent of all breeds. You can't bull them around, you can't beat it into them with a two-by-four. You have to know horse psychology and plenty of it for them to respond and want to work willingly with you."

"I'm in total agreement," Jordana said. Nervously, she gulped down the rest of her coffee. Slade seemed ready to give her his final decision. Never had Jordana wanted something more than this. Thor was an exceptional mustang in every way. She now understood why he was the top endurance breeding stallion in the country. Just having the privilege of riding him once was enough to make her appreciate Thor on so many more levels.

"If I let you ride him in the endurance contest, Jordana, you have to agree to take the prize money *if* you win it."

Stunned, she sat up and pushed her mug aside, holding his flat, stubborn gray stare. "No, that's not what we agreed to do. You *need* that prize money, Slade. I'll do my darnedest to win it for you, but I don't want it."

"You're not in good financial straits either," he pointed out.

"That's true," Jordana murmured, "but I'm not as bad off as you are."

Slade winced over her words. Jordana was right. "Out here in the West, a man's word is exactly that. If Thor wins, you win the money. That's it."

Frustrated, Jordana sat up, her eyes blazing. "No way, Slade! I love this ranch!" and she jammed her index finger down at the tile floor. "You're such a wonderful teacher and I've learned so much from you in such a little time. This ranch and you *deserve* to not only survive but thrive. I know I lack experience riding at this level, but I think you can see that I can handle Thor and he's responsive to me. That," she whispered rawly, "is what gives us a chance to win that money for you. You *must* see that!"

Slade sat back as Jordana's passionate argument struck him. Her cheeks were flushed red, her eyes blazed with righteousness, and, God help him, she was incredibly beautiful in that moment. Jordana lived in the world of her heart, he realized, unlike him who was locked up tighter than Fort Knox. That is what touched Slade: her unbridled passion for life, for living with her sense of morals and values. The competitiveness was in her eyes, and he liked what he saw. "I do see all of that," he countered. Opening his large, callused hands, he said, "But there's no way I'm taking free money from you."

"Then," Jordana exploded with frustration, "look at it this way. You're *paying* me to ride Thor! If I win that ten grand, it's yours. You can set out a training program for me here at the ranch so I can continue to learn from you, Slade. I don't care what money you assign to it, either. Don't you understand that I feel more than paid by getting to ride Thor in that competition? Some things," Jordana said, her voice dropping, "can't be bought with money. If you give me permission to ride Thor, that's all I want. This isn't a money issue for me. What endurance rider wouldn't give his or her right arm to ride your remarkable stallion?"

He sat back, digesting her emotionally fueled arguments. Staring at her, Slade smiled a little. "You're a regular bantam rooster when you get your feathers all riled up. You know that?"

Chuckling a little, the tension flowing out of her because she saw the warmth and care burning in Slade's eyes for the first time, Jordana said, "Funny that you said that. My mother raised bantams and sold their eggs.

My dad always called me 'Banty Rooster,' because I would fly into a tantrum when I didn't get my way as a four- and five-year-old."

Slade could see that. Her black hair was mussed. Without thinking, he reached over and pushed some of the errant strands away from her face. He saw her eyes grow large with shock over his gesture. Removing his hand, he saw her soft mouth part. Wanting to kiss her, but knowing it wasn't right under the circumstances, Slade muttered, "I can believe it."

"Will you let me ride Thor, Slade? And if I get lucky and win any of the prize money, it goes to you. And then you can arrange repayment in the form of riding lessons for me and Stormy once she gets well."

"That's fair," he nodded. "Only Stormy isn't going to be ready for a year."

"I realize that," Jordana said. "I know you have other endurance prospects in your training stable. Maybe you can let me ride one of them instead until Stormy is ready?" She understood the importance to Slade of being fair about this. Slade could have the money. She wanted the advance training only he could give her. That was worth everything to Jordana.

Mulling it over, Slade said, "Okay, you got

a deal." He thrust out his hand toward her. "Out here, we live by our word and a handshake."

Giving a whoop of unfettered joy, Jordana stood up and gripped his hand. "You got a deal, Slade!" And then, she released his hand and followed her heart. Swiftly leaning over, Jordana pressed a chaste kiss to his cheek.

Startled by Jordana's unexpected enthusiasm, his flesh tingled wildly where her soft lips had grazed his cheek. Before he could react, Jordana had slid her arms around him, hugged him hard and immediately released him. Slade's mouth opened, but nothing would come out of it. Jordana stood there, her blue eyes glinting with joy, her hands clasped between her breasts.

"Slade," she promised breathlessly, "you won't regret this! I *promise* you!" Her heart pounded to underscore his decision. And she had kissed him. And hugged him! What was Slade drawing out of her?

Sitting back in the chair, Slade soaked in her happiness that trickled through him like hot lava awakening his heart and lower body. What was there not to like about this small, feisty woman? His cheek still tingled. Slade was in shock over her warmth and unexpected kiss. Was this Jordana, the doctor who hugged her sick patients? He thought so. She was just letting him see more of who she really was. Inwardly, Slade wished her kiss and hug had been more personal, more private . . . woman to his man. Harshly, he warned himself that was a crazy whim at best. No woman wanted a man with a ranch floundering on the edge of foreclosure. Further, Jordana was a physician. He was merely a horse wrangler and trainer. Their two worlds were so different, just like Isabel and himself had been. Isabel had been rich and well-off. She hadn't known what it took for Slade to keep his ranch above water and then had pouted when he didn't spend his time with her instead.

"I won't disappoint you, Slade," she went on quickly. "If you'll set out a training schedule, I'll work my other jobs around it. I really want to be ready for this ride. I know you can help me get there." Jordana wanted to hug him again but thought better of it. Oh, how she'd wanted to kiss that masculine, powerful mouth of his, but she didn't dare. And the shocking look in his gray eyes told her he hadn't expected her warmth and enthusiasm. But this was who she really was, and Jordana couldn't apologize for her childlike reaction to getting to ride Thor.

Would Slade hold it against her? Jordana didn't know.

"Sit down," he ordered her.

Jordana sat, barely able to stop from squirming with joy. She tried to put on a serious expression to match Slade's somber look. Shocked by her own spontaneity, Jordana wondered if her two-year hiatus without a serious relationship had made her kiss and hug Slade. Unsure how he took her enthusiasm, Jordana knew she couldn't be the playful puppy that she really was. "What now?" she asked in a solemn tone. Slade *had* to know she was not only serious about this but equally responsible. Those qualities were important to him — and to her.

Running his fingers through his hair, he scowled and thought. "Thor's used to thirty-mile runs twice a week." He looked up and out the windows where he could see the beautiful, jagged Tetons in the distance. Turning, he held her gaze. "You've never ridden the fifty-mile contest here."

"No, I haven't."

"Then we need to get you on that trail so you memorize it in every way. There's places to run Thor, there's others where a fast trot will be all you can get because of the rockiness of the area. There's places where it's high meadow water and you can't plunge him through that muck and mud or you'll pull a tendon on him."

Nodding, Jordana hung on his every word. "Draw me a map?"

"I wish to hell I could ride it with you," Slade muttered, frowning. "Then I could show you the hazards and challenges, but I can't."

Jordana forced herself to remain quiet. "You draw me a map," she told him quietly. "And I'll do the fifty miles at half pace. I have a small camera I carry around my neck. I can take photos. I can memorize these situations, Slade."

"You only have a month," he said in a heavy tone. "Only a month. The people you're up against know this trail like the back of their hand. They know how to gauge their mount, themselves and throwing themselves against this harsh land. You don't. You're on a new horse and had never traversed this trail."

"Horses memorize," Jordana pointed out. "I'm *sure* Thor knows these places."

"He does, but you have to *trust* him if he slows down or speeds up. That's where you two are not in sync."

Nodding, Jordana said, "But if I can take the trail once a week as a tune up with

270

Thor? Could we make up the difference, Slade?"

Hearing the low key excitement in her husky voice, he said, "I don't know. That's the unknown." Sitting back, his brows slashed downward. "And then there's Curt Downing. . . ."

"Oh," Jordana murmured, "I forgot about him."

"Yeah, he's going to be a real burr under your saddle. And once he finds out you're riding Thor, his gloves will come off. He'll do *everything* in his power to unseat you from Thor, Jordana. He's a sonofabitch with a crop. Thor hates crops, and if Downing gets near enough to use it on my stud, I don't know what he'll do in reaction to it." Slade shook his head. "Worse, I worry for you."

Reaching out, her fingers wrapping around his lower arm resting on the pine table, Jordana whispered, "Slade, don't worry about me. I'll have a helmet on and I'll be wearing a Kevlar vest. I know how to fall off a horse. I'll be all right, so don't worry about me. My focus is on Thor and keeping him sound and out of trouble. That's where my focus should be." Hesitantly, Jordana lifted her hand away. She saw a glint of hunger in Slade's expression as she'd spontaneously touched him once more. Her womanly core stirred hotly to life. She recognized that look: A man starving for his woman. He wanted to kiss her. Or? Make wildly passionate love to her? Here and now? Shocked by what she saw, Jordana avoided his fiery look. Her world rocked, suddenly unstable and dangerous. Slade wanted her. In *every* way.

Jordana tried to quell her need of him. Yes, Slade was ruggedly handsome. And he stirred the fires of her sensual womanhood, too. No question about it. Gulping, Jordana tried to push her own desires for Slade away. Now was not the time to get into a tangled relationship with him. She knew he was still hurting over what Isabel had done to him. And he had his problems with Griff, too. She couldn't see her way clear to embrace Slade on that level as badly as she wanted to. Yet, as Jordana lifted her eyes and met his stormy gray gaze, all the reasons melted hotly and disappeared. What was she going to do?

CHAPTER FIFTEEN

Curt Downing couldn't believe his ears. He was having hundred-pound gunnysacks of sweet feed carried out to his Chevy pickup when he overheard the two workers talking to one another. Standing on the wooden dock of the loading area, the truck parked up against it, Curt gestured to red-haired Sandy Jenkins, a twenty-year-old who worked at the store.

"Hey," he called, "what did you just say?"

Sandy threw the last gunnysack of feed into Downing's truck and straightened.

"I heard from my boss this morning that Dr. Jordana Lawton is riding Thor in the endurance race." He wiped his brow with the back of his sleeve.

Stunned, Curt growled, "That's crap, Sandy. No one rides Thor except McPherson."

Grinning, Sandy sauntered over, his body lean like a whippet. "Where have you been,

Mr. Downing? Three days ago Slade got gored by his bull, Diablo. It knocked him out of the competition. My boss said he talked to Dr. Lawton about the rider change this morning."

"I've been out of town," Downing snarled. Mind spinning, he couldn't believe his good luck. "So, McPherson can't ride?"

"Yes, sir, that's what the doctor said. He tore a major artery in his thigh and had to have emergency surgery. Dr. Lawton said he was grounded from riding for six to eight weeks."

A slow grin of delight crawled across Curt's face. "Well now, isn't that too bad?"

Shrugging, Sandy said, "I thought you might like that news."

"And Dr. Lawton is going to ride Thor instead?" Curt demanded.

"Yes, sir," he murmured, running his sweaty hands down the sides of his Levi's.

Snorting, Downing muttered, "She's *never* ridden in a level one endurance ride. She'll finish dead last." And his mind churned around Slade losing his ranch to foreclosure. He was that much closer, then, to buying it from the bank.

"I dunno," Sandy said, watching as he leaped off the lip to the ground. "She's got pretty good endurance riding credentials."

Laughing, Curt moved to the front of his truck and opened the door. "Thanks, Sandy. See you around." He slid into his truck and decided to go visit his good friend, Frank Halbert, the head of Wyoming Bank. Glee filled Curt as he drove slowly out of the feedlot area. The sky was cloudy with a mix of white and gray clouds. It might rain, which was good thing for this hot summer.

"I want you to put the screws to McPherson," Curt told Frank Halbert in a low tone. They sat in his large office on the third floor of the bank. During the recession, Wyoming Bank had been not only bailed out, but had received a flush of money from the government. Right now, Halbert, in his fifties, balding and wearing silver-rimmed bifocals, was richer than hell. And Curt knew the wheedling, manipulative bastard could sink McPherson once and for all.

"Well, Curt, he's up to date on his mortgage payments."

Downing gave the fat banker a cutting smile. He didn't like Halbert. The banker was easily led by his money. Curt had used him many times in the past. He was slowly buying up ranches going into foreclosure. He also had his eye on the Bar H south of town, as well. It, too, was in dire straits. He needed the hundred acres of the Bar H as a place to establish a larger breeding facility. By getting McPherson's fifty acres next to him, he was able to enlarge his training program. The fact that he has bought half a million dollars into Halbert's bank meant if he wanted something done, the banker would do it, no questions asked. "So? Change the rate on him."

Studying the computer screen that had Slade McPherson's data on it, Frank murmured, "He does have a floating loan percentage."

"Then," Curt said, "make it go up."

Nodding, Frank said, "I can, but I have to justify it." He wiped his brow with his linen handkerchief.

Halbert reminded him of a pig. He had close-set brown eyes and a pug nose. His round face only emphasized his chubbiness in Curt's eyes. His patience thinned as Halbert kept clicking the keyboard looking at various elements of McPherson's long-term loan on the Tetons Ranch. Hands moving slowly into fists on the arms of the over-stuffed brown leather wing back chair, Curt barely held his impatience in check.

"Well," Frank murmured, looking up from his computer, "it's done! I've raised it a quarter of a percent. We'll send out a letter today to him notifying him of his new mortgage payment."

Rising, Curt said, "Excellent. Thank you, Frank," and he turned on his heel and strode across the wooden floor to the door. A frisson of joy flowed through Curt as he walked to the elevator and pressed the down button. Mentally, he was rubbing his hands. If McPherson had the added pressure of a new, higher mortgage payment due October first, it would put him in a helluva bind. Unable to ride Thor and putting a green-horn on the stud instead would be enough stress. The elevator door whooshed open and he stepped inside and pressed the button. The doors closed.

By the time he'd left the bank and headed for the parking lot behind the three-story building, Curt was walking on air. There were plenty of ranchers in the area who were hanging on by a thread because of the deep recession. Curt knew that McPherson was counting on winning that ten grand, but now, he wouldn't. There was no way Dr. Lawton could win on Thor. She simply didn't have the experience necessary.

Approaching his truck, he gave a short, sharp laugh. Curt now saw that not only was he going to win, he'd do it easily with McPherson removed from the competition.

There was no one at the top of the endurance riders who could beat his Arabian stallion, Shah. Thor had been his only worry, and now, he could breathe and relax. Sliding into the truck, Curt pulled the door shut. He snickered to himself as he drove out of the parking lot. Raindrops began splattering across the windshield. The sky had turned dark above the cow town. He turned on the wipers. Right now, he'd give *anything* to see McPherson's face when he received that letter from the bank and the higher monthly mortgage bill.

"What the hell," Slade muttered as he stared at the bank letter. He was sitting at the kitchen table. Shorty had just brought in the mail from the box sitting on a post near the highway.

Jordana was at the sink washing dishes. She had just come in from a thirty-mile ride on Thor. It was the second of the week. Slade's leg was still bothering him, and she knew he liked to keep a clean, neat house. Her hands in suds, she turned and saw the dark look on his face. "What is it?" she asked. Feeling energized and hopeful because of the second ride on the stallion, Jordana felt them beginning to get used to one another.

"My floating mortgage rate just went up a quarter of a point," he muttered unhappily.

"Does that mean you owe more monthly?"

"Exactly. Five hundred dollars more." Where was he going to get it? Slade charged a high price for each endurance student. They helped cover his mortgage. But now . . .

Jordana wiped her hands on a towel and walked over to the table. Little by little, Slade was letting her into his world. And it was a stress-filled one from what she could see. She saw his broad shoulders slump and defeat come to his face. "Five hundred a month is a lot," she murmured.

Griff came through the door into the kitchen. "Slade, we got that hay moved to the main barn," he said, walking to the cof-feemaker and pouring himself a cup of cof-fee.

Irritated by his brother's lighthearted mood, Slade snarled, "Fine."

Turning, Griff frowned. He looked at Jordana silently, asking why his twin was in such a funk. She barely shook her head and moved her gaze toward the front door. Okay, he got the message. Never mind that his hands had blisters on the palms even with the protective leather gloves. Or that they burned like fire. Griff had tried putting

Band-Aids on them before the work started, but it did no good. Shorty had laughed when he'd bitched about his hands having blisters. The wrangler had no pity for him. Griff thought telling Slade what he'd accomplished might make him feel better. But Slade was obviously in no mood to hear it. Feeling proud of himself that he'd actually done some physical labor and done it well, Griff turned and left.

The door shut. Slade lifted his head and glared toward the foyer. "I wish to hell he'd leave," he told her.

Jordana saw and felt the tension in Slade's face. Every time Griff came in, she saw his armor come up and his face go expressionless. That didn't mean he wasn't feeling anything because by now, she knew he felt plenty. The twin was a burr under his saddle. Griff was not motivated like Slade. If Slade didn't kick his butt and give him orders to do something specific, Griff was on the computer looking for Wall Street jobs for hours on end. Griff was not earning his keep, and she knew Slade was in a constant angry stew over the situation.

Moving closer, she placed her hand on Slade's slumped shoulder. "If we win the ten thousand dollars, will that get you over that extra monthly hurdle?"

Slade sat back, relishing her soft touch. There was such calmness and clarity about Jordana. More and more, he found himself wanting her around. He counted the days until she'd be out for half a day at his ranch. They were his only time-outs from the present financial situation threatening to overwhelm him and his ranch. "Yes, it would give me the breathing room I need." He felt like crying. His whole world was crumbling before him. Slade knew in his heart that Jordana would never win the race. He was going to lose the ranch. *Oh, God . . .*

"Slade," she whispered, coming around and sitting down at his elbow, "don't give up!" Jordana gripped his hand that was curled into a fist. "Listen to me, will you? I *know* I can win this for you!" She clung to his dark, hopeless gaze. His mouth was thinned, the corners drawn in because he was in pain. Fingers tightening on his fist, she said urgently, "Slade? You have to have faith."

He cut a glance toward Jordana. Her hand soothed some of his pain, but not all of it. She was the pinnacle of faith and hope. "Listen, I've been in such bad straits with this ranch for so many years that this feels like the last bombshell that is going to destroy it." There, he'd said it. Slade didn't ever confide his real fears to anyone, but Jordana's hand on his triggered his admittance.

"No, it won't destroy it, Slade," she said solemnly, holding his dark gaze. He looked as if he were going to cry. Slade swallowed several times as if choking back the tears. Her heart burst open with such pain for him. "You've done everything right," Jordana whispered. "And I can't believe the cosmos is going to take this ranch away from you."

Slade didn't have the heart to tell her she didn't stand a chance of winning. Hell, she'd be lucky to finish the race at all because it was such a wicked and challenging one. Instead, he rasped, "I can."

Shaking her head, Jordana said, "I wish I had the money, Slade. I'd give it to you. This ranch is beautiful and you've worked hard to keep it in good condition." She couldn't imagine what he would do if he lost it. Yet, it looked as if he would. Her heart tore more for him. Slade was suffering so much, struggling to keep how he really felt away from her.

"You're as poor as I am," he reminded her. Slade knew she was living from paycheck to paycheck. Yes, he'd lowered her training rate to one thousand dollars a month, but that put him into an even worse financial hole.

"I can loan you that extra thousand dollars a month," she told him, a fierceness in her husky tone. She gripped his hand hard. "Slade, for once, take some gifts from someone else. You're not alone in this fight!"

He grunted and pulled his hand away from hers. Because if he didn't, he was going to kiss her until she melted into him. It was driving him hard, and Slade was too anxious about the loss of his ranch staring him in the face to divide his energies right now. "I've been alone since my parents died in that damned car accident, Jordana. Every day is a fight. You're around here enough to see that." His nostrils flared as the shock of losing his ranch was imminent. Nothing had hurt so bad as this. He wadded up the bill in his right hand and threw it on the pine table.

"Oh, Slade," Jordana whispered, "this isn't over! I can loan you the money. I have a thousand dollars a month. I won't charge you interest —"

"Dammit, Jordana, I can't do that!" he exploded. Slade shoved the chair away and stood, fighting back a real need to sob. He swallowed hard, the lump in his throat being pushed down once again.

Standing, Jordana heard the cry of anguish in his growling tone. No longer was she afraid of his irritable and snarling disposition. She'd come to realize that when Slade was under pressure, he was that way. But she'd seen him when he wasn't, and he was a man that any woman would desire. Without thinking, she threw her arms around his shoulders and pressed herself to him. The startled look in his eyes told her he wasn't expecting this. Well, that was fine because she was being driven to pull him out of the throes of his anguish.

Leaning up, Jordana pressed her lips against the hard, flat line of his mouth. Instantly, Slade groaned, and he rocked her hard against him, his arms moving like steel bands around her slender torso. The breath was crushed out of her. Jordana kept her eyes closed, her arms tight around Slade, and rocked his lips open. There was a tremble that rolled through him as her soft mouth pleaded with his to open and allow her entrance. Something primal and raw pushed Jordana. Her world melted into a fiery heat as his mouth turned mobile and hungry, and he took her with savage intensity.

An explosion of incredible heat tunneled through Slade. Kissing Jordana was the last thing on his mind in his crumbling world. Yet, the soft insistence of her mouth, the movement of her full lips gliding teasingly against his dragged a volcanic and animal response from him. It had been years since he'd kissed a woman. Her breath was moist and caressed his cheek. He'd shaved this morning, but already his beard was growing back. Her face was like velvet, and he was starved for her touch. Slade's mind melted, and all he focused on was her breasts pressed against his massive chest, her mouth wet and hungry against his, her breath moist and the scent of pine in her silky hair.

Moaning, Jordana surrendered fully to Slade as a man. His arms were powerful, his mouth starving against hers. The texture of his beard against her cheek was proof of his masculinity. He swept his hand down her back, his fingers memorizing the curve of her spine. Sliding his hand over her hip, Slade pressed her insistently against him. Jordana became aware of just how much he wanted her. She relished the incredible virility of him. Slade's mouth was hungry, and so was hers. She couldn't get enough of him, enough of his mouth ravishing hers with an animal-like need. Wasn't she needy? Oh yes, it had been too long without a man who stirred her heart and her body. Slade did both. As his hand ranged up her spine, Jordana trembled inwardly. He was strong, and yet he didn't hurt her. He was monitoring the strength of his touch. When his hand moved across her back to graze the curve of her breast, she moaned. The sound echoed between them.

What was happening? Slade felt drugged, his mind turning into useless mush, his body throbbing with white-hot need of Jordana in every way. He wanted to lock himself into her willing body, feel every curve and valley, drawn in by the throbbing heat as he plunged into her welcoming depths. If he didn't stop, he'd haul her into his arms and carry her off to his bedroom. And he'd love her until she moaned with utter pleasure. As Slade tore his mouth from hers, he opened his eyes to mere slits. His breathing was harsh and ragged, but so was hers.

Jordana moaned as the kiss abruptly ended. Lips throbbing from the power of his searching kiss, she wanted more. No . . . she wanted Slade . . . all of him. Her mind whirled, and she felt as if she were floating in a way she never had with a man. Slade was incredibly masculine in a way she'd never experienced. And the boiling tension in her lower body ached to pull him deeply into her and consummate something Jordana felt was inevitable. As she forced her lids open, she burned beneath Slade's predatory look. Here was a man who was as raw and untamed as the wilderness he lived within. She felt his hands roaming across her back and hips, as if remembering her and burning every curve of hers into his mind.

Slade pulled away. He didn't want to, but he had to. Jordana was too willing, too beautiful, and he was in such a hell of a mess with his ranch and life right now that he couldn't take this on, too. His mouth tasted of hers. She liked to chew peppermint gum when riding, and he could taste it now. "We can't do this," he growled unsteadily. "Not now, Jordana." *Not ever.* All Slade saw was another Isabel Stephens debacle. "There's too much at stake," he managed in a raw whisper. "I don't want to lose my ranch. I have to focus on that . . . not . . . us."

Hurting for Slade and knowing her spontaneous kiss was healing to him on one level, Jordana understood. She touched the strands of hair against her cheek and pulled them aside. "Sure, Slade. I understand."

The quaver in her husky voice tore at him as nothing else ever had. He saw disappointment and hurt in her large blue eyes. She was guileless, Slade realized as he stood before her, tense and unmoving. His heart told him Jordana was not another Isabel Stephens. His mind shouted at him that she was. Every woman was a temptation because he'd gone so long without real nurturing from one. Pushing his fingers through his hair, he said, "I appreciate your care, but right now, I need to focus on a way to keep my ranch."

Her whole body was burning and throbbing like a flame flickering in the wind. How badly Jordana wanted to consummate their relationship. She saw the raw hunger and anguish in Slade's narrowed gaze that never left hers. "It's tough to balance off financial stuff against a new relationship," she acknowledged in a hoarse tone. "I do understand, Slade." Jordana lifted her chin and held his stare. "But I'm not sorry I kissed you."

She had such guts, Slade decided in that moment. Jordana was a fierce warrior, afraid of nothing. "I'm not either," he confided more gently. Opening his hand, he offered, "But right now, I can't, Jordana. I'm sorry." And he was. God, how sorry he was. How could he explain that he distrusted her because of Isabel? That he saw all women as waiting to steal his family ranch from under him? Yet, Jordana had offered him a thousand dollars a month to make up that difference. Pride wouldn't let Slade accept that offer.

CHAPTER SIXTEEN

"Are you ready?"

Jordana nodded. She was holding the reins on Thor tightly because he was pawing and ready to get on with the fifty-mile run. Slade stood next to her. They were at the beginning of the actual endurance starting line. His hand was on the slope of the stallion's shoulder. It was barely dawn; and she could just see the trail ahead. "I am."

Worried, Slade knew his stallion was more than ready to do a test run across the entire course. This was the first time Jordana would take the route. "You got your iPhone with the maps?" They had worked a week to input the information into her Apple iPhone so that it would be on her, and she could use it during the ride.

Patting the iPhone strung around her neck and hidden beneath her sweater and Kevlar vest, she said, "Got it."

"Okay, take it easy. Don't let him run full-out. I'll time you, but don't try and push him."

"Right," Jordana said, excitement thrumming through her. She smiled down at Slade. Since the unexpected kiss, they'd danced around one another, never really mentioning it. The past two weeks, she'd ridden three times a week on the thirty-mile circuit on the Elkhorn ranch, fine-tuning Thor's endurance and preparing him for the race. How badly she wanted to speak to Slade about their kiss, but he'd withdrawn since then. Jordana tried not to be hurt by it. After all, neither had expected it.

Patting Thor's taut, arched neck, Slade murmured, "Okay. We'll be in constant contact by radio," and he pointed to the one hooked on his belt. "At every five miles when you hit a point, you call. If you don't call, I'll know you're in trouble."

Nodding, Jordana knew he was nervous for her and his horse. "I'll do it, Slade. And I'll be okay." She wanted to reach out as she had done before the kiss, but after it, he'd really retreated, and Jordana had forced herself to stop touching him from time to time. The race and learning the trail and handling Thor was paramount right now. Jordana wanted to win that money for Slade. And nothing else mattered at this point. They could talk about their kiss after the race.

"Okay," he said, holding up the stop watch, "take off. . . ."

Thor heard his master's voice and reared, fighting the bit.

Jordana laughed and eased the reins. Instantly, the stallion dug in with his hind legs, dirt and rock flying as he hurtled down the path strewn with rocks and grass. The wind sailed past her as she settled into a fast trot with Thor. Very quickly, they were swallowed up by the thick stands of ever-greens across the slope of the mountain. The trail started at six thousand feet and quickly climbed to ten thousand. Thor snorted violently, continuing to fight the reins, but Jordana held him at a ground-eating trot.

Slade watched as the pair disappeared up the winding, twisting trail. The last two weeks had been hell on him in so many ways. As he walked back to his truck at the trailhead, he was glad to be rid of the damned cane. Climbing in, he felt his leg that was still tender and sore. He'd never realized that a puncture wound of this size could cause so much havoc. Cursing Diablo under his breath, Slade started his truck. He would drive to the first checkpoint twenty miles into the ride. It was a high meadow at nine thousand feet and was accessible by vehicle. It would be there that the first vet station check would occur for all riders.

Even though he wasn't a vet, Slade knew what to look for. Thor would come into the station, and Jordana would dismount. The vet and assistant would check Thor's pulse, his blood pressure and look over each leg very carefully for any signs of injury or swelling. Shorty would walk Thor for twenty minutes, cooling him down. Thor would then be checked again by the vet team. He would be given water to drink. If Thor's pulse and blood pressure had settled to a normal rate and his legs passed inspection, Jordana would be given permission to continue on for the next twenty-mile leg. This time, Slade would be doing the checking.

As Slade drove slowly out of the huge, oval gravel parking lot, he knew he had to have Jordana run the fifty miles at least three times before the actual race. There were plenty of other horse trailers and pickup trucks around, signs that other endurance riders were familiarizing themselves with the challenging trail. What he didn't like was seeing the bright red trailer owned by

Curt Downing. He was already on the trail ahead of Jordana, but Slade didn't know how far ahead. Worried, he hoped they wouldn't meet. And Slade knew that every one of these riders would have assistants waiting at the first checkpoint.

As he drove down the long, flat graveled road within the Tetons National Park, Slade's mind and, if he were honest, his heart, centered on Jordana. He'd dreamt every night about that unexpected kiss that had exploded between them. And then, his torrid dream would melt into the nightmare of his past with Isabel. The last year of their marriage had been a daily donnybrook. She would scream, curse him and call him a loser. Slade had taken it all, and he'd felt relief when Isabel had finally had enough, packed her bags and flown back to her rich parents' penthouse. He'd felt even more relief when the divorce papers had been served on him. Cutting Isabel out of his life had been like getting out of prison to Slade. Rubbing his unshaven chin, Slade braked at the stop sign. At five on this August summer morning, few tourist cars were on the highway. Turning left, he kept the truck at the twenty-five mile an hour limit. It would be no time before he was at the vet check meadow.

The sky was turning pink as sun rose in the east. Herds of elk were here and there near the highway. One thing about the Tetons, the wildlife was not afraid of park visitors. And one had to be careful about driving this time of morning because all the deer, elk and moose were grabbing their last grass meal before settling down to sleep during the daylight hours. Often, they were near the road. Too many crashes at dawn had occurred because of this situation.

What was he going to do about Jordana? Clearly, she liked him. Hell, he liked her. Slade knew he was in no position to start a relationship as bad as his body and heart keened for it. Isabel had just done too much damage to him. His brows fell. Finally, Slade admitted he was afraid. Afraid of another failure. Oh, no question there was a chasm of difference between Isabel and Jordana, but his mind balked anyway.

Soon enough, the exit came up for the twenty-mile stop. Slade turned and drove slowly down the six-mile gravel road that would end at the trailhead parking area. When he arrived, he saw about fifteen teams waiting for their riders to come in. Parking, Slade knew every one of them. Some waved to him. He waved back. His gaze moved across the large, oval meadow. It had been mowed, so it was easy to work with incoming endurance riders and their sweaty mounts. Wearing a red T-shirt, Chuck Merced, Curt Downing's assistant, stood away from the other endurance crews, his wrist held up as he looked at his stopwatch.

Climbing out of the truck, Slade knew that twenty miles at a trot would bring Jordana and Thor in at a certain time. He was content to lean against the front of his truck and watch because she'd been the last of all these riders to start the trail. When had Curt Downing started? That worried him to no end. What if Jordana came upon him and that black Arabian stud of his? Stallions, when together, automatically wanted to fight one another. He'd repeatedly warned Jordana about this. She'd never seen two studs go at it, but he had. It was visceral, primal and brutal. Stallions fought to win, and their intent was to inflict as much damage upon their competitor as they could.

"Hey," a male voice called, "Slade! How are you?"

Turning to his right, Slade recognized red-haired Bart Peters. He was the husband of Bernadette, a champion endurance rider.

"Hey, Bart," he said, greeting the forty-year-old man with thick glasses with a smile.

"What time did Bernadette start the course?"

Walking over and smiling, Bart looked at his stopwatch. "She started off at the trail-head thirty minutes ago."

Nodding, Slade said, "And how's her mount?" He knew her Arabian gelding, Smithy, had been retired last year. They had bought one of Thor's offspring from him, a part mustang and part Arabian gelding called Checkers.

Leaning against the truck front with Slade, Bart said, "Checkers is doing great. You know he placed fifth in the Tevis Cup?"

"Yes, I heard. That's damn good for a first timer." And it was. Thor's stamina and endurance being passed on to his offspring was well known. People brought their Arabian mares to be bred to him. The resulting offspring had shown consistently in the past ten years that Thor's genes were winners.

Bart grinned. "It sure was. Bernadette was surprised. So was I." His green eyes danced as he held Slade's gaze. "Your stud is remarkable. We'd always heard how good he was, but Checkers is just blowing us away. He's six years old and just starting his career. It's hard to believe he took fifth place in the Tevis."

"That was a combination of Bernadette's

riding skills and her horse," Slade murmured. One could have a great horse, but if the rider wasn't up to snuff, there would be no winning anything.

Smiling fully, Bart agreed. "Hey, we were really sorry to hear you aren't competing this year. We heard on the circuit one of your students, a woman, is riding Thor instead? We never thought you'd let anyone ride that stud of yours. What changed your mind?"

"Dr. Jordana Lawton is riding him," Slade said. He didn't want to tell anyone.

"This is the first female student you've had, isn't it?"

Uncomfortable with the fact that his business as a teacher and competitor was public knowledge, Slade frowned. "Yes, it is."

"She must be exceptional," Bart said, watching the other teams going out to the meadow with buckets, brushes, stethoscopes and towels in hand.

"She is," Slade agreed.

"Is she new? Bernadette and I haven't heard of her being on the circuit before."

"She's competed at the lower levels for many years and is moving up."

Red brows raising on his long, narrow face, Bart murmured, "Wow, she must be a heck of a rider then. We know how much of a handful Thor is." And he laughed.

Grinning, Slade said, "Dr. Lawton has a strong dressage background coupled with a decade of endurance riding under her belt."

"Ah," Bart said, nodding his head, "dressage. Well, we all know a good dressage rider is pretty capable. How's Thor getting along with her?"

"Actually, very good," Slade told him. He enjoyed Bart's company. There were many times that Bernadette would be in the first ten riders on this particular endurance ride. They were a husband and wife team, and it was their love of the sport that kept them trailering around the United States on the national circuit rides.

"Amazing. We all thought that feisty stud of yours was a one-man horse only."

"Well," Slade said with a smile, "he's got more facets to him than I thought. I didn't think Dr. Lawton could handle him, either, but he's completely surrendered over to her." And then Slade wanted to add, *just like I have.* Thinking better of it, he remained silent.

"Wise horse," Bart laughed.

"Hey, did you see when Downing left the trailhead?" Slade kept his voice nonchalant and the worry out of it.

"Yeah, he was driving in his trailer just as

I was leaving. Bernadette started the trail at 4:30 a.m."

"I see," Slade murmured. In his head he was calculating the difference. "He probably took off at 4:45 a.m., then." The horse had to be saddled and bridled, and that took a few minutes.

"Yeah, I'd guess about there. I'm worried he and that black devil of his are going to catch up to Bernadette." Shaking his head, Bart lowered his voice and muttered, "I always worry about her when Downing is around. He's known for his tricks."

"I know," Slade said in a low tone. Everyone on the circuit knew Downing's maneuvers could harm other horses and riders.

Looking at his stopwatch, Bart said, "I'd better get out there. Bernadette should be coming in any minute. I'll look forward to seeing Dr. Lawton on Thor. That has to be a sight to behold." He eased away from the truck.

"Later," Slade murmured, watching his friend carry the water bucket and sponges toward the meadow. Every team had to do a lot of things when a rider and horse came into a vet check station. Bart had several white towels draped over his left shoulder. In another bucket he had liniment, dressings, bandages and medications. There was a long garden hose strung from the parking lot out to the check area where teams could fill and refill their buckets with water for the horses. After twenty miles, every horse was thirsty. The animals would gulp down one to three buckets at one stop.

If Downing were fifteen minutes ahead of Jordana, Slade mentally calculated that they would not meet. But if Jordana wasn't pacing Thor correctly, letting him run when he should be trotting, it was possible the two might encounter each other. He hoped to hell they didn't. Jordana had no way to counter Downing's deceit out there away from prying eyes. Did Downing know that she was riding Thor? Most likely — because it was common knowledge between the top endurance riders. It wasn't a secret. Worry ate at Slade. He rubbed his jaw. The sun was just starting to peek over the mountains in the east. The sky was a light blue and cloudless. It was a perfect day for a test run on the course.

Thor was galloping along on the part of the trail where Slade had wanted him to trot. Jordana's hands and arms ached from holding in the athletic stallion. She reasoned on this trial run, on one of the few flat areas that was a mile long, it was all right to open him up a little. Thor was bursting with such robust energy that it shocked her. It seemed that every upward, winding mile along the dirt and rock trail within the tree line made him stronger, not weaker. His coat was gleaming with sweat, foam around his mouth from chomping constantly on the bit because he wanted to be let go to gallop at full speed.

She saw no other riders ahead of her, although they had passed three already. What harm was there in letting him run a little? Jordana knew on this section that Slade had wanted him at a trot. But Thor was so full of himself and she'd been fighting him so hard, she needed the rest. Leaning forward, she knew her weight would signal to the stallion that he could run. She loosened the reins just a little. Instantly, Thor surged out of the trot and into a ground-eating gallop. This one-mile run was across a high altitude meadow filled with dried yellowed grass.

The wind whistled past her. Jordana wore the helmet and Kevlar vest. Her thin leather gloves were soaked with sweat. Thor thundered down across the meadow with such fierce strides it took her breath away. Jordana knew from the map on her iPhone, that the trail suddenly turned wicked at the other end as it disappeared once more into the evergreens. Checking Thor at a half mile, she fought him back down to a trot by the time they hit that twisting, winding trail upward.

Shaking his head, angry, Thor fought her as he easily climbed up the switchbacks. They were at nine thousand feet. In no time, they broke out of the evergreens that stopped at the ten thousand foot level. Jordana saw the radiant slats of sun just cresting the eastern horizon. She didn't have time to enjoy the beauty of it. The trail turned very narrow, and they climbed more. Thor was breathing evenly, snorting and still wanting to run.

As they crested the last switchback to the trail that now lay between millions of boulders and loose rock at ten thousand five hundred feet, Jordana saw another rider just ahead of them. It was Curt Downing and his black Arabian stallion! Surprised, Jordana automatically felt her gut clench. Slade had warned her so many times about this rider. What should she do? Pull Thor up and bring down his stride to not meet up with them? Her mind ranged over the options. This trail went on for five miles and then curved down through the forest to nine thousand feet where it emptied out on the vet check meadow.

Gripping the reins hard, Jordana watched the pair flying across the rocky expanse. There was no question the black stallion was powerful and fast. But Thor was equally swift. She also knew that there was no possibility of passing on this narrow trail. There was no way for another rider to move over so she could pass. If anyone got off this trail, it would be disaster. This trail had been carved out of the scree that lay on the slope of the mountain. To get off would be to invite injury of both horse and rider.

Her intuition told her to rein Thor in. She couldn't expose him to possible injury. This was just a test run, not the actual race. And once they got off this high altitude trail, she didn't know if the thousand foot drop provided a place wide enough to pass, either. This was why she was riding; to understand the lay of the land and where she could and could not safely pass another rider.

She saw Downing look back. She was close enough to see his surprise and then rage cross his face. He knew Thor when he saw him. Continuing to rate Thor's pace and slow him down so that he didn't run up on the other stallion, Jordana focused on keeping the distance between them. *Damn.*

Of all things. She had passed three other riders, and they had easily moved aside to allow her transit. Slade had warned her that Curt wouldn't move. More than one rider had been forced to stay behind because he bent and broke the rules where judges couldn't see him do it.

"Easy," she whispered to Thor, "just take it easy, big boy," and she watched his ears flick back and forth over her crooning voice. With her arms, legs and hands, she slowed the mustang even more. Slade wouldn't be happy to see them arriving in the meadow one after another, Jordana thought.

Slade's eyes widened as he stood out in the meadow. He saw Downing burst out of the tree line, his black Arab stallion surging at a wild gallop toward the center of the meadow. It was a mile-long run. And right behind him came Thor and Jordana. The mustang wanted to run, he saw, but Jordana was fighting to keep him at a floating trot instead. Realizing what was going on, he waited for Jordana to pull up the horse.

"Whoa," Jordana told the stud. Thor came to a halt, shaking his head. She saw Slade's frowning face as he walked up to her and took the reins.

Dismounting, Jordana took the reins back.

"What the hell happened?" Slade demanded. He put the stethoscope to Thor's sweaty chest and listened. Once he got the information, he went and took the horse's pulse. Writing down all the statistics, he timed the horse's breaths for fifteen seconds and then multiplied it by four.

Jordana waited until he'd finished writing down the information. "I came up to the rocky trail at ten-five and saw Downing ahead of me."

Scowling, Slade gestured for her to take Thor over to the waiting pail of water. "You must have been pushing faster than you should have. Downing left the trailhead at four forty-five a.m. You left fifteen minutes later."

Grimacing, Jordana heard the anger in Slade's growling tone. "I was fighting him so much, Slade, that I let him move out faster." She held up her leather-gloved hand. "My fingers, wrist and arms ache from holding him in." She slipped the halter around the stud's neck and removed the bridle. Bringing the blue nylon halter over his head, she led him to the water.

"Doesn't matter. You *have* to rate him properly or he won't have any gas left for that five-mile run at the last." Slade took the bridle from her and hung it on the saddle horn. As the horse drank in great, gulping drafts, he unsaddled the stallion. For the next ten to fifteen minutes, Thor would be walked around. When his resting heartbeat was reached, the vet would give the signal for the rider to resaddle the horse and take off.

Chastened, Jordana brought over a second pail of water to the thirsty stud. "I never expected him to fight me like that." She was amazed that anyone could force Thor to keep up a steady, ground-eating pace. Slade had. Her respect for him rose even more than before.

"He's a competitor," Slade warned. He looked ahead to where Downing and his crew were. Anger stirred in him. He returned his gaze to Jordana. She was flushed, her eyes bright and filled with joy, despite the rugged ride on Thor. And God help him, he longed to be in her company. Gaze automatically moving to her mouth, Slade swore he could taste Jordana on his lips once more. His lower body throbbed to life, much to his chagrin.

"What do you want me to do tactically now that Downing is here with us?" she asked. Lifting a third pail to Thor's water-dripping nose, she watched him thrust his muzzle into it.

Slade moved to her, his voice low. "Let's see whose horse leaves first. Knowing Downing, because this isn't an official vet check, my experience tells me he isn't going to wait for his stud to get to his resting heart rate. He'll take off a lot sooner because he knows Thor is here."

Eyes widening, Jordana said, "But that hurts his horse if he does that."

Shrugging, Slade said, "Downing doesn't care. He thinks that stud of his can make up the difference. He won't want you moving out ahead of him."

Sure enough, as Jordana continued to walk Thor in a large circle to cool down, she saw Downing resaddling his stud five minutes later. Shaking her head, she saw Slade watching the pair. Who would harm their horse like that? Endurance riders prided themselves on horses first, contest second. She lifted her hand and patted Thor's neck. The horse was a lot less feisty right now. He was more tractable. Twenty miles was a lot for any horse. And she hoped that when she resaddled him and took off for the next twenty, that he would be less of a handful.

The meadow was filled with horses and riders coming and going. It was always exciting for Jordana. Slade's leg had healed up enough so that he could walk on the other side of his horse with her. She walked ahead of Thor and said, "How are *you* doing?"

Heat surged through Slade. Jordana's care extended to him even during the competition. Maybe it was the E.R. doctor in her. He didn't know. "I'm fine," he groused. Watching Downing galloping out of the meadow, he felt some relief. "My leg is fine, if that's what you're asking."

Nodding, she smiled a little. Slade had on what she termed the "bad cowboy look" of the perpetual scowl. He hadn't shaved this morning, and the beard made him look primal. It appealed to her as a woman. Did he know how handsome he really was? She didn't think so. "That's good," Jordana said. "Let's go over things I need to remember on this next twenty mile stint." Because if she didn't, Jordana knew she'd start thinking of that hot, ravishing kiss all over again. Oh, for sure, she wasn't going to confide in Slade her nightly amorous dreams in which they made wild love with one another. Jordana blushed just thinking about it. Still, he made her feel good. She was always happy when she was around Slade. What kind of relationship was maturing between them? Where would it lead?

CHAPTER SEVENTEEN

It was late afternoon when they arrived back at Slade's ranch. Shorty had unloaded Thor and was taking him to the bathing facility. Jordana was helping by unloading the saddle, bridle and other items to be placed in the tack room. As Slade entered the ranch house, the phone rang.

"Slade here," he answered. His leg was aching. Grabbing a chair in the foyer, he sat down.

"Slade, this is Charley."

Brows raising, Slade's heart took a little skip. "Hey Charley, do you have good news for me?" Two weeks ago he'd put in a bid with the U.S. Forest Service at the Tetons Headquarters to supply them several pack-horses. It was an open bid system and Slade had always gotten these contracts from Charley, who was the head ranger of the Tetons district. He hoped he had, because every source of money was vital to keeping the ranch above financial disaster. This particular bid was for ten horses, and that wasn't a small amount of money. It could mean close to eight thousand dollars for him. Unconsciously, he held his breath. Whoever the winner of the bid was, they received a phone call from Charley to seal the deal.

"I'm afraid not, Slade. Listen, your brother Griff was over here yesterday."

Scowling, Slade muttered, "My brother? What the hell was he doing over there?" His mind whirled. Slade recalled filling out the contract bid one morning when Griff was sitting and having his breakfast with him. Slade had explained the system and how important it was to put in the lowest bid so that that individual would be chosen and, therefore, hired or paid for their services.

"Yes," Charley said gruffly. "I'm hard-pressed not to report this, Slade."

"What are you talking about?"

"You didn't send him over here to talk with me?"

Frustration came out in his tone. "Charley, I don't have a *clue* as to what you're referring to. I never told Griff to go over to your office."

"Griff came over, out of the blue, and demanded an appointment to see me.

Lucky or unlucky, I happened to be here and told him to come on in."

Slade heard the tense tone in Charley's voice. He'd been supervisor of the Tetons for five years. "What did he come to see you about?"

"Your bid," Charley warned heavily.

"*My* bid?" Slade sat up, his brows moving upward in complete surprise. "How can that be? I didn't send him over to talk to you."

"Well, he alluded that you did, Slade, and that's why I'm calling you direct. Your brother sat here and told me that if I would choose your bid over all the others, that you would throw in another horse for free."

Rage exploded through Slade. Instantly, he was on his feet. Pain shot through his injured thigh as he did so. "What?" He nearly shouted the word. His hand tightened around the phone, his other hand curled into a fist. Slade knew that no one could do something like this. His heart sank. His brother had just scuttled his chances of getting that badly needed contract!

"It was a bribe, Slade. Your brother seemed to think that by throwing in an extra packhorse for free that it was obvious that I should choose your bid over the others."

"I *never* sent him to do that, Charley." Breathing hard, rage filling him, Slade tried to fight down his anger enough to think clearly. His entire connection with Charley and the U.S. Forest Service was now in jeopardy. Griff had stupidly blundered in, and now Slade knew that Charley could report him. And then, because this was clearly a violation, Charley could bar him from ever bidding again on a U.S. Forest Service contract. *Sonofabitch!*

"That's why I'm calling you, Slade. We've worked together for five years, and you've never tried to influence a bid before."

"I'm sorry, Charley. My brother is from New York City and a Wall Street type. He's stupid for trying to do this behind my back. He's got the morals and values of a sidewinder. That stuff might sell in the east, but it don't out here."

"That's what I thought. Your brother appeared to be completely clueless about the bid system. I had a good talk with him, and it became clear he was ignorant."

Closing his eyes, Slade felt sweat pop out on his brow. "What are you going to do about it?" he asked in a rasping tone. Slade knew he could be turned in and blacklisted from future bids — forever. The Tetons put out three to four bids a year, and Slade would lose a valuable source of income. Money was hard to come by in ranching, and Slade counted heavily on winning at least one or two bid contracts a year from Charley.

"I could turn Griff in for bribery."

"Yes," he said tightly, "you could."

"But if I did that, the only person it would hurt would be you, Slade. I know from experience that you are trying to keep your ranch out of foreclosure. You've never attempted to influence a bid with me — ever."

Rolling his eyes, Slade knew that if Charley turned in Griff, there would be an arrest and charges against him. His stupid brother didn't realize the damage he'd just done. "No, I would *never* do that, Charley."

"Right," he said. "I know that from dealing with you for five years now, you're a man of your word."

"What is going to happen? Are you calling the sheriff to pick Griff up and charge him with bribery?"

"No, I don't want to do that, Slade. I think if you talk to him and make him understand what he did, that will be sufficient." Charley hesitated, his voice lowering, "But I can't allow your bid to be chosen, Slade. You had won the bid, and I was getting ready to call you. Your brother screwed you royal. Now, I have to pick the next highest bidder, and he will be awarded the money instead. I can't, in all good conscience, let your bid win. Griff came in here and destroyed that chance. I'm sorry. I know you were counting on this money."

Hanging his head, gripping the receiver, Slade rasped, "I understand, Charley. Thank you for being fair-minded about this."

"I wish I could overlook Griff's bribe, but I can't."

"No, you shouldn't." Slade smarted because it was his good name that was being dragged through the mud. Sucking in a breath of air, Slade finally asked, "Are you barring me from further bid lists, Charley?"

"No, I'm not. And I'm basing that on your good name, Slade. But don't *ever* let that brother of yours come in here again and try to bribe me. Okay?"

"Thanks, Charley. I'll take care of him when he gets home."

"Good. Again, I'm sorry I can't award you this bid, Slade. You were the lowest."

Mouth tightening, he rasped, "It's just deserts under the circumstances, Charley. Thanks for not tarring and feathering me with the same brush as my younger brother."

Jordana walked into to the ranch house as Slade hung up the phone. He felt a wall of rage boiling inside of him. As he turned to look at her, she looked tired from the grueling fifty-mile test run on Thor. Choking it all down, he said, "Everything taken care of?"

For a moment, Jordana hesitated. Slade's eyes were black with rage. Who had been on the phone with him? "Yes, I just brushed Thor down and he's in his paddock rolling." Tilting her head, she reached out and said, "Slade? What's wrong? You look really upset."

The touch of her cool fingers on his lower arm nearly unleashed his rage. Shaking his head, Slade pulled his arm away from her. "It's nothing. Why don't you get going? It's been a long day for you."

Just then, Griff entered the ranch home.

"Hey, you're back," he hailed, taking off his tan Stetson and hanging it on a wooden wall hook near the door.

Jordana felt rage explode around Slade as he snapped his head up and glared at Griff. She stood between them, feeling the blast of anger leaping from Slade toward his twin brother. *What* was going on?

"You," Slade ground out, and he took three steps around Jordana, grabbed Griff by the collar of his shirt and shoved him hard against the wall. "Sonofabitch, you just cost me a bid!" he snarled into Griff's shocked

features.

Automatically, Griff threw up his arms and broke Slade's hold on him. "What the hell has gotten into you?" he yelled, backing toward the door.

Jordana opened her mouth and then shut it. Slade looked like a volcano ready to spew out lava as he strode toward Griff. She felt as if she were in a corral with Diablo. But Slade was the enraged bull this time.

Griff dodged Slade's outstretched hand and moved into the living room. He hunched over, waiting for another attack. "What the hell is the matter with you?" he shouted. Why was his brother looking as if he was going to kill him? Griff simply didn't understand his sour brother at all. What had he done?

Moving swiftly to the living room, Slade roared, "You stupid bastard! You just cost me an eight-thousand-dollar bid contract with the U.S. Forest Service. *That* is what you've done!" He punched his index finger into Griff's chest.

Peddling backward, Griff kept the pine coffee table between them. "What are you talking about?"

Slade stood there, breathing hard, his breath rasping. "You went to Charley at the Tetons headquarters and tried to *bribe* him.

That's what you did!" Slade rounded the coffee table, wanting to punch his twin in the face.

Moving quickly, Griff avoided Slade and kept the coffee table between them. "Bribe? You're insane! I didn't bribe Charley! I just went in to make a deal with him."

Jordana entered the room. Both men were roaring at one another. She stood there, helpless to interfere. Griff's expression was one of confusion and then surprise. Slade looked as if he wanted to kill Griff.

"A deal?" Slade roared. "Don't you know *anything* about bids? Once they're entered into the system, you don't contact the party about it! You went sallying into Charley's office today and offered him a bribe."

Nostrils flaring, Griff yelled, "Like hell I did! I was just sweetening the pot was all. One extra horse would seal the deal!"

Shaking his head, Slade snarled, "You might wheel and deal on Wall Street like that, but that kind of crap doesn't fly out here in the West. You got me deleted from this bid." Slade held up his hand. "I had the bid, dammit! Charley was going to call me tomorrow morning and tell me I had it."

"That's good," Griff muttered. "So I don't see why you're so pissed off at me."

"Because," Slade thundered, "Charley saw

your little visit as a bribe and I got removed from the list because of it." Slade's face reddened with rage. "Damn you, Griff, you just cost me eight thousand dollars I needed to pay on the ranch mortgage. You interfered and screwed me and my ranch." He jammed his finger down at the pine floor. "You stupid jerk, you just put this ranch in a financial hole! What you did is a *bribe!* Do you get it?"

Breathing hard, Griff glared at his enraged brother, who was hunkered over him like a bull ready to gore him. "It was not a bribe! We do deals like this on Wall Street all the time! It's not a bribe. It's just part of what we do. No one calls it a bribe. Damn, you're crazy, Slade!"

Jordana saw Slade start to move. She knew he was going to grab a hold of Griff and beat him. Racing forward, she gripped his left arm with both hands. "Slade! Calm down! You need to take a walk." She tugged insistently on his arm. He didn't budge, his focus on his white-faced brother across the coffee table. Using all her strength, digging in her heels, Jordana jerked Slade hard.

Snapping his head to the left, Slade saw Jordana's grim face. Her full lips were tight, her eyes hard and insistent. Trembling with fury, he felt the strength of her small hands around his thick upper arm. The look in her eyes told him that she meant business. For a second, his rage cooled. He wasn't angry at her. But he sure as hell wanted to beat Griff to a pulp.

"Come *on,*" Jordana insisted, tugging on his arm again. "Walk with me outside, Slade. *Now!*"

Hesitantly, Slade nodded. He glared over at Griff. "You sonofabitch, you get the hell off this ranch. *Now.* I don't care where you go, but don't *ever* step foot back here. You understand?"

Glaring back, Griff snarled, "This is my ranch, too! You can't kick me out of here!"

"Watch me." Slade made a move to go toward Griff.

Instantly, Griff leaped away, ran to the door, jerked it open and left.

Jordana sighed and released Slade. "You can't hit him, Slade. Calm down, please." She used her best soothing tone, the one she'd use with a traumatized patient at the hospital. She saw the anger leave and, in its place, anguish return. "Let's go to the kitchen. I'll make us some coffee. Come on. . . ." She tugged at his hand that was still folded in a fist.

His rage began to dissolve by degrees as Slade opened his hand and entwined it within Jordana's fingers. She might be small, but she was gutsy coming between him and his brother. "Okay, coffee," he whispered, defeated. He walked her to the kitchen.

"Here, sit down, Slade. Your leg has to be hurting you."

It was, he realized. "Yeah, it's throbbing a little."

Nodding, Jordana went to the counter and made coffee. "You've been on it all day. It's bound to be achy." Her hands flew knowingly over the counter to get the coffee beans and the other items she'd need. "Can you tell me what happened?" she asked, turning and giving him a gentle look.

Slade sighed, rubbed his face with his hands and told her the whole conversation with Charley. He ended it by saying, "I can't believe Griff doesn't know what the hell a bribe consists of. Charley and I sure know what one is."

Placing two heavy ceramic mugs on the table, Jordana said, "Maybe things are different on Wall Street, Slade. He looked confused when you charged him with bribery."

Shaking his head, he pulled the empty mug over to him. "That's a load of crap, Jordana. Bribery is bribery. That's why this nation is in shambles is because of the very mindset my brother has. He no longer knows right from wrong. To him, this was just another deal making session. But in the West, a man's word is his bond." He looked over at the counter where Jordana was plugging in the coffee-maker. Just having her around was like a wet blanket to the fire he felt. His rage was rapidly receding in her quiet, calming presence. She had that kind of effect on him.

"Griff grew up in the east," Jordana offered. She sat down at his elbow. "I can't believe he'd purposely go to Charley to sandbag your bid. Do you?" She looked him squarely in the eye.

Shrugging, Slade muttered, "I don't know Griff. We rarely saw one another. He's from a different planet, Jordana. His world is a world of no morals and values. He doesn't *care* what effect his decisions have on others." And then, he closed his eyes. "Damn, I was counting on winning that bid. I knew I was low enough to get it."

Placing her hand on Slade's arm, she whispered, "What does this mean?"

Opening his eyes, Slade looked blankly at the wall of the kitchen. His hands tightened around the mug. "Charley usually has four bids a year for services at the national park.

I have been winning two of them every year for the last five years he's been the supervisor. I provide packhorses and mules to him for his construction crews. I also provide good horses for the rangers to ride, too. It was enough money to help keep me out of foreclosure." His mouth moved downward. "This bid was the one I was really counting on because the bank has upped my mortgage payment."

Frowning, Jordana said, "Can the bank do that?"

Snorting, Slade growled, "A bank can do anything it damn well wants. The president doesn't like me. I was informed that my bill is going up with the October payment."

Nodding, Jordana knew that homes across America were in what was termed an upside down mortgage, thanks to the antics of Wall Street destroying the finances of millions of people. Because Slade's ranch was right on the border of foreclosure, she had read that banks were now forcing such owners to either pay up or lose their home. In this case, Slade stood a very real chance of losing his family ranch; a ranch that was his lifeblood. Moving her fingers in a grazing motion cross his forearm, she asked, "What can I do to help?"

He gave a harsh laugh and sat up. "Win

the endurance race. But that's not going to happen, Jordana. That ten-thousand-dollar award could mean all the difference right now." The anger went out of him, and Slade rested his elbows on the table. Head falling forward, he muttered, "I'm screwed. Griff just put this ranch into foreclosure. The bastard . . ."

Tears gathered in Jordana's eyes. She whispered, "I know you don't think I can win this race, Slade, but I can. I just rode Thor for fifty miles. I know the trail better. If I ride it one more time before the actual race, I *know* I can win! There's never going to be another horse like Thor. He's one of a kind, Slade." Gripping his hand, she forced him to look into her eyes and whispered fiercely, "Slade, I can do this! I know you don't think I can, but you don't really know me!"

Jordana released his arm. "I'm made out of titanium steel inside, Slade." She poked at her chest. "But you don't know that yet. How do you think I made it through medical school and seven years as an intern? Trust me," she said, lowering her husky voice, "that really separates the men from the boys. I made it to become a doctor because I *wanted* it. I have terrific focus and drive. You'll see it come out in that race. I will win that money for you."

Shaking his head, Slade said in a dull tone, "Jordana, I appreciate everything about you, but you won't win. Curt Downing is going to take it. He knows this trail inside out, like the back of his hand. You don't."

"Well," Jordana said, allowing some anger into her voice, "your horse sure does! Thor will make up the difference. I'll let him guide me."

"I want to believe you," Slade told her gently. Reaching over, he gripped her hand. Slade saw the feisty quality in her blue eyes and the way her mouth was set. "You're already a champion to me, Jordana. I know you mean well and want this for me, but the truth is, you're going up against Downing. You're not used to his dirty tricks and he'll sandbag you. I know he will."

Sitting up, Jordana gripped his hand. "Now, you listen to me, Slade McPherson! I'm not going down without a fight! I'm not a quitter and neither are you! Stop looking like you've already lost, because you haven't!" She released his hand, got up and brought over the coffee. Pouring the steaming liquid into each of their mugs, Jordana added, "You have never seen me in action, Slade. And because of that, you don't know my capabilities in the saddle. I've won plenty of second level endurance races and I win them consistently. Put a little faith in me?"

Jordana placed the coffee on the counter. Turning, she held his sad gray eyes. How badly she wanted to wrap her arms around Slade, hold him and tell him to have hope. Sitting down, she added cream and sugar to her coffee and stirred it.

The silence was thick and strained. Slade sipped his coffee. It burned his tongue. Frowning, he set it down and wrapped his large hands around it. Jordana looked fierce right now; something he'd never seen in her before. Admiring her spirit, he found nothing else to say. The kitchen hung with pregnant silence.

"I'll do it, Slade. I promise," she said grimly, holding his stare.

CHAPTER EIGHTEEN

Curt Downing smiled as he watched his groom, Brodie Myers, brush his black Arabian stallion, Shah, until he gleamed. He watched the quick, sure motions of the fifty-year-old man who had always taken care of his horses. Shah snorted in the ties, defiantly lifting his head as he impatiently pawed the concrete. The horse had large dark brown eyes, small, refined ears and a dished face, typical of the Arabian breed.

Hearing a car pull up, he saw it was Frank Halbert, the president of the bank. "Finish him up, Brodie," he ordered the groom, "and then wrap his legs."

"Yes, sir," Brodie sang out, brushing the stallion's long, flowing black tail.

Moving down the breezeway, Curt wondered why the banker was coming here. Usually, he saw Halbert in town. The man looked happy as he emerged from his black Mercedes-Benz. Walking down the slope, his curiosity piqued, Curt saw Halbert smile when he caught sight of him.

"I have good news," Halbert said without preamble as they met down on the flat.

"Oh?" Curt said, lifting his hands and placing them on his hips.

Grinning, Halbert said, "I just heard something today you need to know about."

"Go on," Curt said. He saw a number of his wranglers herding a group of horses into one of the many pipe rail corrals.

"I was out at the Tetons headquarters working with Charley, the U.S. Forest Service supervisor. He'd left the room and I saw all the bids on his latest packhorse contract." He could hardly keep the joy out of his tone as he continued in a whisper, "You're getting the bid, Curt!"

Brows raising, Curt said, "Really?" He knew that Slade McPherson usually won two out of the four yearly contracts. His bid wasn't the lowest, and therefore, he hadn't expected to get it.

"Yes." Frank looked around to ensure no one was listening. "I saw a hand-scribbled note on McPherson's bid." He grinned a little. "Griff McPherson, his twin brother, had called and tried to bribe Charley."

"What?" Curt frowned. "A bribe? Are you kidding me?"

"No, no, I'm not kidding!" Frank raised his hands and smiled fully. "Charley had a note on the bid saying it was declined due to Griff's interference. How about *that?* Slade's brother is an ace in the hole for you."

Shaking his head, Curt muttered in disbelief, "A bribe? Charley wouldn't put up with that. What's this twin doing that for?"

"He was a Wall Street banker who lost his job when his company went broke," Halbert explained.

"I'd heard rumors of McPherson having a twin in town, but I hadn't ever seen him myself."

"Yes, he's around, and you do realize what all this means?"

The gleam in Halbert's eyes reminded him of a coyote getting ready to pounce on his victim. "It means," Curt drawled, "that I'm not an idiot. He's lost out on money he could have sunk into that ranch of his. It puts him closer to foreclosure."

"Exactly!" Frank said excitedly.

"And McPherson knows his monthly mortgage has gone up?"

"Oh, yes," Frank said, satisfied. "I raised it another five hundred dollars."

"Damn, so the only thing between him and foreclosure is this endurance ride," Curt murmured.

"Exactly," Frank said with enthusiasm. "And then, when it goes into foreclosure, you can snap it up. I'll make damn sure no one gets a bid in on it before you. I know you want the land so you can expand your operations."

Nodding, Curt said, "I'm desperate for more land," he agreed. And it wouldn't hurt that this new land gotten by the foreclosure would butt up against the biggest ranch in the valley, the Elkhorn Ranch. "I've *got* to expand my breeding facility. I got more people wanting to breed to my stud than I have room to accommodate them. I'm losing a helluva lot of money because of this situation. I've been looking at the Bar H south of town. They're about ready to go belly up. That's a hundred acres where I could move my entire breeding facility down there and keep this place for student training."

"I understand," Frank murmured. "But you know Gus Hunter, who's a pistol in her own right, isn't going to sell her family ranch to anyone."

Nodding, Curt muttered, "Old Gus is a firecracker. She's eighty-four. A tough old buzzard. I'm going to wage a war against her soon. She's alone and she's in poor health and can't continue to handle that ranch by herself."

"True," Frank said, "but I hear from Gwen Garner over at the quilting shop that her granddaughter, Valerie Hunter, is coming home to take up the reins of running the place."

Snorting, Curt muttered, "Buck Hunter was a mean bastard. He beat the hell out of his wife, Cheryl, and his daughter, Val. Cheryl's dead now. And Val left for good. She hated her father and hated the ranch. I have a hard time thinking she's leaving the Air Force to come back to the scene of the crime and try to save it."

Shrugging, Frank murmured, "That's what I heard. Gwen is never wrong."

"Well," Curt said with a frown, "I think I'll go visit Old Gus and see what I can persuade out of her."

Chuckling, Frank said, "You won't get anything out of Gus. She's a bona fide pioneer woman. Tough as they come."

"Maybe. But Valerie Hunter will be more than ready to dump that broken-down old ranch into my hands two months after arriving home. I'll just have to bide my time. In the meantime, my sites are set on Slade McPherson's ranch. It's mine. He just doesn't know it yet."

Looking around, the banker straightened

and said, "It's just a matter of time, now, Curt. I'm sure you'll win this contest. You're taking McPherson's last chance to save his ranch away from him. You did hear that, because he got gored by his own bull, that Dr. Lawson is riding his stallion for him?"

"Yeah, I saw her out on the trail two weeks ago." He didn't add that Lawson was a helluva better ride than he thought. No sense in letting Halbert know anything. Curt didn't trust the banker any further than he could throw him. His thoughts about Lawson and Thor were known only to him.

"And?"

Shrugging, Downing muttered, "She was fighting that mustang stallion all the way."

Chuckling, Frank said, "I'm surprised McPherson let *anyone* on that mustang's back. That's a one-man horse."

"Yes, Thor is," Curt agreed. He switched topics. "Tell me more about Griff McPherson."

"He came in last week and filled out a résumé to work at our bank. Of course, I have no openings."

"Not for him you don't," Curt growled.

"I would never hire a McPherson," Frank told him in a confidential tone.

"So, he's looking for local work?"

"Yes. I interviewed him myself. He's lost everything. His job, his millions he had in derivatives, and he has nothing but a dwindling savings account."

"Really?" Curt said, his mind spinning. "Those two twins split up when my father killed their parents. I never did know where Griff went."

"Back East. His uncle was a big-time Wall Streeter. Griff grew up, went to Harvard and got an MBA. He worked for his uncle's company until it collapsed. Now, he's destitute like thousands of other Wall Street brokers."

"Too bad," Curt murmured. "But that's good for me. Griff can't loan Slade money to save his ranch."

Chuckling indulgently, Frank said, "You've got that right. When I interviewed him last week, he had two hundred dollars left to his name."

Grinning, Downing said, "I saw a help wanted ad at McDonald's. They're looking for help."

Joining in the laughter, Frank said, "Oh, I don't think he'll lower himself to that level. Too much pride."

"Pride goeth before a fall," Downing said, enjoying this piece of unexpected news.

"He's got a *lot* of pride," Halbert agreed.

"You won't find him working at a burger joint. He tried to come in and sell me on the fact he's got an MBA from Harvard. And that he can make my bank a ton more of money. I told him if he was so good, why had he lost his entire job and livelihood?"

"Right on," Downing said. His brows fell. "One thing I *am* worried about is Dr. Lawson. What if she loans McPherson money?"

"Oh, that won't happen," Frank consoled him. "Her account is at my bank. She's got a thousand dollars in her savings and only two thousand in her checking."

"She's a doctor. I thought they were all rich."

"I spoke to her two weeks ago. She did come in to try and get a loan. I knew it was for McPherson, but she didn't say that. She said it was to build an addition on to her home." Snorting, Halbert said, "She's not a very good liar. You can read her face like a road map."

Laughing softly, Downing said, "You're full of all kinds of good news, Frank." He clapped the banker's rounded shoulder. "How much was she trying to get out of you?"

"Ten thousand."

"That's a lot. But that's exactly the amount McPherson needs to dig him out of potential foreclosure. It gives him breathing room."

"Correct," Frank murmured. "And I knew from that moment on, it wasn't for any house addition."

"Does she have a credit score to get such a loan from the other bank in town?" Curt asked, worried.

"No. She's had plenty of debt and lost everything two years ago. Right now, she's trying to rebuild, but it's slow. Don't forget, she's still paying off loans for her medical schooling."

Rubbing his hands together, Curt grinned. "You've really made my day, Frank. I thought those two were getting a little close. And I figured she might try to loan that bastard the money."

"She can't," he said with finality. "No bank right now, in this recession, will loan her a dime."

"Have you put out the word that Griff McPherson shouldn't be hired?"

Frank, who had loans on every business in town, smiled. "Not to worry. I've already done that. Griff won't find *any* job open to him except for a burger joint." He snickered.

Curt liked using Halbert. He was a fat slug of a man, but he was wily and knew where money power was at. "Well, under these circumstances, I'm going to buy more stock in your bank, Frank."

Eyes widening with pleasure, Frank mopped his perspiring brow with a white linen handkerchief. "Why, that's mighty good of you, Curt. I didn't expect that."

Mouth lifting into a slight smile, Curt murmured, "You're my eyes and ears on the McPhersons, Frank. And you're doing a good job. I'm just showing my appreciation."

Nodding, Frank stuffed the handkerchief in the back pocket of his gray pinstripe suit pants. "Good, good."

"Wish I could be a fly on the wall and watch Griff McPherson squirm."

"I heard that Slade kicked him off the ranch."

"That's even better. I like Slade in such a state. It will keep his mind off trying to win this endurance ride."

Shaking his head, Frank murmured, "Oh, I doubt Dr. Lawson can even come in among the top ten riders."

"I agree," Curt said. "She's never raced in a level one event. I don't care how good Thor is, it's the rider who sets the pace and knows how far they can push their mount, and when."

"My money is on you," Frank chortled.

"I'll be there at the finish line to see you and your black stud coming in first."

Downing's mind was elsewhere. If Griff McPherson was in town, kicked off the ranch, he wondered what he was going to do. This had to weigh on Slade. And that was good. Very good.

Griff sat in McDonald's nursing a cup of coffee. It was a busy place with plenty of tourists in town. Sitting alone, smarting under Slade's rage, he tried to think of a way to get a job. The sky was a bright blue, but white clouds over the top of the mountain rose above the town. It looked as if it might rain later in the day. As he sat watching families, hearing laughter and seeing the smiles, he felt even more depressed. They had money. They had a home. They had family who loved them. . . .

The coffee, although hot, tasted bitter. He knew it was him, not the brew. Yeah, he was damned bitter. After he'd been sent to his Uncle Robert, life had turned out well for him. At first, he'd missed his parents and Slade terribly, but his aunt and uncle had taken over as his parents. They'd loved him. Maybe not as he remembered his own parents doing so, but he'd been loved. Slade had slowly disappeared from his life. Looking up, he saw a family of five sit down next to his table. All he could afford was a cup of coffee. With only two hundred dollars in his pocket, he had to be very careful how he spent what was left.

Would Slade let him back on the ranch or not? Smarting beneath the attack by his angry older brother, Griff turned the paper cup around and around between his long hands. What if he wouldn't? What next? Going into the county welfare office and asking for food stamps? God, he didn't want to do that! Shame flowed through Griff. He'd never thought he'd ever be poor. Not *ever.* Now here he was drinking a cup of coffee from McDonald's and not from Starbucks. He never came to such a place. No, he'd ate eaten the best five-star restaurants that New York City had to offer. The maître d's had known him instantly and had always saved the best table for him.

Not now. What am I going to do? Had it been a mistake to come West? Griff had already tried to get at least twenty positions along the East coast, but no one wanted a Wall Street has-been. After all, many interviewers reminded him, *he* was the reason the economy had crashed worldwide. His greed. His lack of care for what derivatives might do to the middle class of America, never mind the rest of the world.

Mouth turning downward, Griff stared blackly into the steaming cup of coffee. Right now, he was a pariah. He'd found it an error to tout his resume. People blackballed him and saw him as part of the reason why the economy was failing. It was *his* fault.

His gaze fell on a sign in the window: help wanted for night shift. Moving uncomfortably, Griff didn't want to try for a job that was so far below him. A hamburger turner? Was that the only job open to him? He opened his hand and looked at it. When he'd first arrived, he'd had soft palms. Now, there were a few calluses from working daily out at the ranch with Shorty. Ranch work, he'd discovered, was damned hard, always ongoing and never finished. Animals needed to be fed every twenty-four hours. There was no dispensing machine that could feed them. And he was exhausted after mucking out box stalls and hauling old hay and horse turds to the compost bins. Some of the horses, like Thor, hated him. The stallion would charge the box stall door every time he walked past him. Shorty had to clean Thor's stall, instead. There was no way Griff was going to get bitten by that ornery stud.

Even horses hated him, Griff glumly

decided, sipping the coffee and feeling sorry for himself. Slade certainly hated him. How was he to know that by offering to throw in an extra packhorse that Charley considered the gesture a bribe? In his business, they were always wheeling and dealing like this. It wasn't wrong; it was just the way things were.

Pulling over the local newspaper, Griff turned to the want ads. There were pitiful few of them, as usual. And all of them were either for cleaning hotels, burger joints or janitorial work. There was nothing that appealed to him. Yet, as he sat there, he had no house to go to. Rents were high here, he'd discovered. Too high for the likes of him. So, where was he to go? At least at Slade's he'd had a room at the main ranch house. What could he do about this?

Angry, Griff dropped the paper on the table. This was all Slade's fault! He hadn't meant to bribe Charley. It was all a misunderstanding. Obviously, they didn't meet or agree on much of anything. How badly he missed his penthouse apartment. It was gone. Everything was gone. And his brother had kicked him off the property.

Just as he looked up, he saw Dr. Jordana Lawton enter. She saw him, waved and smiled.

Griff waved back, feeling at least she didn't think he was a bastard as Slade did. He watched as she stood in line. Would she avoid him, too?

"Hey," Jordana called as she got her salad and walked toward Griff, "can you use some company?" She felt sorry for the younger twin who looked terribly sad.

Griff stood and said, "Hi, Jordana. Come and sit down."

"Thanks," she said, smiling and sitting opposite him. "I didn't expect to see you here, Griff." Jordana unwrapped the plastic fork and poured the salad dressing across the salad. "How are you doing?"

Sitting down, he grimaced. "Not good, to tell you the truth. Is Slade still pissed at me?"

Jordan speared a slice of grilled chicken breast on top of her salad. "He didn't say anything about you this morning."

"I didn't mean what I did as a bribe," he said.

"I'm sure you didn't," Jordana said. "You don't strike me as a weasel, Griff."

Feeling a bit of relief, he tried to explain his actions to Jordana. She nodded, ate and looked sympathetic. Just encountering someone who was at least neutral about the situation helped Griff a lot. He wondered what she saw in his dark, over-responsible brother.

"I don't think Wall Street and the West can meet on similar ground," Jordana told him after the explanation. "I'm sure you meant well, Griff."

"Thanks, I needed to hear that." He stared down at his cup. "Do you think Slade meant it?"

"What?"

"That I can't come back to the ranch?"

Giving him a pained look, Jordana said, "I don't know, Griff. That's something you have to talk over with Slade."

"I was hoping you could put in a good word for me."

Jordana wiped her mouth with the paper napkin. "Slade and you have to settle this. I'm not getting between you."

"Actually, a smart, strategic choice," Griff told her, a slight smile hooking one corner of his mouth.

"He's under a lot of pressure right now," Jordana gently offered him. "I can't believe he really means it, Griff, but now is not the time to test the waters. If I can't win that ten-thousand-dollar purse on this endurance ride, he's going to lose the ranch."

"*Our* ranch."

"Okay," Jordana said, frowning, "but

Slade doesn't see it that way and you know that." She felt sorry for Griff. He was literally like a fish out of water here in Jackson Hole.

"Yeah, yeah, I know," he muttered unhappily. "I've been trying to find a job ever since I got here. I've been on fifteen different interviews here in town. I never told Slade that because I know he's worried about our ranch. I can't seem to get a job," Griff said, frustrated. "If I could get a job, I could help Slade pay that mortgage."

Sympathetic to Griff, Jordana said, "Maybe you should have kept Slade in the loop and told him you were interviewing for jobs. If you don't tell him what you're doing, Griff, how can he know any different?"

"I know, but I was hoping to surprise him. A good surprise, for once." His voice fell in disappointment.

Seeing the sadness in Griff's eyes, Jordana said, "Look, I think if you offered to come and help him at the race, he might look upon that favorably. Slade needs a team of people. He's got Shorty, but he's a person short. If you could run errands, fetch water, towels and brushes, I think Slade would jump at that. Right now, his leg is hurting him, and he's not as fast and nimble as he hoped to be."

"You think he'd go for that?" Griff knew he could run errands.

Shrugging, Jordana picked at her salad. "It's worth a try. But, Griff, I'd give him a few days to cool off. He desperately needed that bid contract."

Nodding, Griff said, "I get it — now. I just thought I was helping. . . ."

"Easterners have a different mindset, I know, because I came from New York City myself. This is the first time I've been out West. And in the two years I've been here, I've seen remarkable differences. Stunning, sometimes."

"Yeah, it sucks. But I need a real job, Jordana. I'm really frustrated. No one wants me. . . ."

Sipping her coffee, she offered, "Griff, I can go to our human resources department and see if they need a medical orderly."

"I don't know anything about medicine," he protested.

"You don't need to. Nursing assistants do a lot of clean up. They mop, sweep and change bedcovers and such. It's a good wage, too."

Griff looked at working at a hospital as slightly above flipping burgers. "Could you? I'd really appreciate it. I'm not afraid of work, Jordana."

Hearing the hope in his voice she said, "My shift is tomorrow morning. I'll go see Cary and find out if she has any openings, Griff. If she does, I'll give you a call on your cell phone?"

Embarrassed, Griff admitted, "I'm losing my cell phone coverage in a month. I don't have the money to pay for it any longer." It hurt to admit that to anyone. He saw Jordana's blue eyes go soft with understanding. No wonder Slade was in love with her. Jordana was special.

"Okay," she murmured, giving him a slight smile, "I'll do what I can. In a hospital, people are always coming and going. And assistants are always needed."

Relief started to trickle down through him. Griff whispered, "Thanks a lot, Jordana. This means a lot to me."

"I know it does. Let me see what I can do."

CHAPTER NINETEEN

The endurance contest was only one day away. Slade felt a twinge in his thigh where Diablo had gored him. Watching Jordana as she walked out of the training barn after putting Thor away, he felt his heart open. Her hair was mussed, and she looked beautiful in her jeans and yellow tank top. He ached to hold her, kiss her and most of all, make slow, exploratory love to her. Such were his dreams that were mixed in with nightmares of losing his family homestead.

Jordana smiled and tucked her damp, thin leather gloves into her belt as she approached Slade. The sun was starting to set. Tomorrow was the big day. Her heart raced as Slade's eyes revealed raw desire for her. When had their relationship changed? She wasn't sure. All Jordana knew is that she wanted to get past this race and see where the chips would fall. Her desire for Slade was visceral.

The last rays of the sun slanted across the wide, oval valley, the peaks of the Tetons turning pink.

"I have a surprise for you," Slade told her as she came to a halt.

"Oh?" Jordana grinned and saw a slow smile work its way across his mouth. What a mouth! To kiss Slade again would be as close to heaven as Jordana thought she might ever get. And she warmed to his dropping that mask and being human with her. As the month had worn on toward the race, Slade was no longer the man behind the armor. Now he was allowing her to see him as he really was, and it was breathtaking.

"I'm taking you out to dinner tonight," he said. "You want to get a shower and into some clean clothes?"

Surprised, Jordana said, "Really?" Was this a date? Or, more than likely, Slade's way of thanking her for riding Thor tomorrow. Looking deeply into his eyes, Jordana saw happiness gleaming in them. That wasn't something she saw often in Slade with the pressures haunting him.

"I'm trying to be more social," Slade admitted wryly as he walked with her toward the ranch house. "So be kind to me on my first try?"

Laughing, Jordana asked, "And did someone put a bee in your bonnet about this?" She loved the way Slade walked with a boneless kind of grace. He was a man in his prime in every way.

Chuckling a little, Slade slid her a glance. "Guilty as charged. I was in Gwen Garner's quilt shop the other day. I was buying some soft fabric to wrap your knees in for the ride. She gave me an earful."

Slade opened the back door for Jordana, and she walked into the mudroom. He enjoyed simply absorbing her small, athletic form. She sat down on a wooden bench and pulled off her boots.

"So, Gwen suggested this?"

"Yes," he admitted with some hesitancy. Taking off his Stetson, Slade hung it on a wooden peg near the door. "She asked me how I was repaying you for all the hard work you're putting into this race. I told her about our agreement that if you picked up any of the prize money that it would go toward future training for you."

Sitting there, hands in her lap, Jordana laughed. "I'll bet that went over like a lead balloon."

He sank into her soft, wide smile. Jordana's blue eyes danced with deviltry. Slade had to stop himself from reaching out and tunneling his fingers through her soft, mussed black hair that lay about her shoulders. "Yes. She wagged her finger in my face and you know how short she is."

Getting up, Jordana padded in her sock feet toward the door to the kitchen. "Gwen's my height," she laughed, opening it and stepping inside.

Slade followed and closed the door. The kitchen was neat and clean. Ever since Griff had gone, the ranch had settled down to a fixed routine that Slade needed. "Yes, she is."

"And she said?"

"I should take you out and wine and dine you. It was the least I could do, and I agreed with her."

Jordana stopped and looked up into his weather-beaten face. Heart warm with the unspoken care she held for Slade, she reached out and touched his arm. She knew that he was saving every penny he could for the coming mortgage payment that was due a week after the race. "Listen, you don't have to do this, Slade. Just the fact you'd do it is plenty good enough for me."

Her fingers were strong and caressing on his upper arm. Slade wished things were different. But the pressure of the coming race tomorrow morning took his attention.

"No, I'm taking you out to dinner. We're going to Red's Steakhouse on the southern end of town. You ever been there?"

Allowing her hand to drop back to her side, Jordana shook her head. "No, but I've heard they have great steaks."

"Yes, and I'm buying you one," he promised firmly. "Now, go get cleaned up and put on that other set of clothes you brought with you."

How badly she wanted to step into Slade's massive arms. He looked handsome in the dark blue long-sleeved cowboy shirt and Levi's. His chest was broad, and she ached to explore what was beneath that material. "Okay, I'll be out in about thirty minutes," she promised, turning and heading out of the kitchen.

Slade stood there after Jordana was gone. The kitchen suddenly seemed sterile as if the life had gone out of it. Such was the sunshine nature of Jordana, he thought. Looking down at his dirty Levi's, he walked toward his bedroom. He had to get cleaned up, too. As his boots thunked hollowly down the hall to the master bedroom, his heart sang. Grateful to Gwen Garner, Slade realized he had to learn to get involved with people and society once more. He couldn't keep hiding out like a polecat. But life had

made him that way. Now, Jordana bright-
ened his life and was changing it in a good
way. And that was something Slade wanted
equally as much as he wanted to keep his
ranch.

Jordana sat in a black leather booth with
Slade. Red's Steakhouse wasn't loud and
raucous as she had thought it would be.
Instead, Nashville music drifted softly in
the background while waiters and waitresses
zipped smoothly between the many tables.
The booth was hidden in a darkened corner,
and it felt intimate to her. Slade sat opposite
her looking handsome in a clean white
cowboy shirt and Levi's. He wore a red
bandanna around his throat, his hair recently washed and gleaming beneath the
lamplight suspended above the table.

"I like the fact we can be here in working
clothes," she admitted. The waitress who
was serving them was an older woman in
her fifties. She set down two glasses of water
and a basket of freshly baked bread and
cornmeal muffins.

Slade thanked the waitress who smiled
and left. "Gwen suggested this place because
I didn't want to go anywhere that demanded
a suit and tie."

"Oh," Jordana teased, picking up a warm

cornmeal muffin, "that would be The Aspens. It's a five-star restaurant."

Nodding, Slade watched her long, graceful fingers as she buttered the cornmeal muffin. What would her fingers feel like moving across his body? He squelched the thought for now. "I've never been there," Slade admitted. It was too pricey, for starters.

"I've been there," Jordana admitted, setting the buttered muffin on the small white porcelain plate near her dinner plate. "The Aspens is nice, but stuffy. The senator's wife, Clarissa Peyton, goes there all the time."

"She's a good person," Slade murmured, picking up a piece of sourdough bread from the basket and buttering it. "The senator is in prison in Washington, D.C., on murder charges. I felt sorry for Clarissa throughout that godawful public trial of Carter Peyton. She was the innocent in that mess."

Sad, Jordana said, "Yes, she was."

"Have you ever had lunch with her?" Slade wondered.

Nibbling on the muffin, Jordana said, "I have. Clarissa has brought in a lot of donations to our hospital. She's a national charity organizer and very good at it."

"Clarissa has a big heart. I don't blame

her for divorcing Senator Peyton and taking back her maiden name, Renard, after the trial was over."

Nodding, Jordana added, "Clarissa got the house here in Jackson Hole as part of her divorce settlement. Right now, her little sister, Nicky, is living with her. Her son, Bradley, just went off to college this year."

"She looks happier than I can recall," Slade said. "She's raised money to protect the mustangs out in Nevada. I liked working with her because she's the real deal."

"A Wyoming native like yourself," Jordana pointed out.

Smiling a little, Slade murmured, "Wyoming bred and Wyoming tough. Clarissa is beautiful, talented and intelligent. But she doesn't suffer fools for long." He chuckled.

Laughing with him, Jordana said, "That's so true. And I'm glad to see her getting back her life now that the trial is done and her divorce is final. She deserves a break." And, Jordana thought, so did Slade.

Slade chewed on the warm sourdough bread. Red's knew how to make it right. He gazed over at Jordana. Her black hair was still damp from the recent shower, the strands curling around the collar of her pink blouse. Jordana always brought along a clean pair of clothes after riding thirty miles.

It was hot, dusty work. He liked the cream-colored slacks she wore because they showed off her long, beautifully tapered legs.

"I think this dinner is a pre-celebration, Slade. I *know* that Thor and I can win."

Shaking his head, Slade smiled at her passion. "I wish I had your faith, Jordana. I'll feel good that you and Thor will complete the ride without injury." And Slade knew there were plenty of places where she could fall off and injure herself. Even more, he worried about Thor's legs. Jordana was competitive but not foolish. He knew she'd take care of the mustang stud and not put him into a potentially injurious situation. The only fly in this ointment was Curt Downing. Slade had nightmares about the bastard.

"Ye of little faith," Jordana teased with a laugh. "We've gone over the fifty-mile trail twice. I've worked hard to memorize all of it."

"Especially the parts where you trot Thor or canter him?"

"Absolutely," Jordana said, seeing the worry creep back into his eyes. "I'm not a risk taker, Slade. I won't put Thor into a situation where he could be hurt. You know that."

Slade impulsively gripped her hand for a

moment. "I could lose him, but I can't lose you, Jordana." Shocked over what he'd just blurted, Slade pulled his hand away from hers. He saw the sudden widening of her eyes and then her mouth going soft and kissable. Clearing his throat, he looked down at the table and muttered, "I've come to like you a lot, Jordana." Slade forced himself to meet her gaze. "You're unlike my ex-wife, Isabel. You might come from New York City, but you're a Westerner at heart. You love the land and the animals. You aren't afraid to get your hands dirty. . . ."

The words came hard from Slade but they made her fast-beating heart melt like hot butter in a skillet. Jordana sat there savoring his admittance. How like Slade to be all bottled up and then suddenly explode with the truth. Gently, Jordana said, "I like you, too, Slade. I admire your honesty and work ethic. You always tell the truth, no matter how tough it is. When I first met you, you scared me to death." Jordana managed a sour smile. "You bluster a lot and I had to get past that. It was easy to do because of the way you treated Stormy. You might be a bit rough around the edges with people, but you have a kind heart."

Heat ran up from his neck and into his face. To Slade, who wasn't used to blushing, it felt as if he'd stepped into a patch of stinging nettles. It was Jordana's husky tone, the longing look in her blue eyes, that tore loose the rest of Slade's hidden truths. "I'm not one for fancy words," he managed awkwardly. Opening his hands, he added, "Isabel always called me stupid. I knew I wasn't stupid. Gwen would tell you I lack some social skills, but I'm far from dumb."

Digesting his painful admittance, Jordana saw a little six-year-old boy struggling to make sense of his parents' sudden deaths. And then, to be handed over to his aunt and uncle. She couldn't appreciate all that Slade had gone through. Losing his parents had put armor around his shredded, grieving heart. At eighteen, she knew Slade had taken over the ranch. He'd struggled ever since then. Nothing had come easy for him. He'd earned every bit of money he got. "Social skills," she murmured, "are something you can add to your repertoire as you see fit, Slade."

"They call me a loner," he finally admitted. It felt so right to just let all the poison out of his soul and share it with Jordana. He knew now that she could handle the worst-case scenarios and not flinch. "And I guess I have been. At least . . . until lately."

She saw the little boy in the man's eyes.

He was so scared to admit all of this to her. Reaching over, Jordana grasped Slade's hand. She felt the toughness of his flesh, the hard calluses earned by unrelenting work in all kinds of weather conditions. "Slade, you lost everyone you loved. You did the best you could. I don't know of too many eighteen-year-olds who could walk into a ranch situation and keep it on its feet. You don't see yourself, but I do." Her fingers caressed the back of his dark-haired hand. "Slade, you're an incredible person. I'm absolutely in awe of you. I know I couldn't have done what you did and kept your ranch solvent."

Her words were warmth to his wounds and scars. He saw the sincerity in her darkening eyes and the gentle expression across her face. "I've made some stupid decisions doing that," he admitted. "Isabel stepped into my life and I lost control of my world. I couldn't think straight, I couldn't be realistic. I guess I was lonely. . . ."

Hearing the pain and personal censure for his actions in his gravelly tone, Jordana leaned forward and whispered, "Slade, stop gigging yourself. You WERE lonely. When did you have an opportunity to date women after the ranch got hung around your neck? All you did was focus on keeping the ranch viable. That doesn't leave a lot of time to date and be social."

He lifted his other hand and captured hers. Although her hand was small, her fingers were long and elegant looking. The warmth of Jordana's hand heated him up from his heart down to his throbbing lower body. Forcing himself to look deeply into her pleading gaze, Slade said, "Do you always give people a long length of rope to run around on instead of hanging them with it?"

A grin tipped her mouth. Holding Slade's hand and having him respond like that was salve for her soul. Somehow, Jordana had never seen who she might fall in love with, but Slade fit her dreams. "Always. People get stressed out, traumatized and in shock by what goes on in their lives, Slade. I see this all the time in the ER of the hospital. Life isn't easy on anyone. And it's been especially rough on you."

How badly Slade wanted to kiss her. Right now. Here. He didn't give a tinker's dam about who saw him do it, either. Unable to reach across the length of the table, he squeezed her hand gently between his own. "I want to think we have something to build on after this race?"

Nodding, Jordana whispered, "Yes, there's

a lot there to work with, Slade."

The waitress arrived, and they released one another's hands. In no time, large oval platters filled with T-bone steak, baked potatoes with all the fixings and buttered peas sat before them. Slade thanked the waitress, and she left.

"Wow, this is a *lot* of food!" Jordana said, giddy over Slade's admittance. "I don't think I have a stomach big enough to hold all of this!"

Grinning, Slade picked up his knife and fork. "Listen, stuff yourself because tomorrow you won't be doing much eating, just guzzling water at the vet stops."

He was right, she realized. "It looks delicious, Slade."

So did Jordana, but Slade didn't dare say that. "Just enjoy it."

"I'm enjoying *us*," Jordana parried with a smile.

Again, that hot sensation moved to expand his heart, which was beating double-time. Slade had never felt what he felt for Jordana. As he focused on cutting up his steak, he found himself hungry — for her. Where would this all lead? He was afraid to dream because of his less-than-glorious past.

"Have you ever been married?" he wondered.

Stunned, Jordana's fork halted halfway to her mouth. "Er . . . no."

"You never found someone? I find that hard to believe."

Jordana popped a piece of steak into her mouth. Slade's bluntness was, at times, unnerving. With a slight smile, she said, "Let's put it this way, Slade, when you're a resident, there's no time for anything. I would sometimes work twenty-four hours straight and stagger back to my apartment and sleep the sleep of the dead. I would put in a minimum of twelve hours a day at the hospital. I never had a day off. I found it hard to do all the other things that needed to get done, never mind having a man in my life. There just wasn't room."

Slade tried to imagine her world as a doctor-in-training. "But you had time for riding. I know you rode in endurance contests."

"Yes, that was my only gift to myself," Jordana agreed. She spooned up some peas. After eating and swallowing them she added, "What you have to understand is that riding was my outlet. If I could throw my leg over a horse, no matter how bad my hospital life sucked, I was free for those hours. And it helped me deal with my boss, who was a sexual predator."

Brows raising, Slade set his hands on the table. "What are you talking about?"

Jordana confessed to her her six years with the physician she'd had to work under. When she finished the sordid tale, the court drama and final judgment for her, she said, "I was so burned out by the whole thing, Slade, that I left the East Coast to come out here and start a new life. I didn't want to be known. I wanted to have a good career as a physician and still be able to ride endurance races." With a shrug, she said, "And the last two years, I didn't have time for a relationship. Oh, there were some guys, that's true, but I wasn't swept off my feet by any of them."

Giving her a heated look, he asked, "Do I sweep you off your feet?"

The question was thickly spoken and pregnant with promise as it hung between them. Jordana stopped eating and looked up. She felt her heart expand powerfully as she held his warm, gray gaze. "Yes, you do, Slade."

Nodding, he said, "I'm glad to hear that." His world spinning and wobbling inwardly, Slade tried to tamp down the sudden joy that sizzled through him. Jordana liked him! And God knew, he liked her more than he had any woman he'd ever met. Frowning, he glanced up and asked, "Do you think it's possible that a doctor and a cowboy can get along?"

Laughing softy, Jordana said, "Haven't we so far?"

"That's true," Slade admitted in a deep tone. All he wanted to do now was bring Jordana home, take her to his bed and make love to her until dawn rose. But none of that could happen. Tomorrow, long before dawn, they would be out at the beginning of the fifty-mile endurance ride. Reality crashed like cold ice upon Slade.

"I feel like Alice in Wonderland," he told her. "This date with you is good, but when I look at my watch, I know it's not going to last. At four-thirty a.m., we're going to be out in that meadow and you're going to be riding Thor."

Hearing the disappointment in his voice and seeing it reflected in his sad looking eyes, Jordana reached out and squeezed his hand. "Yes, and I'm going to ride him to win, Slade. That ten thousand dollars is yours."

Shaking his head, Slade couldn't believe her. He wanted to, but he knew the dangers, knew Downing and knew that she or his horse could be injured or killed tomorrow. Jordana simply refused to believe that she could be harmed. But she didn't know Downing and he would be gunning for her. The first thing he'd do is take her out one way or another. Thor was his only competition. Suddenly, the magic of their intimate dinner dissolved into sheer terror for Slade.

CHAPTER TWENTY

"Are you ready?" Slade asked Jordana as he checked Thor's cinch one last time. Dawn was a thin, gray line on the eastern horizon. Bright lights had been set up around the huge staging area so horses and riders could see what they were doing.

Jordana nodded, pulling on the Kevlar vest that would protect her torso should she fall. Her heart was doing a slow pound. "I am," she told him. Around them were a hundred other horse trailers, riders and their nervous, frisky endurance charges. The meadow was a controlled bedlam of a sort. Jordana had seen this before, but not as a level one endurance rider. Slade held Thor's reins. The stallion snorted and pawed, more than ready to get on with the race. Slade handed her the black, protective helmet she'd wear.

Slade looked around. The start line was about a hundred feet from where they were parked. Thor, because he'd won last year's endurance ride, would be the first to leave the starting gate. He'd get a five-minute head start, and then Curt Downing and his black Arab stallion would be next. Worried, he said, "Remember, let Thor gallop. Don't hold him back on this first mile. It's flat and even. This is where you want to make up time between you and Downing."

Strapping on the helmet, Jordana nodded. "I've memorized the trail, Slade. I'll do what you told me to do. Don't worry." And she gripped his hand and gave it a firm squeeze.

Slade saw Downing on his black stallion, Shah. In Arabic, shah meant "king." And indeed, the black stud who was rearing and pawing the air in anticipation was all of that. Shah was nearly equal to Thor. But there were subtle differences that would determine the winner and loser. Slade watched Jordana wrap an Ace bandage around each of her knees. The tape would stop the chaffing of rough material against her skin that always occurred over long-distance rides. It would stop the skin from being rubbed off. If it did happen, it made riding excruciatingly painful and sometimes took a rider out of the race because so much tissue damage occurred. She was quick and professional about it. Some of his anxiety dissolved. Everything about Jordana was confidence and focus. It entered Slade's mind that maybe, if she was lucky, she *might* finish in the money. Second place was five thousand, and third place was two thousand dollars. Any money would be better than none, but he knew she had her sites set on winning. His heart opened with such a rush of startling emotions, he blinked. He'd never felt this way before. What *was* it? Slade had no time to figure it out.

"I'm ready," Jordana announced. She looked up into Slade's dark and shadowed face. How handsome he was! How utterly rugged as the Tetons was this man that she felt such a powerful love for. Jordana no longer tried to explain how she felt toward Slade. She didn't know when she'd fallen in love with this iconic cowboy, but she had. It was her secret — for now. After the race was over, she'd have the time to speak of it to Slade. How would he react? Jordana wasn't sure. "And," she whispered, throwing her arms around Slade's broad shoulders, "I need a kiss for good luck!"

Taken aback by Jordana's bold move, Slade automatically curved his free arm around Jordana's slender form as she leaned up to kiss him. Startled by her assertiveness, he leaned down and captured her smiling lips. Her mouth was warm and inviting as she surged against him. Groaning softly, Slade melted into her lips, tasting the coffee she'd had earlier. She was all woman, all sensuality in that moment. The scent of her briefly dizzied him. And just as suddenly, she pulled away. The kiss was over far too soon.

"You're my luck," she told him in a husky tone. She saw Slade's narrowed eyes smoldered for her. Jordana felt every cell in her body tingle over that raw, hungry look. "Help me mount!" She turned and took Thor's reins from his hand.

In moments, Slade had boosted her up on the stallion. Thor moved sideways, full of himself, vital and like a powerhouse ready to explode. Slade grinned and settled his hands on his hips. Despite his stallion's aggressive nature, he immediately answered to Jordana's quiet hands and guiding leg pressure. "Okay, be careful out there."

Smiling down at him, Jordana heard the horn blast. That meant she had to get Thor up to the start line. "I will." She blew him a kiss. "And we have some important things to talk about after the race," she called, whirling the mustang around.

Standing there, Slade watched her move the sunbonnet stud in and around the horse trailers. The first ten riders were mounted. Every five minutes, one would be released in the order they'd earned from other races. Pride sifted through Slade. As he stood there watching Jordana guide Thor up to the start line where two judges and a timer stood, he smiled faintly. The feeling he had was one of intense love for her. Even in the semidarkness, the dawn barely crawling over the horizon, Slade felt the immense power of love avalanching through him for this feisty, petite woman. Thor was a huge, rangy stallion, and Jordana literally looked like a jockey on his broad, long back. He was chomping on the bit, tossing his head, his brown-and-white mane flying like spun candy around his neck and withers. Jordana was focused on a judge who came up to speak to her. He would ask her name, the name of her horse, double-check the number pinned on her back and the number spray painted onto the rump of the horse. Everything had to match and it did. He shifted his gaze to a woman with a red flag standing fifty feet inside the start line. When the male judge lifted his hand, she brought the flag down. That meant, "go!"

Jordana didn't need to do anything as Thor saw that flag whip downward. Instantly, he launched off his powerful back legs, dirt and rocks flying from beneath his hooves. He knew it was the signal to run! Hunching down on him, her face close to his neck, her hands steadying the thundering stallion as he surged forward for the one-mile run to the slope of the Tetons, Jordana felt a thrill unlike anything before. Thor knew he could run here. His legs stretched, and she felt him establish a ground-eating stride. All she had to do was look ahead for holes, branches or anything else that might make him stumble. As the rider, she was always looking ahead. The wind whipped past her, her eyes watering as the stallion gained even more speed. It was dizzying! The dawn light was there, but she still had to squint to see a few hundred feet ahead of the stallion.

By the time they reached the trail that would eventually twist upward toward ten thousand feet, Thor had gotten his initial burst of energy expended. Jordana didn't look back. She knew that Downing would be galloping as hard and fast as he could to catch up with them. As they entered the thick forest, the path well marked with red-orange flags every quarter of a mile, Jordana negotiated with Thor. The stallion still wanted to run, but it was impossible as the trail twisted upward. In some spots, there were tight, ninety-degree turns. In others, there were logs fallen across the path and they had to jump them. The best she could do now was throttle Thor's nuclear power down to a steady, hard trot. He hated it, snorted and tossed his head. Laughing, Jordana sang softly to him. Ears flicking back and forth, Thor stopped chewing on the bit and got down to the business of trotting.

It would be impossible to know how close Downing was to her. The trail was wicked, steep and she could barely see twenty feet behind her. Slade had told her to just keep Thor moving at a fast trot and negotiate all the tight, demanding turns. There were pullouts about every quarter of a mile on this narrow portion of the race, where a rider could move over to allow another to pass, but that was all. Jordana keyed her hearing behind her. Now that Thor was trotting, the wind wasn't tearing past her as it had out on the meadow run, and she could hear very well. The light grew as the dawn became stronger. The path was tricky, full of rocks sticking out of the soil along with roots that grew across it. She wondered how close Downing was to her.

Curt cursed softly as he took the whip he

always carried and let it hang on his wrist. Shah was snorting hard, his black nostrils wide open and showing red deep within them as they hit the beginning of the trail. How far ahead was Jordana and that damn stud of McPherson's? Gouging his heels into his black Arabian, Curt forced the horse to canter up the path until he couldn't do it anymore. No horse could gallop around tight, ninety-degree turns. He cursed, trying to see ahead. It was impossible on this part of the trail. It was narrow, thickly wooded, and while it was a switchback trail that wove back and forth across the slope of the Tetons, it didn't allow him to catch sight of his competition. The only thing he could do is take advantage of every straight spot, which were few, and canter his horse. Every stride meant a second of time and Curt knew that. And sixty seconds made a minute. And one minute could determine the difference between winner and loser. He pushed Shah as much as he dared. Inwardly, Curt knew he could overtake the woman. Thor might know this trail, but she didn't. Women were conservative riders compared to a man. She would be slowing down on this weaving, narrow trail, not urging Thor as he should be pushed. Grinning, Curt took his whip and laid it against Shah's rump as a short, straight part in the trail popped up. The Arab grunted and lunged forward, hurtling up it at a dizzying speed.

Slade drove his trailer and pickup to the first stop in the high mountain meadow. He found a parking spot, got out and saw that Shorty was already there and prepared for the vet check. Griff had volunteered to help. Slade had been surprised by the generous offer and told him to help Shorty. His wrangler had driven the other truck up earlier. When Jordana came galloping into the vet check, she'd have to dismount and have the saddle and bridle taken off so that the vet team could check Thor. Shorty would then walk the stud for the vet. After the check and figures were marked down by the team, he would then walk the stallion for twenty minutes. Slade would have time to give Jordana water and talk to her about the race.

Worriedly, Slade looked at his watch and then glanced at the opening into the meadow that was half a mile away. He knew this first section of the race was very challenging. Would Jordana still be in the lead? What if Downing tried to pass her? Would he push her out of the way? Slade knew that there was no cell phone reception on this endurance ride. There was no way for Jordana to let him know what was happening to her and Thor. As he paced and kept glancing at the opening, Slade found himself far more worried over Jordana than her placement in the race. When had he fallen in love with her? Slade knew it was love. It was nothing like he'd felt for Isabel. No, this feeling was like a warm glowing light in his chest. He thrummed with joy he'd never experienced in his life. Jordana made him happy. Just her smiling face, those dancing blue eyes, fed his starving soul in a way Slade had never realized existed.

Thor and Jordana burst out of the forest. By now, the sun had risen. Long, bright slats of light filtered strongly across the flat, oval meadow. Slade breathed a sigh of relief. Jordana was in the lead! Thor looked good. So did she. Where was Downing? A million questions showered through Slade as he walked to where Shorty was standing. Thor was wet with sweat, but there was no foam on his neck or hindquarters, which was good. That would indicate nervousness, which would voraciously eat up a horse's energy and slow him down. Jordana had him at a full-out gallop because this was where she could get time against other riders following her. He enjoyed seeing them flying toward the awaiting vet group. She was so small bobbing on Thor's back. Clearly, Jordana had the stallion in hand, and he was fully listening to her commands. Pride for her abilities moved through Slade.

Jordana brought Thor to a halt. Quickly leaping off, she handed the reins to Shorty. She saw Slade grinning fully as he came around to uncinch the saddle.

"How are you?" he asked, quickly removing the saddle, blanket and breastplate.

Sweaty, Jordana smiled and said, "Fine."

The vet team moved in with a stethoscope and their clipboards that would list Thor's pulse, breathing and heart beat. The stallion snorted, still full of himself even after twenty miles. Within moments, Shorty put the halter over Thor's head and then removed the bridle. Griff nodded to Jordana and helped the wrangler.

Jordana smiled at the twin. She was happy Slade invited him to come along and help.

Slade gripped Jordana's arm and guided her toward the truck. "You need water and food," he told her.

Laughing with relief, Jordana said, "I'm not hungry! We're doing fine, Slade. How's our time?" She walked close to him and he reached out and gripped her hand in his.

Her heart soared with joy. She could still feel the power of his mouth against hers from their kiss earlier in the meadow.

Slade drew her to the rear of his pickup where he had pints of cold water and trail mix waiting for her. Releasing her hand, he picked up a bottle and twisted off the cap. "Drink. You're more dehydrated than you realize."

Nodding, Jordana dutifully took the water bottle from him. The moment their fingers met, she felt a wild and tingling feeling up her arm. Slade looked serious, his cowboy hat drawn down over his brow, his gray eyes narrowed upon her. It was a look she eagerly absorbed as she gulped down a pint of water. As soon as she was done drinking, she watched the vet people work with Thor. They had gotten their numbers, and now, Griff had to walk him for twenty minutes.

"How's Thor doing?" Slade asked, leaning against the tailgate as she munched on the granola and dried fruit.

"Good," she murmured between bites.

"Is he listening or fighting you?"

Grinning, she said, "A little of both, but when it got down to it, Slade, he did exactly as I asked him."

Nodding, Slade absorbed her sparkling blue gaze and the happy smile on her mouth. Strands of black hair had crept out on the sides of her helmet. Perspiration dotted her brow. Her cheeks were flushed a bright red. He knew how strenuous and demanding this part of the trail was. "How are *you* doing?"

"Great," she said.

"Your legs? Any chapping of the inner knees or cramping of your legs yet?"

Leaning down, Jordana checked the duct tape on her knees. "No, I'm fine so far. No burning sensation, no rubbing on my inner knee area. The duct tape is doing its job." She straightened. "Is our time good?" She knew Slade had all the times from past rides on the clipboard setting on the tailgate.

Picking it up, he motioned for Jordana to sit on it next to him. "Your time is actually one minute ahead of what I did last year," he told her, pointing to the numbers. How badly Slade wanted to kiss her. But now was not the time.

Studying the figures, Jordana said, "The next twenty miles is from seven thousand to ten thousand feet. We take that trail across the high, rocky slopes and then come down to nine thousand into our next pit stop."

Nodding, Slade said, "Here comes Downing. . . ."

Looking up, Jordana saw Downing running the stallion full-out across the flat meadow toward the vet check. The horse looked fit and his sweaty body gleaming like polished ebony. She frowned as she saw Downing whipping the horse's rump with that ever-present whip that hung around his wrist. "He shouldn't beat his horse," she muttered, frowning.

Slade looked at the time the horse flew across the vet check line. "No, he shouldn't, but Downing beats everything he owns," he growled. "He's thirty seconds later than his time last year," he added, smiling a little. "And Shah looks good."

Jordana watched Downing's team race over and quickly unsaddle and unbridle the black stallion. Downing was scowling and yelling at his team as the vet came over. "He's pissed about something."

"He's always angry on a ride," Slade said. "He's competitive."

"He should relax while he's got a chance." Jordana was happy to sit on the tailgate of the truck with Slade. She continued to eat. Food and water were necessary for the rider, who was expending a tremendous amount of energy. She saw that Shorty took Thor over to the waiting pails of clean, cool water. The mustang eagerly thrust his muzzle into the first pail, gulping down the contents.

"Downing never relaxes," Slade warned. Sighing, he said, "If he's going to make a move to pass you, it will be on this next stretch. And you have to be ready for him. He'll try and run you off the trail. If you get into those rocks . . ."

Holding up her hand, Jordana said, "Stop worrying, Slade. I know what he's capable of doing. And I'm not going into the rocks with Thor." More grimly, she added, "We'll be okay. How are you doing?"

He smiled slightly. "Worried."

"That's to be expected. Thor's doing fine. He's an old hand at this. He remembers this trail and knows how to negotiate it."

Picking up her hand, Slade kissed the back of it. "I was worried for you, not my horse."

Touched, Jordana clung to his burning gray gaze. His hand was firm and strong around hers. Her flesh warmed instantly as his mouth settled on it, and he kissed it. "Oh," she whispered, suddenly touched by his unexpected gesture. "I'm okay, Slade. Really."

"Well, it's the second twenty miles that you'll start feeling the push and getting tired," he warned, releasing her hand. At that moment, he could have drowned in Jordana's eyes. Slade wanted nothing more than to bury himself into her, take her and love her until she fainted in his arms.

For a moment, Jordana's world swam around Slade. She ached to kiss him again. Tucking away that need, she slipped off the tailgate and gave him a warm look. "Time's almost up." She was ready for the next twenty miles.

Downing whipped his stallion as they raced along the narrow dirt track across the rocky slopes at ten thousand feet. He pushed his Arabian hard to make up that minute of difference between him and Thor. What he hadn't expected was how well Jordana rode the horse. He'd miscalculated terribly, thinking she would never finish this grueling event. So far, he'd been dead wrong. She rode smart, and she rated Thor like a pro, much to his chagrin.

They were coming down from the rocks. Thor flew into the forest at nine thousand feet. He spurred Shah. The stallion grunted and pounded even faster down the trail, eating up the distance between them.

Jordana's full focus was forward. She didn't hear Downing coming up on them until it was too late. The path was wide enough for three horses in the forest. Thor was trotting at this point because a tight turn was rapidly coming up. She suddenly heard the pounding of hooves bearing down on her. Thor's ears laid back. He squealed a warning but it was too late.

In seconds, Jordana found Downing and his black Arabian alongside them. It happened so swiftly, that she was caught off guard. Downing grinned savagely and threw his stud into hers. Instantly, Jordana hauled back on Thor, not wanting to be shoved off the trail and into the trees. Her reaction was wrong, but at the time, it was visceral. Downing flew past them. The Arabian took the sharp turn and disappeared. *Damn!*

"Come on!" she called to Thor. Angry at herself for not dividing her attention between the front of the trail and who was coming up behind, Jordana leaned forward. Thor snorted and plunged forward, thundering down the trail in pursuit of the black Arabian not far ahead of them. Jordana focused on catching up with them. She knew in less than a mile, the trail ended and opened up into another meadow where the second vet check was located. She'd screwed up. Big time. Slade was going to be disappointed when he saw she wasn't in the lead at the next stop. *Damn!*

Slade's brows dropped as he saw Downing whipping his horse to high speed as they burst out of the trail and into the meadow. Worriedly, he stood, holding his breath. Where was Jordana? Had Downing hurt them? Rage warred with concern. When Thor galloped out of the woods, Jordana still on him, Slade's breath exploded from him. Without thinking, he ran toward where Shorty was waiting for her.

Jordana quickly dismounted, handing Shorty the reins to Thor. She saw Slade's dark face and worried look. Trotting toward him, she was angry and upset. "I screwed up, Slade. I let him get around me. I'm sorry."

Slade gripped her arm and brought her to a halt. "What did he do?" he demanded, quickly looking her over. She had no scratches, bruises or whip marks on her arms. Downing had done worse to other riders who challenged him out of sight of the judges. Her eyes were narrowed. The set of her mouth told him how upset she was. "Come on, you need to drink and eat," he coaxed as he led her to the truck.

Jordana told him what had happened as she drank the water. "I'm sorry, Slade. I wasn't paying attention like I should have . . ."

Soothing her, Slade said, "Don't worry about it. The last ten miles of this race is where Thor will excel." He pointed toward the other end of the busy meadow now milling with horses and riders galloping in. "You've got a five-mile steep trail down from eight thousand feet to the final leg at six thousand feet. And then you've got five miles of flat land to make your final run on him. Wait until you get out of the woods. When you're on the flat, open Thor up."

"There's no way to try and make up this thirty seconds on that five-mile trail?" Jordana demanded. How badly she wanted to win that money for Slade! It broke her heart to think that he'd lose the ranch without it.

Shaking his head, Slade muttered, "It's narrow, twisting and few places to pull over to let a horse and rider move past. It's too dangerous, Jordana."

Frustrated, she stared over at him. "But not impossible to do?"

Hesitating, Slade muttered, "No, not impossible . . ." Holding her angry glare, he added, "Listen, I want you to come out of this alive. You can't challenge Downing in that section. He'll eat you alive, Jordana. Don't try it. You'll be putting yourself and Thor at risk."

The grave tone of his voice along with the pleading look in his gray eyes made her contrite. "I won't risk Thor, Slade."

"He's second in importance to you, Jordana. Do you hear me?" He drilled a dark look into her startled gaze. Gripping her hand hard for a moment, he rasped, "Dammit, Jordana, you're important to me. I can lose the ranch. I can't lose you. . . ."

Those words echoed within Jordana as she rode hard down the narrow, steep trail toward the flat plain. Thor didn't like being second, either. She loosened the reins and let the stallion eat up seconds as he inched closer and closer to the fleeing black Arabian. She saw Downing jerking a look back at them every time he could. They were gaining on him! Jordana wanted nothing more than to overtake them! And in the last mile before they hit the flat, she surged Thor forward to do just that.

Downing cursed and saw Jordana make her move. The trail was wide enough. But he was damned if he was going to politely move over! Grabbing his whip, as Thor thundered even with them, he raised it up to slash at the animal's face and force him to retreat.

Jordana saw Downing's face turn livid. As he raised the whip to strike at Thor, she jerked her leg out of the stirrup, leaned to the right and slammed her boot as hard as she could into Downing's leg.

With a scream of surprise, Downing felt her heel connect. It broke the momentum of his whip coming down to strike Thor. Shaken, the Arabian spun to the left. It nearly unseated Downing. Thor charged past. Cursing, Downing got a hold of his startled horse, and he whipped him unmercifully to catch up with them. *Damn her!* He hadn't expected the woman to fight back! Mouth tightening, Curt leaned down across his stallion and urged him to catch up.

Jordana hit the flat at an all-out gallop. Fifty feet behind came Downing. They had five miles to go! The dust tore up under the pistonlike surge of Thor's hind legs as he lunged forward. His nostrils were wide open. He was sucking up and blowing out explosive drafts of air. The wind screamed past Jordana's bobbing head. She looked back. Downing was gaining on her! He was unmercifully whipping his stallion. Leaning down, riding Thor for all he was worth, Jordana began to use her hands, legs and weight to push him just a little faster. The stallion gamely responded.

Out of the dust, Slade saw Thor and Jordana in the lead. Not more than twenty feet behind was Downing on his foaming black stallion. Cheers began from bystanders standing on either side of the course the last half mile, urging the riders on. Watching through his binoculars, Slade swelled with pride for the woman who rode his sunbonnet stallion. Jordana had proven so many times before that she was a champion in every way. He never, in a million years, thought that she could win this race. But there she was, riding Thor, the two of them flying across the sagebrush plain toward the finish line.

Jordana heard the hoof beats of the black Arabian approaching from behind. Her eyes were tearing so much from the wild run that she could barely see. Thor was hitting the ground hard and swiftly, his mane constantly whipping and stinging her face. She had to win! Slade's ranch was at risk! Looking over, she saw Shah's black head slowly edging up toward her. She saw a maniacal look in Downing's eyes, his mouth lifted in a snarl at her. She knew he couldn't hit her or do anything at this part of the race. The judges would see it.

Her legs were tired, and she felt herself loosen the grip she needed. Understanding that the first forty miles had taken more of a toll on her than she'd first believed, Jordana dug deep. There was only a half mile to the finish line! They were now neck and neck!

Mouth thinning, Jordana moved her hands firmly against Thor's neck. She called out to him. Instantly, the stallion's ears went back. He stuck his nose out, grabbed the bit and surged ahead.

Slade couldn't believe his eyes as Thor pulled away from Downing in the last quarter mile. His stallion was literally flying, his mane and tail furling outward like a flag, Jordana was barely a bump on his back, her hands and arms pushing him forward with every massive, ground-eating stride. Cries of triumph erupted from the crowd as Thor and Jordana passed the line into first place. Shorty came over and leaped up and down, slamming Slade on the shoulder.

"She did it! She did it!" he screamed, throwing his hat into the air.

Stunned, Slade stood there watching as Jordana and Thor galloped across the finish line. His ranch would be saved! God help him, he loved her with a need that engulfed him. As he walked toward them, slightly dazed by the unexpected turn of events, a crooked grin of triumph began to spread across Slade's face.

CHAPTER TWENTY-ONE

"Ready to go home?" Slade asked. Slade knew the winner would not be honored or the check given out until tomorrow morning at the awards ceremony. Riders would be coming in until dusk. The late-afternoon sun slanted across the valley, the Tetons reflecting the light.

Jordana grinned, turned and threw her arms around Slade. Shorty gathered up Thor's reins, and Griff began to unsaddle him for the final vet check. "We did it!" she whispered against Slade's ear, feeling his strong arms slide around her. Closing her eyes, Jordana didn't care who was watching them as she leaned up and kissed Slade fully on his smiling mouth. She felt as if she were floating on a cloud of pure joy as he returned the swift, quick kiss.

Releasing her, Slade knew many were watching them. Some had shock written on their faces. No one had suspected there was a brewing relationship between them. Grinning down at her as she removed the Kevlar vest, he said, "You did it. You and Thor. I was wrong, Jordana. You're a champion through and through."

Feeling heat crawl into her face as she lifted the helmet off her head, her hair mussed, Jordana smiled up at him. "I knew you'd realize that sooner or later," she teased. When Slade smiled, it did something warm and wonderful in her heart. It was so good to see Slade smile! A number of people came over to congratulate them. In the distance, Jordana saw a fuming, angry Curt Downing glaring at them. Both Thor and Shah were being walked to cool down after being vet checked. She wondered if he was going to charge her with a foul.

Turning to Slade, she whispered what had happened on the trail. His brows instantly fell, and his gray eyes turned angry.

"He won't say a word," Slade muttered, lifting his head and glaring at Downing in the distance. "I'm sure he was surprised you fought back."

Taking her vest and helmet to the pickup truck, Jordana tucked them into the area between the seats. She was hot, sweaty, dusty and in dire need of a shower. "He had a surprised look on his face," she told Slade with an elfish grin. She followed him to the rear of the trailer.

Slade saw Shorty bringing a tired Thor toward them. The stud had earned a nice, cooling bath when they got home. Opening up the one side of the trailer that Thor would be led into, he smiled a little over at Jordana. She looked beautiful, her face streaked with dust, her black hair gleaming beneath the late afternoon sun, the strands showing reddish highlights. His lower body tightened with screaming need of her. Jordana was such a brave, fierce warrior. Why hadn't he seen that in her before?

As Slade pulled down the ramp and placed the rubber mat over it so Thor wouldn't slip walking into the trailer, he knew why. Jordana was nothing like his ex-wife, Isabel. But he hadn't seen the difference until now because he'd allowed Isabel to color his view of all women.

Thor was damp and dusty as he obediently climbed into the trailer. Shorty tied the rope to the bar and gave the stallion a pat. "He did good, Boss. He won with five minutes to spare. That's a new, personal record for him."

"It is," Slade agreed. Shorty left the trailer, and they closed it up. Shorty and Griff would take the other truck after putting all the supplies in the back of it.

Jordana waited for Slade. Once he climbed in and started up the Chevy, he drove slowly down the dirt road toward home. Leaning back, she closed her eyes. "It's over. We did it, Slade. We won that ten thousand dollars for you."

He reached over and gripped her hand resting in her lap. "You've got a lot of lessons coming," he told her.

Opening her eyes, she met his warm gaze. "I'm looking forward to them, Slade. Stormy is slowly healing and by the time next year comes around, we'll bring her back to her original shape." She absorbed the strength of his hand around hers. He divided his attention between driving and her. She wanted Slade fully focused on driving and released his hand. What she had to say could wait until they got home. *Home . . .*

"Stormy has a good chance to fully recover," he agreed.

Jordana went to shower immediately upon arriving at the ranch. Shorty unloaded Thor and took him to his showering facility. The stallion would be bathed and then turned out into his own paddock with some well-earned sweet feed as dessert along with his hay for winning today. Slade went to the master bedroom. Everyone was dirty and sweaty from the endurance contest. Jordana scrubbed her hair with almond and spice shampoo from her favorite soap company, Herbaria. The scent of almond and cinnamon encircled her like a magical potion.

After drying off, Jordana tucked the fuzzy pink terry cloth bath towel around her body. Today was the day. And she hoped Slade agreed. Padding down the pine hall, she saw Slade's bedroom door was ajar. Feeling a bit of anxiety, Jordana allowed her heart to do the talking.

"Slade?" She knocked lightly on the opened door.

Slade had just come out of the bathroom, a cream-colored towel wrapped low around his waist. When he heard Jordana's voice, he knew. "Come on in," he called, walking toward the door. Slade saw her round the door. Her hair was damp, uncombed and fell around her face. Seeing the shining love in her blue eyes, he reached out for her. Without a word, Slade drew her gently against him, rested his head on her damp hair and felt her arms twine around his waist.

"This is what I needed," Jordana whispered softly, lifting her face to meet his narrowing gray gaze. "I need *you,* Slade. I have for a long time. Maybe since I first met you." She moved her fingers down his powerful back, feeling his muscles leap, tense and respond to her grazing movement.

"You're a bold little thing," he told her, taking his hands and framing her upturned face.

Jordana grinned mischievously. His roughened hands were warm, and he smelled of the pine soap he always used. "I learned that in residency. He who doesn't move first, gets nothing." She lifted her hands and caressed his unshaven face. Her fingertips tingled as they flowed across his sandpapery flesh. "Slade, I love you. I don't know when it happened exactly, but it has."

The words flowed over him like a hot, beckoning shower. His heart flew open. "And how long have you been hiding this little secret?" he murmured, leaning down and brushing his lips against hers.

"Mmm," Jordana whispered against his mouth, "probably ever since I met you. Looking back on it, I was always wanting to come out here just to be near you. I loved the riding lessons, but I began to realize the highlight of my day was simply sharing time and space with you, Slade." She became serious and held his stormy-looking gray gaze. "I know what love is. I know what it means." She framed his face with her hands. "Do we want the same thing, Slade? Or is it one-sided?" Jordana held his suddenly serious look. His hands gently moved across her damp strands. Inwardly, Jordana shook. She'd waited a long time to feel that kind of loving caress.

A sensation of trembling began in Slade's core. Drowning in her blue eyes was like being given the keys to heaven. With great gentleness, Slade placed a series of kisses across her hairline and her brow and whispered near her delicate ear, "We want the same thing. I love you, Jordana. Like you, I don't know when I fell in love with you. I only know that I did. . . ." Slade melded his mouth to hers. She tasted of toothpaste, the peppermint mingling with her sweetness as a woman. She pressed herself against him, her lips opening, allowing him deeper entrance into herself. Groaning, Slade leaned down, picked Jordana up in his arms as if she were nothing but a feather.

Slade placed her on the bed. Jordana opened her eyes and smiled up at him as he divested himself of the towel. He dropped it to the floor. Truly, he reminded her of a Greek god, his body solid, heavily muscled and athletic in every way. As her gaze drifted down in appreciation of him as a man, it was clear he wanted her. That sent a white-hot need lancing through her lower body. Pulling the towel off herself, Jordana felt the burn of his gaze as he memorized every inch of her exposed body. Beneath Slade's heated gaze, she felt her breasts grow taut, the nipples hardening and her belly beginning to glow with anticipation. He hadn't even touched her, and she was responding to him! Such was the power of mutual love, Jordana realized, as she reached up, gripped his fingers and pulled them lightly across her body.

Slade moved slowly. He weighed enough that he didn't want to crush Jordana beneath his body. As she guided him over her, he turned on his side, slipped his arm beneath her neck and with his other hand, placed it on her hip. In one smooth, unbroken motion, he pulled her against him. As he lay down, holding her liquid blue gaze that had gone misty with what clearly was love for him alone, Slade allowed himself to feel every inch of her pressed against his hard body. Her breasts were small but firm, teasingly moving against his dark-haired chest. Where her hips met his, he began to ache until he thought he'd explode. When she wrapped her small, fine legs around his thick, hairy ones, he closed his eyes and gripped her. His lips pulled away from his gritted teeth, and he sucked in a sharp breath as she moved suggestively against him.

When Jordana's mouth settled on his, Slade felt her hips nestle against his. He took her mouth commandingly. She responded with hungry nips and her tongue slipping into his mouth. There was nothing sedate or conservative about Jordana now. Slade was getting a taste, literally, of her as a strong and powerful woman. Her hips ground demandingly into his. Slade smiled beneath her lips. She was heat, softness and hunger all wrapped into one. Without realizing it, Jordana had lifted and slipped herself over him. A tortured groan rolled out of him as her wet confines enveloped him. Stars exploded behind his tightly shut lids. Slade buried himself into her heated depths.

Every bit of Isabel and his doomed marriage dissolved beneath the heat of Jordana's lithe, athletic body. Any questions he had about comparing the two of them disappeared forever. Her mouth was wanton, searching and assertive. He liked Jordana's fierceness as a woman wanting her man. She made him feel as if he were the king of the world as she began to move sinuously against him.

Jordana shuddered as Slade moved his hands down from her damp shoulders, slowly exploring her long back and then covering her hips. He raised his and thrust hard into her, establishing a wild rhythm that made her moan with pleasure. In seconds, he had lifted Jordana so that her thighs straddled him. As he brought her fully against him, she cried out with joy, her back arching, her hands spread across his chest. The world tilted and spun into the boiling heat gathering deep within her. As Slade rose up, his lips feathering her taut nipples, she moaned and wanted more of him.

He lavished his attention to each of her throbbing breasts and puckered nipples. Jordana felt the boiling cauldron deep within her explode. She froze, cried out, her fingers digging deeply into the taut flesh of his chest. Slade ground his hips, rocking against hers, prolonging the delicious sensation and orgasm. Light-headed, her eyes shut, Jordana whirled in light and heat in those precious moments as Slade guided and deepened the experience for her.

Slade could no longer withhold his own need of Jordana. As she collapsed against him, her lips parted in a whisper of pleasure, he took her fully. He released his love into her. Her hips moved in delicious rhythm with his, designed to pull every bit of energy out of him. Throwing his head back, teeth clenched, Slade sank into the throbbing fire. For molten, wonderful moments, he was spun out into a sensual, black world that enclosed him as her arms wrapped around his neck. As her mouth met his, Slade surrendered to her searing lips. The heat releasing in his lower body surged and melted within her.

Groaning and satiated, Slade relaxed. So did Jordana, resting her head in the crook of his neck. Both breathing raggedly, their hearts in pounding union as they lay against one another, Slade managed a sliver of a weak smile. He moved his fingers in a grazing motion against her damp flesh. Tracing the length of her strong, straight spine, he absorbed every delicious inch of her. Memorizing Jordana's firm body was easy. His mind had no other thoughts except to absorb her into him in those moments after they'd surrendered to one another. Inhaling her sweetness, the almond scent in her drying hair, Slade murmured, "I've died and gone to heaven. . . ."

Barely opening her eyes, Jordana lifted herself just enough to meet Slade's gaze.

She whispered, "We're heaven for one another, Slade."

Caressing her shoulders, Slade drowned in her barely opened eyes. They were a deeper blue, he realized, and she looked like a satiated mountain lion. Grazing her lips, he whispered, "I love you, sweetheart. You're all I want."

Warming to his nickname for her, Jordana moved off him and snuggled at his side. "You are surely a stallion among men, Slade," and she smiled into his stormy gray eyes, seeing pride flash in them over her whispered compliment. Leaning upward, Jordana kissed Slade once more, cherishing that strong mouth of his. She wasn't disappointed as Slade smiled his very male smile and returned her tender kiss.

Slade whispered, "Marry me?"

Jordana sighed and relaxed fully against him. She nestled her head against Slade's jaw and shoulder, content. "Yes, I want more of what we have, Slade. I want to be your partner and best friend."

"So do I," he murmured, nuzzling her soft, nearly dry black hair. "I have an idea. . . ."

Pulling away to look up at him, she said, "Yes?"

"Tomorrow morning when we go back to

the meadow to pick up the trophy and money, let's announce our engagement." He saw joy leap into her face, her cheeks redden even more.

"I like that idea," she murmured.

Slade caressed her jaw and placed a light kiss on her smiling mouth. "The town will rock with shock. Gwen Garner will be miffed because we didn't tell her first so she could tell the whole town."

Laughing softly against his mouth, Jordana said, "Gwen Garner will have a *lot* to gossip about anyway." They laughed together over that thought.

The moments filled with silence, and Slade appreciated the woman he held tenderly in his arms. He was amazed at Jordana's strength, her fierce love for him and the devotion he'd seen in her eyes for him alone. Moving his hand down across her shoulder to her hip, he rasped, "I don't know what I did to deserve someone like you, Jordana. I honestly don't."

Leaning up on her elbow, her breasts brushing against the wall of his chest, she said, "You wouldn't, Slade. But I do. You're a man with incredible morals and values. Your word is your bond. You work hard, long hours . . ." She slid her hand across his dark-haired chest. "You're humble, Slade, about everything. Maybe it was the way you were raised. I don't know." Jordana leaned down and whispered against his lips, "That just makes me love you even more, darling. Pride doesn't run you like it does a lot of other men. You're a complex man, Slade." Jordana placed a nibble on his ear and then lifted her head. Meeting his smiling expression, she added, "And I like a complex man. I want my life to be entwined with yours. We share so much already."

"We do," he admitted, liking the way her drying hair curled softly about her flushed features. "You've given me so much already."

"Well," Jordana said in a wispy voice, "I wouldn't have it any other way, Slade. We share an equal partnership."

"That money you won will go to saving our ranch."

Nodding, Jordana said, "And now, once we get married, my money will be mixed in with yours." She looked around the large bedroom. "Not only is the ranch saved, but so are we."

Nodding, Slade drew her back into his arms. Her long leg crossed his. He savored the warmth and womanly strength of her body against his. "I never thought I'd ever fall in love again." And then Slade amended,

"Now, I realize I never really loved Isabel. It was all about sex. Once we'd burned through that phase, there was nothing left to replace it. We were like strangers. What I loved, she hated and vice versa." His mouth thinned, and he cupped Jordana's shoulder. "It taught me a good relationship is like a cake recipe. Everything has to be there to make it work for the long-term."

Laughing softly, Jordana said, "I like your idea about a relationship being like a recipe. You're right," she murmured, touching his hard, unyielding jaw. "Something that you want to last forever is a mix of many things. Among them, being friends. You really have been a dear friend to me whether you realized it or not."

Hearing the sudden choke in her voice, Slade turned his head and dissolved into the tears he saw in her eyes. "I didn't know what a friend was until I met you," he admitted in a roughened tone. "I've got a lot to learn about a healthy relationship, Jordana." His mouth lifted a little, "But I've got a sense you're going to help teach me about the rest of that recipe."

"Not that I'm an expert," Jordana protested with a breathy laugh. "The key is we both want this to work, Slade. *That* is the difference. There's going to be a lot of compromises, but I love you and I'm willing to make them."

Touched deeply, Slade shook his head. "I don't know what I've done to deserve you, but I'm a grateful man."

Nodding, Jordana rested her head on his chest. She felt the wiry hair against her cheek and heard the drumlike beat of his powerful heart in his massive chest. There was such strength to Slade. As she closed her eyes and simply absorbed the moment, Jordana promised herself that she would show him over time why he was a man worth loving. "You're no longer a loner, Slade. You have me. . . ."

The next morning at the awards ceremony, Slade stood with Jordana. They were surrounded by everyone who'd been either a spectator or contestant after the final horse and rider had finished the endurance ride yesterday evening. And after he'd announced their engagement, the entire crowd gave a collective gasp. And then cheers and applauding broke out. He stood with his arm around Jordana's small shoulders, the rope of Thor's halter in her other hand. The stallion, who stood next to her, his bare back gleaming in the early morning sunlight, tossed and snorted as if to agree with the happy crowd.

"Well," Judge Amy Talbot said into the microphone with a smile, "I'd say this is a marriage made in heaven, Slade. Now, we'll have *both* of you on the pro circuit to watch out for!" Everyone burst into good-natured laughter.

Jordana grinned and looked up at him. Slade looked so ruggedly handsome in his tan Stetson drawn down across his serious features. He wore a black leather vest this morning, gussied up for the ceremony. The red bandanna that was always around his thickly corded neck was in place against the clean, pressed white cowboy shirt. He'd even put on his best pair of Levi's and his fancy ostrich hide cowboy boots he wore only for special occasions.

Slade gave the crowd a sheepish grin. Taking the microphone from the judge, he said, "I hadn't thought of that, Amy."

The forty-year-old red-haired woman shook her head and took back the mike. "Well, *we did,* Slade!! You two are going to be double-barreled trouble out there on the circuit. It used to be we only had you and Thor to worry about, but now, Jordana has shown she's got the moxie to win equal to you." She handed him the microphone.

"That's true," Slade said. He handed the

mike to Jordana and said, "Tell them about Stormy."

Jordana told the crowd about her mustang mare who would show up on next year's circuit. She saw the merry crowd laugh and clap some more.

Amy said, "Well, let's give Jordana her due, Slade." She handed over the ten thousand dollar check. "Congratulations, Jordana. You earned every cent of this!"

Taking the check, Jordana saw Curt Downing standing nearby. His brows were puckered, and he was clearly still angry about the loss. She held it up in the air, and the group applauded more. Turning, she handed it to Slade. "With this money, Slade's ranch will be safe from foreclosure," she told the crowd, her voice growing raspy. "I rode Thor for him to try and save his home. I just want to thank Slade for having faith in me that I could do this," and her voice cracked. She turned and gave Thor a pat. "And this horse ran his heart out for me. They're *both* champions!" The crowd roared with approval as she turned and gave Slade a quick hug. He embraced her, his eyes suspiciously bright.

As Jordana drew away, she saw Griff McPherson hovering on the edge of the crowd. She hadn't seen him before. He was looking around, as if hunting for someone in particular. That was strange. Her heart went out to the younger twin. Looking up, she saw Slade had spied him, too. Some of the happiness faded from his eyes. He led her off the stage so second and third place riders would receive their accolades and checks. As they stood to the right of the stage, they both clapped for Downing, who was not happy. He took the check and stalked off the stage without a word. There were some catcalls and boos from the crowd. Slade shook his head. Downing was always a sore loser.

After the ceremonies, there was hot coffee, hot chocolate and Danish pastries for the crowd of one hundred and fifty people. Slade and Jordana were the focus of the crowd, and well wishes came from everyone. Andy Patterson, who had won third place on his half-Arabian gelding, called out, "Hey! When's the big day, Slade? When you going to get hitched?"

Jordana laughed and looked up at Slade. "We are, Andy," she said.

"How about you make the date the same as the Tevis Cup ride? That way, someone else gets a chance to win it!"

The crowd rocked with laughter and applause. Slade grinned. "Now, Andy," he chided, his voice booming over the crowd, "I was thinking that *after* the Tevis Cup Ride, we'd get hitched."

Groans collectively rose from the crowd. Andy smiled and called out, "Hey, that's a *great* idea, Slade! You're gonna have to send all of us invites because we're all gonna be there to try and beat you and your bride!"

Never had Jordana felt so happy or fulfilled as right now. The endurance riders were a small, tight-knit community. Everyone knew everyone else. She saw how happy they were for them. Slade nodded and promised to send the invitations. It was a joyful celebration.

As the party finally broke up around ten that morning, Slade finished shaking hands with the last of the well-wishers. He and Jordana walked toward the truck.

"Slade?"

Turning, he saw his twin coming up. Griff looked nervous. Automatically, Slade put his arm around Jordana and drew her close.

"Griff?"

Griff halted in front of them. "I want to just say congratulations to both of you," he began, his voice sincere.

Jordana knew what it cost the twin to say that. After all, he still legally owned half the ranch. Reaching out, she touched his arm and whispered, "Thank you, Griff. We appreciate your care." And she did. Glancing at Slade, however, she saw no change in his frozen, dark features. There was still a war going on between the brothers. Her heart ached for both of them.

"Well, I just wanted to let you know I got a job."

"Really?" Slade growled. "Where? McDonald's?"

Griff stiffened a little but held on to his anger. "No, brother. I was just hired as a wrangler for the Horse Emporium. I'll be moving hay and feed for them. And I found a room for rent in town, so I'll be moving out today."

"Good," Slade bit out. He was relieved but wasn't going to say so. Griff looked like a cowboy to others. But he doubted he had the spine to stay the distance. "Being a wrangler is nothing but hard, constant work."

Nodding, Griff said, "I'm willing to do it."

Relieved, Jordana released his arm and said, "That's great, Griff. Stay in touch with us?"

He gave Jordana a slight smile. How like her to be the peacemaker between them. Tipping his hat, he murmured, "I will.

Thank you. And congratulations on your engagement. I'm really happy for both of you."

Slade stood there tense and unyielding as his twin turned and walked away. He felt Jordana's warm hand moving slowly up and down his back as if to soothe him. "I'm okay," he growled, walking to the truck with her.

"I know you are," Jordana said lightly. "The good news is Griff has a job."

"The better news is he won't be at our ranch," Slade bit out, opening the truck door for her.

Sliding in, Jordana said nothing. As they slowly drove the horse trailer with Thor out of the meadow, she watched as Slade began to relax. There were such untended wounds between the brothers. And they wouldn't be healed quickly. As they moved out onto the highway that would take them back to the ranch, Jordana slid her hand across Slade's massive thigh.

"Give yourself time with Griff," she counseled gently. "He's hurting like you, Slade. There are a lot of bridges to be rebuilt between you two over time."

Shrugging, Slade's hands tightened on the steering wheel. "He doesn't belong out here, Jordana. He never will. And he wants the ranch. I know he does."

"Don't be so sure," she whispered, patting his thigh. "I think he's going to try to make it out here on his own, Slade. There's no job for him on Wall Street anymore. The country is in the deepest recession it's ever seen since the Great Depression. He looked happy to get that job. I feel he'll make a go of it."

Mouth tightening, Slade said, "You're kinder to him than I am."

"I don't have the family baggage you two do, that's why."

Giving her a quick look, he saw the peaceful look on Jordana's beautiful face. His anger was snuffed out. Reaching out, he gripped her hand and gave it a squeeze. "We'll cross those bridges as they come. Right now, all I care about is loving you. If I have you, I have everything."

Nodding, Jordana understood. She returned the squeeze to his large, powerful hand. "Life is never easy, Slade, but it got easier for us because we love one another." And then she added, "Forever."